PRAISE FOR *OVERKILL*

'Vanda Symon's fast-paced crime novels are as good as anything the US has to offer – a sassy heroine, fabulous sense of place, and rip-roaring stories with a twist. Perfect curl-up-on-the-sofa reading' Kate Mosse

'This was an excellent read. It wasn't just the setting that made the book stand out. Symon is wonderful at characterisation, and the supporting characters spring to life from the page' Sarah Ward

'Finally, UK readers get to discover New Zealand's own Queen of Crime. Vanda Symon is a big talent and everything she writes is fast, intelligent and utterly gripping. In Sam Shephard, Symon has created a compelling series lead, and her treatment of small-town New Zealand is superbly atmospheric. This one's a cracker' Liam McIlvanney

'One of the best in this genre that I've read in years' Trena Marshall, *Waikato Times*

'A rollicking good read' Kim Knight, *Sunday Star Times*

'Symon nicely balances action, character and story in a well-drawn rural setting, and realistically speckles the book with light-hearted moments and humour throughout' *Wild Tomato* Magazine

'*Overkill* marks a bold beginning for a new voice, and a new hero, in crime fiction' Crime Watch

'Sam Shephard does not disappoint, and she is one of my favourite heroines' Steph's Book Blog

'One of the best female protagonists ever to come out of New Zealand, Sam Shephard (Shep) is a delight. As she treads her own investigative path, she ends up literally and metaphorically knee deep in shit as the tension rises and we fear for her safety as she makes one questionable decision after another … *Overkill* is written with pace and verve; it really flows well and is both engrossing and highly enjoyable. The characters stand out and I identified with Sam to the point that I was literally shouting at her to watch out as the final scenes played out. Verdict: a great start to a series I want to read more of and a ballsy protagonist I already love to bits' Live and Deadly

'A wonderfully evocative sense of place plus an engaging and intriguing main protagonist means *Overkill* is a must read' Liz Loves Books

'*Overkill* moves at break-neck speed, plunging the reader and Sam into a mystery that is cleverly thought out and impeccably told. The tense atmosphere and the multiple twists and false leads make this a breathtaking and compelling read' Random Things through My Letterbox

'Symon has a wonderful writing style; her vivid descriptions of settings conjured such crisp images in my head … There is an incredibly "real" feel to this book. The way that the plot pulls together is superb and leaves you with a satisfying conclusion' The Quiet Knitter

'A taut, atmospheric and page-turning thriller, *Overkill* marks the start of an unputdownable and unforgettable series from one of New Zealand s finest crime writers' Bloomin' Brilliant Books

'Sam Shephard is quite an engaging and attractive character … The rural setting is very well described, and the book is written in a smooth style that makes it a page-turner' A Crime Is Afoot

'The relentless pace of the story carries us along, with short chapters that are long on action. I didn't want to put down my copy' Richard Fernandez, Café Thinking

'A wonderful page-turner. Sam Shepherd is a gritty character, persistent, intuitive, a lateral thinker' Mysteries in Paradise

'I loved this crime thriller from the moment I started reading the chilling prologue, through every spellbinding chapter and right through to the shocking ending. *Overkill* features short, snappy chapters, which move the plot forwards at a fast pace, with great literary writing. Tension and emotion spill from every page, and I found myself whizzing through from beginning to end. I genuinely couldn't stop reading, addicted not only to the gripping, twisty plot but also to its great sense of place and range of believable characters – a perfect combination' Off-the-Shelf Books

'Sam Shepherd is a likable and engaging character. She reminds me of Sue Grafton's Kinsey Millhone in many ways. She shares the doggedness and disregard for her own safety in the pursuit of answers and can also be a little childish, to her own detriment … the last third of the book was quite a page-turner and the ultimate resolution was both well crafted and very credible. Overall this was an entertaining debut novel and I will certainly look for the next in the series' Reactions to Reading

'Massively addictive and compelling. Vanda Symon has written something very special here: an intense and powerful thriller told with a combination of prose and narrative that elevates *Overkill* head and shoulders above the pack and makes it a serious contender for one of the year's best reads' Mumbling About...

'With one of the most chilling prologues I've ever read, *Overkill* had me gripped from the opening paragraph' Joy Kluver's Blog

'A really enjoyable story, I loved Sam as the lead character and I warmed to her straight away. I thought she was excellent and was rooting for her throughout' Donna's Book Blog

'An intense and atmospheric procedural which vividly evokes a sense of place and a powerful new personality' Murder, Mayhem & More

'Of the many admirable aspects of Symon's storytelling, chief is her creation of Sam Shephard, a protagonist you want to follow; headstrong, passionate, and flawed. A talented detective, but not infallible. Shephard puts herself out there, cares, makes mistakes … She's human, real, and well rounded … a great read. Symon populates a good story with great characters, and unique touches in a distinctly Kiwi setting' *NZLawyer* magazine

'Sam is in a race against time and a white-hot violent battle to save herself and her friends ensues. And as a backdrop to all this, the tight-knit community, cadence and usages in the New Zealand dialogue, references to local plants and wildlife and the rural way of doing things round everything off nicely and make *Overkill* all the more readable. We'll look forward to the next in the series because, with the author's storytelling skills, the first is a pleasure to read' Crime Fiction Lover

OVERKILL

ABOUT THE AUTHOR

Vanda Symon is a crime writer and broadcaster from Dunedin, New Zealand. Books in her Sam Shephard series have hit number one on the New Zealand bestseller list, and she has been a three-time finalist for the Ngaio Marsh Award for Best Crime Novel. When she is not writing, Vanda can be found busy in the garden, or on the business end of a fencing foil.

Follow Vanda on Twitter *@vandasymon* on Instagram and visit her website: *vandasymon.com*.

OVERKILL

VANDA SYMON

ORENDA
BOOKS

Orenda Books
16 Carson Road
West Dulwich
London SE21 8HU
www.orendabooks.co.uk

First published in New Zealand by Penguin Books (NZ) in 2007
This edition first published in the United Kingdom by Orenda Books 2018
Copyright © Vanda Symon 2018

A catalogue record for this book is available from the British Library.

ISBN 978-1-912374-27-4
eISBN 978-1-912374-28-1

Typeset in Garamond by MacGuru Ltd
Printed and bound by CPI Group (UK) Ltd, Croydon CR0 4YY

For sales and distribution, please contact *info@orendabooks.co.uk*

OVERKILL

For Mum

Prologue

The day it was ordained that Gabriella Knowes would die there were no harbingers, omens or owls' calls. No tolling of bells. With the unquestioning courtesy of the well brought up, she invited Death in.

Death politely showed his identification and explained that there had been a telecommunication problem in the area. He then requested Gaby check if her landline had a dial tone.

She left him on the doorstep under the watchful gaze of Radar, hallway sentinel, and turned back into the house. She recalled she had left the phone in the bedroom after her usual morning chat with her mother, and smiled at the memory of her mother's excitement when she told her about Angel's first faltering steps.

The distant clatter of plastic told her that Angel was happily strewing Duplo around the lounge floor.

Gaby picked up the phone and pressed the 'Talk' button: sure enough, no dial tone.

'You're right, it's dead,' she said, as she walked back to the door. 'It was fine an hour ago when I was talking to Mum. Are everyone's phones down?'

'Just the homes in this block. It seems to be a localised fault,' he said.

'How long will it take to fix?'

'Well, if I can come in and check each of your jack points, we can eliminate them as the problem.' The man bent down to pick up a large black tool bag. 'In any case, we should have it sorted out within two hours, so you won't be without a phone for too long.'

Gaby opened the door wide for him. 'Oh sure, come in. But would you mind taking your shoes off? We've just got new carpet and I'm still a bit precious about it.'

'Of course.' He put the bag down and leaned over to untie his work boots. 'We've carpeted recently too. Where are your jack points?'

She walked down the hallway and pointed into the bedroom.

'There's a phone in there, another in the dining room through here,' she waved her arm to the right, 'and one in the bedroom straight ahead. I'll shut the dog away so he doesn't hassle you.' She grabbed Radar by the collar.

'Thanks for that. I'll start in there,' he said, and indicated the main bedroom. He shifted his bag out of the way and closed the front door. Gaby watched him for a moment as he found the jack point in the bedroom and began to unzip the bag.

'I'll leave you to it,' she said.

She deposited the dog in the end bedroom and went back to the lounge, where Angel was sitting on the floor amid a riot of coloured plastic. She bent over and kissed the top of her daughter's wispy blonde head, then continued through to the laundry to empty the machine and put on the next load. It never ceased to amaze her how much extra washing one kid could produce. She had just tossed in the last of the towels when she heard footsteps approach. She turned and was surprised to see the Telemax man carrying Angel on one hip.

'Oh, you found my Angel. Come to Mummy, poppet,' she said, and stepped through into the kitchen, arms outstretched to take her.

But the man backed away into the dining room, putting the table between them.

'Sit down,' he said.

'No, no, just pass her straight to me, she'll be fine.' Again, she reached out for her Angel.

'Sit down at the table,' the man said, all pleasantness gone from his voice.

'What are you doing? Just give her to me.' Gaby was moving around the table. Unease weighted the bottom of her stomach.

'Sit down. Now.' His tone made it clear there was no room for discussion, and his right hand drew what looked like a flick knife from his pocket. 'You've got such a pretty girl here. It would be a pity to have to spoil that face.'

Gaby lowered herself onto the chair; her legs no longer had the strength to support her. She could feel her heart hammering in her chest and struggled to hear over the pulsating, rushing noise in her head. The world had started to turn grey around the edges. She sucked in a deep breath and thought, Don't faint, don't faint. Think. Look for something – a weapon, anything. But she couldn't tear her eyes from her daughter who, oblivious to the threat, was smiling in the stranger's arms.

'We can make this easy or we can make this hard. It's up to you,' he said as he adjusted Angel's weight on his hip. 'I need you to write a note.'

'If it's money you want, my purse is in the bedroom. Take it, take anything, just give me back my daughter.'

'Ah, money. Well, no. It's not that simple.'

Gaby watched him gently tease Angel with the flick knife, tickling her under the chin. Angel giggled and kept reaching out, trying to grab at it. Gaby felt her gorge rise, and swallowed back hard. She could not allow herself to retch or faint. She had to keep a cool head. With her eyes she begged Angel not to hit the damned button by accident. Then her anger flared up, momentarily breaking through the fear. She leaped to her feet.

'What do you want, you fucking sick bastard! If you hurt her, I will kill you, I fucking swear—'

'Well, I'm afraid I'm not the one who's going to be dying today.' A contemptuous grin spread across the man's face. 'Like I said, we can make this easy, or we can make this hard. It's up to you. Me, I have a job to do. I don't personally like hurting children, so if you cooperate, we can just get this done and your daughter will be fine. If you make any trouble…' With a lightning-fast action he activated the flick knife and deftly removed a lock of Angel's hair.

Gaby flopped back onto the chair, fighting the urge to vomit as she watched the curl drift down to the floor. Her hands flew up to her face, to physically hold back the need to scream. It took her several seconds to regain control. She forced herself to lower her hands back to the tabletop, to battle the constriction in her throat.

'I'll do anything,' she whispered, and then looked up to meet his gaze. 'Just don't hurt my baby. For God's sake, just leave her alone.'

He looked at her, appraising, then reached down and pressed the blade of the knife on the table. The click as it closed made Gaby flinch.

'Now get a pen and a piece of paper. I need you to write that note.'

Gaby reached over and grabbed at the pen and pad she kept by the telephone; she almost dropped them, her hands were shaking so much. 'What do I have to write?' she asked.

'Oh, I think we'll keep it simple. "Sorry, Honey, I love you" – something like that.'

'What?'

'Let me spell it out for you. You are going to die. I want you to write a simple, fitting suicide note. That's it. It's not that hard. Now write.'

His words hit like a blow to the stomach. A gasping sob escaped her and she grasped the edge of the table to steady herself. The man was tall, muscular and probably twice her weight. He had Angel, squirming now, tired of being held and wanting her mother's arms. Disbelief surged up, and Gaby found herself banging her fists on the table. A keening noise escaped her mouth.

'Don't be so bloody childish, lady. It's not going to help you or your daughter. I'm going to get my bag. You, pull yourself together. Try anything, and it's the girl who will pay.' He turned, still carrying Angel, and walked out into the hall towards the bedroom.

She had only a moment; she had to think. There was no way she'd let people believe she'd killed herself, no way she could leave that legacy for Angel or Lockie. Quickly, and with a badly shaking hand, she scrawled a note on the pad, then ripped the piece off, screwed it up and flung it into a pile of old newspapers in the kitchen. Maybe, just maybe, he'd miss it.

She could already hear the man's footsteps returning. She breathed heavily. Her heart still raced, but suddenly, Gaby felt strangely calm, almost disconnected, a mere observer. A thought entered her head and as soon as it solidified her lips formed the question.

'Why?'

He came back into the room and swung the bag up onto the table with one arm, making a heavy thud.

'Why?' she asked again. 'Why are you doing this to me? What did I ever do to you?'

'To me? Nothing. I'm just doing my job, lady. Shit happens.' He hoisted Angel up where she'd slid down from his hip. 'Now get on with writing that note before I get pissed off.'

Gaby picked up the pen again and tried to think of a way to get the message across – this was not her doing, not her in control. There was no way she would dream of committing suicide. The last few months had been hellish, but she loved her husband and she lived and breathed for her daughter. Surely Lockie knew that. Her mother would know it too. She would know Gaby could never leave her Angel.

Gaby made herself stand up. She watched the man's muscles tense, then relax when he realised she was reaching across the table to the box of tissues by the window. She looked outside, but there was no one there, no hope of rescue. It was up to her. Tissues in hand, Gaby sat back down, then blew her nose hard. She shoved the used tissues into the pocket of her track pants, and cursed herself for not putting the secret note in there too. Too late now. Or maybe he would have found it anyway.

She took a deep breath and set her mind to the note. She wrote the words with deliberation, and managed to minimise the shaking of her hand. She only hoped it was enough. Enough for Lockie to know it wasn't right, wasn't her.

'There you are, you bastard. One fucking note.'

'I'm glad you've decided to play the game,' he said, and moved around beside her.

Gaby held her breath as he looked the note over.

'That'll do the job,' he said. 'See, it wasn't so bad.' He patted her on the head as if she were a pet puppy, and she flinched away from his touch.

Angel had started to writhe and grizzle. She lurched over, arms outstretched for her mother. Gaby reached up to take her, but the man pulled the child back against his body, moved around to the other side of the table and set Angel down in the chair opposite.

'Now what?' Gaby asked, voice flat. She sat, shoulders hunched, hands limp where they had dropped in her lap. The black tool bag was on the table between them, another barrier to her Angel.

'Now we get to work,' he said.

He completely unzipped the bag, and she watched as he pulled out a small rolled bag and placed it just out of Angel's inquisitive reach. Then he reached back in and pulled out a large bundle of black fabric. He shook it out to its full size and tossed it down onto the carpet. Gaby's heart leaped in her chest, bile rose up into her throat: she had seen enough movies to recognise a body bag when she saw one.

'This is what you are going to do,' the man said, as he unrolled the first small bag. It contained several syringes, vials and a prescription box of tablets all in their own pockets. 'I am going to give you an injection, but I will make it as painless as possible. If you struggle, if you do not do exactly as I ask, I will kill your daughter and make it look like you did it. If you cooperate and just let this happen, she'll be left alone.'

Gaby looked across the table to where her beautiful Angel was investigating the bag. She blinked back the tears, but this time couldn't halt their path down her cheeks.

'How can I trust you to leave her?' she said in a small voice.

'Lady, what choice do you have?'

Gaby watched as he drew up a dose from the vial with businesslike precision. For a moment she wondered if she could jump him – grab the syringe and stab him in the neck with the bloody thing. But he was too big, Angel too close. He knew exactly what he was doing, and she was just another job.

'Go and get a glass of water,' he said.

Gaby looked up as he moved around behind Angel and pointed the loaded syringe at her shoulder. The child was distracted at play with the empty vial and went to put it in her mouth.

'Uh-uh, Angel, yucky. That's not for eating.' Gaby said it without thought, and stood up, hand reaching out to grab the vial from her daughter's fingers.

'Get the fucking water!'

Her hand dropped.

She went into the kitchen and got a glass out of the cupboard. As she walked across to the sink, her eyes darted to the knife rack on the counter. She looked back up at the man and her eyes met his. He gazed back, eyebrows arched in question, and then combed his fingers gently through Angel's hair. Gaby pulled her eyes away and filled the glass with water. She walked back to the table and sat down with her hand clawed around the tumbler.

He tossed her the box of tablets. She misjudged the catch and they bounced off her chest to clatter onto the table.

'Take some. Five or six will do.'

Her hands shook as she opened the box and managed to pop four of the tablets out of their foil strip into her hand; another slipped out and onto the floor.

'Pick it up.'

She bent down, and the tablet danced through slippery fingers before she managed to trap it. Gaby sat back up and shook off the giddiness that swept over her. She carefully placed the tablet next to the others and glanced at the label on the box before stopping dead. The prescription was in her name.

'What the hell? What have I done? Why is this happening to me? What the hell have I done to deserve this? For God's sake, tell me.'

'I don't know, lady. I just do the job and collect the money. Now shut the fuck up and take the fucking tablets.' He yanked on Angel's hair and pointed the syringe at her exposed throat.

'No!' Gaby screamed and jumped to her feet. Angel had erupted with a screech, her tiny arms flailing desperately at the hand that pulled her hair. She rubbed at her head when finally the man let go, her face a blotch of pink, her mouth dropped. 'I'll take them, I'll take them,' Gaby gasped. She threw the tablets into her mouth and tried hard not to gag as she washed them down with the full glass of water. Then, arms outstretched, she pleaded for her daughter.

'Please let me hold her. Please.'

'Not yet.' He jerked his head towards the lounge. 'Go and lie down on the sofa.'

With barely obedient legs, Gaby walked around the end of the table and into the lounge. How could Angel grow up thinking her mother killed herself and abandoned her? Fresh tears wound their way down her face.

No.

She wouldn't do this, couldn't do this without a fight.

Before her resolve fled, she wheeled around and with a cry launched herself at the man.

The response was immediate and brutal.

He dropped Angel to the floor; she erupted into a scream that tore through Gaby's heart. The massive hands reached out and stopped Gaby dead, wrapped around the fabric at her throat, lifted her off the ground and propelled her backwards, her legs pedalling pointlessly in the air. He threw her into the sofa with a strength that forced the air out of her lungs, and then, with shocking speed, strode back to Angel and yanked her up by the hair.

'You stupid bitch,' he bellowed. 'Do you want me to hurt her? Do you?'

He dropped the pink-faced child, shocked by now into silence, onto the floor again. Then he was standing over Gaby once more, syringe back in his hand, his face twisted with anger.

'Lie down and keep fucking still.'

All fight evaporated.

Gaby's eyes couldn't leave her daughter's as she pulled her legs up and then stretched her body out along the sofa.

'Keep fucking still,' he growled, as he jabbed the needle through her clothes into the flesh of her buttock and then slowly pushed the plunger down. Gaby could feel where the liquid entered, a cold stream against the warmth of her body, a venom commencing its deadly path. The sting lingered well after he withdrew the needle.

It was done.

Gaby looked up to her killer, gazed squarely into his eyes and asked, 'Can I hold her now?'

He turned away and, to her relief, walked over, picked up Angel, brought her over and laid her on Gaby's chest. At last she had Angel safe in her arms. But she knew there was nothing she could do. Already the effects of the drug were apparent; she could feel inertia creep over her as it pervaded her entire system.

She hugged and stroked her Angel as she repeatedly whispered, 'I love you, Angel, Mummy loves you, I'm so sorry, I love you so much.'

Gaby quietly sobbed. Then she buried her face in Angel's hair, and rocked and cried herself to sleep.

1

The cellphone ring snapped me out of my trance. Well, it didn't ring, strictly speaking. It performed an electronic abomination that would have made Bach scream with indignation.

'Ah, God damn it.'

I slowed up, pulled the phone from my running-shorts pocket and gulped in a few quick breaths.

'Shephard.'

'Gore Watch House.'

It would have to be work. They could find you anywhere.

'Hi. What's up?'

'We have had a missing person report come in. Wyndham Road. Are you able to attend?'

Wyndham Road? I knew several people down there. I glanced down at my watch and calculated it would take another ten minutes to run home.

'Yes, I can be there. It could be half an hour, though. You caught me out on a run. What number?'

'One fifty-three. The Knowes household.'

'Knowes?' Lockie? Missing? My heart rate jumped up again.

'Yes, the reported person missing is Mrs Gabriella Knowes. Mr Knowes called it in.'

'Thanks. I'll be there soon.' I hung up, tucked the phone back in, then set off at a jog in the direction of home. My quiet little wind-down after work was out the window.

Gaby Knowes? At least it wasn't Lockie. Curious, though: he wasn't the kind of man to panic if the wife was late home and there was no dinner on the table. And it was only 5.15pm. He must have only just got in from work and called the police straight away.

As the sole-charge policewoman at the Mataura station, it was my lot to be on call more often than not. But call-outs after hours were a rarity now. When I lived at the police house behind the station, I was fair game for the slightest gripe at any hour of the day, or night. The situation had improved only when I moved to a flat and put some distance between me and the job. Nowadays call-outs were usually for a fracas at the pub or a minor car accident – something quick to sort out.

I looked up at the horizon, judged that there were, at best, two or three hours of light left and took off at a trot, preferring the regularity of running on the road rather than on the scraggy roadside gravel and overgrown grass, and having to dodge the matchstick roadside markers. There was only the odd car to worry about, and they generally gave me a big swerve. Occasionally, I'd get some idiot who'd almost force me into the drainage ditch, but they were the exception around here. For the most part, farming folk were very polite. I knew most of the occupants of the houses on the outskirts of town. Molly Polglaise had lost her husband of forty-five years only a few weeks back; her granddaughter had moved in for a month or so as consolation company. The smell of her freshly trimmed macrocarpa hedge reminded me of Christmas. The Mayberry household had a new baby. John, who was out watering the garden, gave me an absent-minded wave as I passed. Considering it had rained the day before, I wasn't quite sure why he was bothering.

Mataura was quintessential small-town New Zealand, although if I was being honest, it was a slightly shabbier and more run-down version of it. Like most towns, it struggled to provide employment and ways to entice the young folk to stay. How could it compete with the excitement of the city? It had a smattering of pubs, stores – mostly empty – and churches: the main ingredients for life in the sticks, although the pubs saw a lot more patronage than the churches. I knew the area intimately, and its residents. That included Lockie Knowes, though I hadn't had more than a passing conversation with him for an age. The fact I'd avoided him probably had something to do with that. Since he'd married the city girl and settled down to do the family thing, I'd pretty much sidestepped any contact – an achievement in itself, given the size of the town and my job. Now it looked like a good dose of professional detachment would be required. I would have to ignore the tightness in my stomach.

I slowed up the pace only when I reached the gateway to my house and its slightly skewiff letter box. Running was my vice – freedom of the road, isolation, being able to tune out everything but the rhythmic rush of blood pumping and powerful breathing. A legal high.

Bugger the telephone.

The sight of Lockie Knowes' house evoked visions of the British Country Living dream – elegant villa, white picket fence, perfectly groomed gardens surrounding a lush lawn, wisteria-draped veranda, bounding dog, radiant wife holding cherubic child. Well, it would have been if there hadn't been a problem with the wife.

I parked the police four-wheel drive on the grass verge and listened to the gravel crunch underfoot as I walked up the driveway. Lockie must have been lying in wait, as I'd barely made it past the letter box when he came out to meet me, his daughter, Angel, resting on his hip. He wasn't what you would call classically handsome, but being tall and muscular, with rugged, well-worn features, his presence demanded attention. He certainly got mine. I was shocked to see the straight-out fear etched in his eyes; its potency overrode any potential awkwardness.

'Lockie, what's up?'

'Something is really badly wrong, Sam. I just don't know what to do. Do I go looking or wait at home? Then there's Angel – what do I do with her?' One hand held a little too tightly on Angel's leg; his free hand tugged at his hair. This was a Lockie I'd never seen.

'Slow down. Tell me from the beginning. I take it you'd just got home from work? What happened?'

'She wasn't here, she was nowhere. I walked in, and nothing. She's always home. What's worse was Angel. She was asleep in the middle of the floor – filthy crappy nappy, and just lying there on the floor.

At first I thought she was dead. My God, I panicked. I grabbed her, gave her a hell of a fright – thank God, she was OK. But no Gaby.'

I guided him back towards the house. 'It's getting a bit cool out here. Let's get inside.' Angel was wearing only a singlet and I could see tiny goosebumps on her arms. 'You've checked everywhere, she hasn't just left a message and…?'

Lockie's face crumpled. 'There was a note.'

'What kind of note?' I hoped my voice sounded neutral.

'I don't know, I don't know what to think. I don't want to think it.'

I kicked my boots off at the door and followed him into the house. The carpet looked new; it smelled new too. The place was a mess. Toys everywhere, clothes strewn – it looked like a hurricane had hit. By the description Lockie had given, it was probably hurricane Angel, left to her own devices. I picked my way through the rubble and followed Lockie to the table. He stopped and pointed at a lone piece of paper on an otherwise clear surface. I moved around to get a look at it.

My dearest Lachlan, I'm so sorry. Look after Angelica. I love you both. Gabriella.

'Shit, Lockie.' Not good. Again, I forced my voice to remain neutral 'This was sitting on the table?'

He just nodded.

'OK. Sit down.'

He sat. He was still holding Angel, as if he feared she too would disappear into the ether.

'Have you rung anyone? Family, friends?' I had a few ideas of my own, but to be honest, I didn't think Gaby Knowes had many friends.

'I rang her mum in Queenstown. She's on her way. I don't know her friends' phone numbers.'

'Has she ever gone off and left Angel before? Been missing before?' I approached that one carefully. I had to ask.

'No, no, she'd never do that, to me or especially to Angel. She wouldn't even leave Angel in the car alone to go into the store; she'd always get her out in case some lunatic stole the car or hit it. She's

always cautious, overly cautious. She would never leave Angel alone.'
He brushed his fingers through Angel's hair and kissed the top of her
head as she nuzzled in closer to him. 'This is so unlike her. Something has happened to her, I know it. This, this,' he gestured around
him, 'it's just not her.'

'What about around the house? Is her car gone? Purse? Shoes?
Where was the dog? Does it look like she popped out on an errand?'
It was a bit rapid fire, and Lockie looked a touch overwhelmed, but
my mind was racing through the possibilities.

'Radar was shut off in the spare room. Made a hell of a noise when
he heard me come home, poor guy.'

'Would Gaby normally put him in there?'

'Well, no, he's got a kennel by the garage. She'd put him in there
if she was going out.'

'So what about her car?'

'It's in the garage. I didn't think to see if her purse was here.' He
stood up and disappeared down the hallway to search.

It didn't look good. That note could have meant Gaby had buggered off and left them, or worse, she'd decided to kill herself – but
that hardly seemed likely. Firstly, she didn't seem the type, if there
was such a thing. Who really knew what was going on behind people's façades? But mainly, she had a great husband and a gorgeous
little girl. You would have to be pretty bloody desperate to leave
that. I scanned the room. Other than the massive toy mess, nothing
seemed to be amiss. Furniture seemed properly positioned and there
were no obvious signs of a struggle, no blood. I looked up as Lockie
came back into the living room. He had a handbag.

'That's her only one?' I asked.

'No, she's got a few, but it's got her purse in it.' His voice shook.

'Cellphone there?'

'Yeah.'

'Shoes?'

'I think they're all there, I'm not really sure. She could have more.
She's a woman, after all.' It was a valiant attempt at humour.

Angel was starting to whinge and wriggle; she pushed her tiny hands against her father's chest to get away from his grasp.

'Have you had a chance to give Angel her dinner yet?' Feeding her might at least stop the whining and distract Lockie for a moment.

'No, I just changed her and gave her a biscuit.' His chin quivered again.

'Why don't you get her some dinner and get her ready for bed while I make a few phone calls,' I said. He looked relieved and headed into the kitchen, talking away quietly to Angel. I guessed to comfort himself as much as her.

The telephone calls didn't serve much purpose. The two people I thought Gaby might contact had not seen or heard from her. If that note read the way it looked, she would not have wanted to see people anyway. She was either long gone or dead already. I looked through the living-room window and could see the light was beginning to fade. Could we mount a search tonight?

'Fuck,' I heard Lockie exclaim.

'What is it?'

He was standing in the kitchen, staring at the sink. From behind him I could see a prescription box and empty tablet strips in the bottom of the sink, next to a large glass. Lockie was frozen to the spot and I had to shove him out of the way.

'Excuse me, I need to get a proper look.'

Hypnovel. A sleeper. I recognised the name: my mum used to take them on the odd occasion. The pills had been made out in Gaby's name and, going by the date, dispensed only the previous day. The box indicated there would have been thirty tablets. This changed things dramatically. I was pretty sure that wouldn't be a good thing in one hit.

'Did you know Gaby was taking sleeping tablets?' I said.

'No, no, she wasn't. She wouldn't have. I would have noticed. Anyway, she's still breastfeeding.' He ran his hands through his hair, intensifying his expression of misery. 'God, she wouldn't have a glass of wine, let alone tablets. She wouldn't have taken anything if she thought it could harm Angel; even Panadol she thought twice about. No, there's no way she'd have been taking those.'

That was emphatic.

'Did she have any medical conditions?' I asked. The image of Gaby lying unconscious and dying under some bush barged its way into my mind, and I made a conscious effort to push it aside in favour of objectivity. Dramatics wouldn't serve anyone.

'No, healthy and, I thought, happy.' He reached out to pick up the tablet strips, but I placed my hand on his arm to stop him. 'Sorry, Lockie, I'll need to keep those as evidence, and also the note.'

I looked around the rest of the kitchen. It was pretty tidy other than the tablets in the sink, some dishes, baking on cooling racks and the beginnings of Angel's dinner on the counter.

'I'm going to pop out to the truck to get my kit and have a look around outside. You get Angel organised and into bed, then we can sit down and plan what to do. You can do that?'

'Yeah.' The strain in his voice was obvious.

Even after all these years, the urge to nurture him overwhelmed. But it was not the time, or the place. I turned, headed for the front door and flicked on the outside light switch on the way past. It would be getting dark soon enough. I jogged down the driveway, and a sense of urgency overtook me. When was the last time anyone had spoken to Gaby? When did she scull those tablets? I collected the kit and torch from the police truck, then methodically worked my way over the yard and surrounds.

The Knowes' house was separated from its neighbours' by 150 metres or so in each direction. There were several large trees, macrocarpa and totara, which acted as a framework for the traditional garden. Rectangular beds of roses and perennials flanked each side of the long gravel driveway; a lavender hedge bordered the veranda. Everything was neat and well maintained. Someone clearly loved gardening, and previous experience told me it wasn't Lockie. He only liked gardening if it involved chainsaws and RoundUp. I didn't get why people would want to emulate the perfect British country garden in New Zealand. Me, I was all for native plants, the sort that drew in the birds – cabbage trees, flaxes, kowhais, toetoe – nothing too prissy, but even I had to admit the Knowes garden was beautiful: structured and open with plenty of well-manicured lawn. From a more practical but slightly sinister standpoint there were no dense areas of bushes or shrubbery that could conceal a person. I moved around behind the house to the garage. Radar was there in his kennel and run. He gave a token woof as I approached, but that was it. I gave him a scratch under his chin as he came up to sniff me.

'You're a great guard dog, I see,' I said in that special voice saved for babies or pets. 'You're just a big lump of porridge. I think you'd lick an intruder to death.' He reinforced my view by giving my hand a thorough cleaning. I scanned the back of the section. Again, the view was unimpeded and visibility helped by a full moon on the rise.

I hadn't realised how close the house was to the water. I walked to the back of the section, through a dense row of agapanthus – standard issue on rural properties – and up to the wire and batten fence. There was only another twenty metres or so of long grass down to the Mataura river. The surface wasn't visible from where I stood, just a dark slash in the dim-lit landscape where it cut its path through the fields, but I could hear its gurgling song. I walked along the fence line until I reached a wooden strainer post and then climbed over. From there it was long grass and the occasional broom bush to negotiate.

Once at the edge there was a four- or five-metre drop down to the water, which, at this point, stretched thirty metres across to the far side. The bank wasn't too steep though. I stood, hands on hips; I watched the rippled reflection of the moon as it marked time in the steady current, listened to the river's accompaniment. It seemed a possibility. Drug yourself up to the eyeballs, then ease down into the river. Drowning was supposed to be a reasonably gentle way to go; numbed by hypnotics, it would be a pain-free way out.

The path from the house to here was not difficult. I worked my way down the slope to the water's edge. There was a slick of dew on the grass, so it took a bit of care not to slip over. Gaby could have made this trip earlier in the day when the grass was dry, so even if the drugs had started to kick in she could easily have managed it. For that matter, she could have walked down to the river, waited for the sleepiness, then slipped in. The fence was the only obstacle, but if I could do it, Gaby, who was half a foot taller again, wouldn't have any problem. I looked around and didn't notice any obvious tracking in the grass to the river's edge, but light was poor and decisions had to be made.

I looked down at my watch. It was just after 6pm. Could I muster up a search party tonight? I crouched down and ran my hand in the water; the ripples' concentric circles fractured the reflected moon. The water was frigid, even for this time of year. If there was even a remote possibility Gaby was still alive, I had to pursue it, and quick.

I'd ring Bill Stevenson to see if he could get a jet boat out onto the water. I knew he didn't take them out in the pitch black, but it was a clear evening and with the full moon visibility might be good enough. The Eastern Southland Search and Rescue group had had a night-training session less than a month ago; they'd be sure to help. With them and some of the locals, we'd have a sizeable search party, and soon.

Still, time was not on Gaby's side.

2

A crisis in a small town and everyone wanted to help; it was one of the beauties of a rural community. Within twenty-five minutes of the call going out, the jet boat was in the water, working its way upstream from near Wyndham, and the pub had disgorged itself of patrons eager to join in the search. I'd also called in for back-up from the Gore police station, thirteen kilometres up the road; my Mataura community station came under its umbrella.

I was now walking knee deep in damp grass along the river's edge. A ballet of torchlight criss-crossed the fields and groves along the bank, a scene repeated on the far side of the dark and now ominous Mataura. I shivered, not just from the chill that seeped through my damp trousers. The river proved difficult to search on foot. Often, we had to clamber back up the bank and over farm fences when faced with a scarp or impassable scrub. At least the jet boat made better progress. The water level was higher than normal, making for an easy passage. Bill had promised one quick sweep of the river while there was still some light, then he'd get out again at first light if needed. But the Mataura was never straightforward to search, with banks of willows, and coal benches which jutted out beneath the water and could conceal a body. I began to hope the gamble of a search of the river wasn't a waste of time. What if there was some other simple explanation?

Despite the oddity of the note, there was a part of me that still fervently hoped Gaby Knowes would turn up at home, returning from a friend's place, having lost all track of time. That all she'd have to do was live down the stigma of having abandoned her child for a few Chardonnays and a gossip session with the girls. It was a futile fantasy. Instinct told me Gaby was already dead and it was now a matter of when we found the body, not if. Bodies that didn't beach straight away invariably popped up after seven days, when the gases from decomposition finally built up enough to make them float in our chilly southern waters. My predecessor had had the task of searching for a couple of people who had died after going into the river off the Mataura bridge.

This was my first.

It was by far the most serious event I'd encountered in the time I'd been on the beat in Mataura. Other than the scuffles of those who worked hard and played hard, life here was ordered and mundane. The country had a gentle rhythm that revolved around the milking habits of its dairy herds, and the shifts at the freezing works. Most of my time was spent in the investigation of farm equipment and vehicle theft. There was a lucrative black market for motorbikes, quad bikes and other small farm vehicles – they were plentiful in districts like this, with the trend towards lifestyle blocks and townies looking for a slice of rural paradise. Down shifters, they euphemistically called them; bloody nuisances was more accurate. And probably a bit harsh, but the locals did take a while to warm to new residents: just look at Gaby Knowes. The rat-race refugees had a standard-issue uniform, which included a quad bike to go with the Aertex shirt and Hunter Wellington gumboots. The bikes were easy pickings for both the opportunist and the more organised criminal element. Fortunately, the latter didn't hit here often. A strong rural Neighbourhood Watch had made a decent impact on theft.

My head jerked upwards in response to a distant report, and my eyes followed the graceful red arc of a flare against the night sky. It would have been beautiful had it not been for the sense of foreboding.

'Shit,' I muttered.

I called across to Dave Garret, who was working to my left. 'That'll be the jet boat; they must have found something. What do you think? That would be a good K away?'

'At least.'

'The terrain is pretty crap from here. I'm going to climb back up there and run along the road till I find them. You and the others continue along the bank, just in case.'

'Yeah, sure, Sam. We'll catch up soon enough.'

I was right: once I'd climbed the bank, the road was only two fences and twenty metres away. I negotiated the fences and set off at a run in the direction of the flare, my eyes straining for any sight of the boat. The road was higher than the river and I was afraid I'd miss it. The moonlight helped to some extent, but it was still difficult to distinguish bank from bush from animal. I didn't like running at night at the best of times, but in these circumstances, and with my breath unnaturally loud in the darkness, I was more than a little creeped out.

At last I caught a glimpse of light down to my right. It had taken just over five minutes to get here. The spot was downstream from an area known as Sam's Grief. Appropriate. I made my way across the paddock towards the bank; the sheep did not approve of my intrusion and flocked to a distant corner. At least they were sheep, and not cattle, or worse, deer. From this distance, I could now see the pools of torchlight that illuminated a prone figure on the bank, as still as the dark hump of the jet boat parked near by. I swallowed hard. It had to be her.

Another realisation hit. Shit, I was on the wrong side of the river. I climbed the fence, then, with as much control as I could muster in the wet grass, slid down the bank to the river's edge. Its once pleasant sound now seemed malicious. A beam of torchlight from across the water struck me in the eyes, then descended to my boots.

'Is that you, Sam?'

'Yes, it's me. Is it shallow enough for me to get across here, or will I have to go back to the bridge?'

'Wait there, I'll come over and get you.'

A portly figure detached itself from the group and walked over to the boat. The roar of the engine ripped the air, and I was startled, even though I had expected it. Bill Stevenson pulled alongside and, with skill, managed to hold the boat steady while I leaped on board.

'Thanks,' I said. That was the extent of conversation. The journey to the other side took mere seconds. I got out, straightened my clothes, drew a deep breath and walked over to the group. I was acutely aware of the squelching sound my boots made as I came near; there were no voices to mask it. Then the circle opened to admit me: I may have been acknowledged, but I had eyes only for what lay at its heart. I knelt beside the pitiful figure of Gabriella Knowes where she lay face down in the sand, her clothes plastered to her motionless body. She had landed in a small shallow, with her head and chest on the silt-covered stones and her hips and legs still in the water. I reached out for her throat and felt for a pulse I knew would not be found. Her skin felt cold and waxen, and I pulled my hand away, repulsed by the touch of death. I had seen dead bodies before, some as a result of violence, but most in their beds, where gentle old age had claimed them with dignity, not crudely like this, strewn as flotsam. I stood up and examined the array of faces around me. Some were solemn and subdued and looked anywhere but at the body. Others stared at her with a morbid fascination that I found disturbing and voyeuristic. I shuddered.

'Gentlemen,' I said, to draw their attention. 'Thank you for coming out tonight to search for Gaby.' Their focus was now on me and I felt an unspoken pressure to say something appropriate to the occasion. 'I know it will be small comfort to Lockie now, but we have found her. He will be able to grieve for her, instead of forever wondering what happened. He will be grateful to every one of you for stepping up to help at such short notice. As you can understand, there will be an investigation as to the exact circumstances of this tragedy. This will be done with as much sensitivity as possible, but this is a small town and everyone knows the Knowes family, so please show them your compassion. They will need it.' I hoped they would get the hint to keep speculation and idle gossip to themselves. 'Who found her?'

'Me. It was me.' It was the quiet voice of Craig Stevenson. Poor Craig. He was only seventeen and, to judge by the bloodshot eyes, overwhelmed by the evening's events.

I laid a hand on his arm. 'Thanks, Craig. That must have been bloody hard for you. We all appreciate it, we really do. Has she been moved at all or is this how you found her?'

'She was lying like that, but we pulled her clothes down over her a bit.' He sniffed back the tears and his dad put a big arm around his shoulders.

'That's OK. She would have appreciated your giving her some dignity. Thank you. I'm going to take some photographs, then we'll cover her over.'

By now more searchers had been drawn to the area, like moths to a flame. The danger was they'd trample heavily over the ground, obscuring possibly vital evidence. The Gore officers hadn't yet arrived at the site – I hoped they wouldn't be long.

'Thank you again.' I spoke as loud as I could, but out of respect for Gaby I didn't want to yell. 'If you can all go straight back to The Arms as arranged, I will be there as soon as possible to say a few words. It's a real plus that we've found her this quick. Now we must do all we can for Lockie and Angel and give Gaby some privacy.'

People began to turn and take their leave. It was a relief to see them go. I scanned the remaining faces for anyone familiar. Bill Stevenson was a responsible bloke; Trevor Ray was there too, a local farmer and community leader who I could entrust with this task. 'Bill, I will need you to stay with her – and you too, Trev, while I go and tell Lockie. The Gore officers will be here soon to take over. Does anyone have a vehicle near by?'

Colin Avery did; he offered to give me a ride back to the Knowes' house. Cole was Lockie's best mate and I knew I'd be glad of his moral support. God knew Lockie would need him.

Meantime, there was a preliminary scene examination to do. I took photographs, careful to cover every millimetre, every angle, as best I could in the dark. Although there were a lot of footprints around, I was grateful the searchers had kept at a decent distance from the body. The body. It seemed such an impersonal way to look at it, but for now I simply couldn't afford to consider the personal side of things. I crouched down and looked closely at Gaby. She had no obvious signs of injury; there was no blood, only a few scrapes, as you'd expect on someone who'd washed up from a river. Her hair and the clothes that were out of the water weren't sodden, merely damp, which suggested she'd been washed up for a while – the dew must have moistened them again. I stood up and looked in the direction of the road. The spot where she lay must have been obscured, otherwise a passing motorist would have seen her. Then I took the lightweight tarp out of my backpack, bent forward and reverently covered her. A prayer or something seemed in order, even though religion wasn't my thing. I whispered a 'God bless your soul, Gaby,' so nobody could overhear. I straightened up and looked at the small group that hovered behind.

'Thanks, guys, for staying here with her. I'll be back as soon as possible, but first I have to break the news to Lockie before he hears it from anyone else. You got enough torches?'

'Yeah, Sam, we'll be right. We'll make sure she's OK,' Trev said.

It was a bit late for OK, but I knew what Trev was trying to say and appreciated it. I could tell from the shake in his hands he was upset by it all. I didn't like to leave the scene without proper police guard – it wasn't exactly protocol – but tonight, Lockie's needs outweighed all else.

'Thanks, guys. We'll all have earned our beer tonight.' I arched over and stretched out my back. A mental checklist of procedures and people to contact worked through my mind.

Who was it who said, 'Be careful what you wish for'? Not that long ago I had yearned for a bit more excitement in my work. Now it had arrived, it wasn't all it was cracked up to be. To break a major crime ring: that was my idea of excitement. The base reality of Gaby Knowes' body in the silt was all too personal. I was from a farming family, where the cycle of life and death played out in a no-nonsense, down-to-earth fashion every day. But even that had not prepared me for this. Still, it was some comfort to be able to slip into the authoritative, take-charge role. It meant I didn't have to examine my underlying feelings – for now, anyway.

3

It was after ten when I finally made it back to The Arms, the designated and pleasantly shabby mustering point. The pub was full, but its usual happy buzz had been replaced by a sombre hum. It had been a hard night for everyone. The on-call doctor from Gore had been called out to certify Gaby's death; the duty funeral director had removed her body. She was to be transported directly to Southland Hospital in Invercargill to await a post-mortem.

Lockie had fallen, sucker-punched. Telling him about Gaby was the hardest thing I'd ever had to do. I was grateful to leave Cole at the house with him, because, to be frank, Lockie's grief was more than I could handle. The last few hours had proven I still felt too much for him, and my calm façade would have given way to stress fractures.

God, I needed a beer.

I waded my way towards the bar through the weary crowd. They were all here, united in community to help one of their own – the search-and-rescue squad, jet boaters, Lockie's workmates and townsfolk who had answered the call for help. A few words of thanks were in order, and a bit of a debrief. I could already see there were some who would struggle to cope with what they'd witnessed tonight, though a few drinks would no doubt take the edge off.

I found the bar and leaned over to Pat Buchanan to ask if I could use it as an impromptu podium. I'd always joked that one day I'd get rollicking and dance on the bar. Well, tonight I'd get to stand on it, for a far more sober reason.

><

'Nice speech, Shep,' Maggie said, as she raised her glass in salute. 'You handled that one well, considering. There were a few tears shed, especially when you talked about the community embracing that poor wee girl.'

'Yeah, Angel and Lockie are going to be the focus of attention for all the wrong reasons. I hope everyone here got the message to keep the rumour-mongering at bay. Small town – all the theories of how and why will come out now. Everyone will have an opinion; I just hope people keep them to themselves. It's the last thing that family needs.'

'One can live in hope. Sit down, girl. You've had one hell of a night.'

'Oh, and you get the understatement-of-the-year award. Bloody hell, they never told us about this in Police College.' Well, actually they had, but naïve little idealists that we were, we thought they must have been talking about what happened in other towns. I slumped down into the armchair opposite my favourite flatmate. Actually, she was my only flatmate, but she was favourite right now because of the beer she'd put on its matching cardboard coaster near by. 'Man, do I need this,' I said, picking it up, 'and several of its mates. I'm still on call, but I'm sure no one will begrudge me. Here's to everyone,' I drank deeply, then made myself set the glass back down before its entire contents disappeared. It was better to pace myself.

'How was he?' Maggie asked, after a bit of a pause.

A flashback of the moment flooded my brain and I couldn't help but shudder.

'Beyond description.' I scrunched my eyes closed, trying to blot out the memory. 'He kept saying I must be wrong, that I'd made a mistake, that it couldn't be Gaby. He wanted me to go and check again. It took a bit to get it through to him. God, I even thought I might have to ring his doctor for a while there – he was distraught to the point of collapse. And the poor sod's got to tell his mother-in-law when she arrives.' I took another swig of the beer. 'Cole's there with him, though. He managed to calm him down a bit. I think he's going to crash on the sofa for the night. Lockie's going to need all the support he can get.'

'And how are you?' Maggie asked slowly.

'Oh yeah. OK, a bit tired, and I've got a lot of work to do tonight yet.'

'That's not what I meant, and you know it.'

I knew where this was going, but wasn't about to make it easy for her. 'What exactly do you mean then?'

'Come on, you've still got a candle burning for Lockie, even after all these years. You can't tell me you didn't have mixed emotions tonight.' Maggie leaned forwards, elbows on knees, and eyeballed me. 'We both know you were jealous of Lockie marrying that girl. You didn't exactly proclaim your approval of his choice of wife. So, get it off your chest: how are you?'

'Put it like that and I sound like a bitch, thanks.'

'I'm only trying to help you clear your head. You're going to need it in the next few days.' She reached out her hand to pat my knee.

I was eternally grateful to have found a friend like Maggie. She was upfront and shot from the hip. She had that wonderful knack of knowing just what to say at the right time. It was not always comfortable to hear, but she was usually right.

'Ah crap, can we talk about this later?'

'I thought you were going to be busy later.'

I had to concede that point.

'OK.' I drew a large breath and then blew it out between reluctant lips. 'At first, when she was reported missing, I thought, yeah, that would be typical – bloody townie girl buggering off and leaving the kid alone. I was pleased in a way, as it proved my opinion of her. It was like, hah, that's what you get for passing up on me. Now she's dead, I feel like a bit of a bloody heel.'

'You still think he should have married you, then?' Maggie asked.

'Of course I bloody do. Didn't everyone?' I drained the last of my beer, and peered with regret at the bottom of my glass. Maggie indicated towards the bar with the universal sign for 'another?' – to which I felt obliged to shake my head. I set my glass back down on the table. 'My parents were so convinced we'd be perfect, they went into a period of mourning when he left. As you can imagine, I was interrogated as to what dreadful thing I'd done to drive him away, as, of course, it was entirely my fault because not only did the sun shine out of his arse, but his farts fixed the hole in the bloody ozone. I must have been seriously defective not to be able to keep hold of the man. Now they've given up on my ever finding a husband and producing offspring, me being twenty-eight and past my use-by date and all. In fact, it's bloody lucky I haven't got a younger sister or they'd be pulling a Shakespearean trick on her: "Sorry, lovey, can't marry you off till we've got rid of the old baggage." They're bloody diabolical.'

Maggie laughed. 'OK, sorry I asked. Bit of a sore point still, huh?'

'Comes up in some way or form in every conversation. They're dependable there. That's why they call them "salt of the earth": it hurts like hell when they rub in open wounds.' I sighed again and slouched further down into the chair.

'If it really bugs you, why don't you tell them to sod off?'

'All that would do is offend them and reinforce their opinion of me. Infuriating as they are, they are my olds and ninety percent lovely. I think they believe that if they marry me off, I'll give up this job, settle down, have brats and conform to the little-wifey mould they always aspired to. Men do the macho stuff, women stay at home – or, if they work, they do nice things like teaching or nursing. They sure as hell don't join the police.' I loved my parents, but their stereotypical views were well and truly entrenched. It didn't help that they were overprotective of their little girl. If I'd been six-foot tall and built like something out of a Scandinavian opera, I'm sure they'd have seen things in a different way. The fact that I just scraped in over five foot and barely made the minimum stature requirements for the police did nothing to reassure them I'd keep safe.

'Well, you can see their point, you being so helpless and all.'

'Yeah. Oh ha, bloody ha.'

I had always been determined never to let my stature be a disadvantage. I'd thrown myself into sports, including martial arts and other forms of self-defence. Coming from a farm, I could drive any vehicle with an engine, including trucks and tractors. And I could hit a target with anything: ball, bullet, knife – hell, even an axe. I wasn't about to let my big brothers beat me. In fact, having brothers was an ideal way to toughen up. I'd had a lifetime of not being taken seriously because I was 'just a little thing' and it irked me something chronic. Sure, I overcompensated a bit with my smart-arse mouth: little-man syndrome. Sometimes it seemed the only way to get noticed. But otherwise I had to rely on feminine wiles and that other piece of equipment that people assumed I didn't possess – a brain. When I joined the police, it was the last thing people expected, which is precisely why I did it. OK, it wasn't the main reason, but it did come into consideration.

'Hello there, anybody home?' Maggie's voice pulled me back from my little reverie.

'Sorry, tuned out for a second there. I better get going – I've got paperwork to do tonight, then tomorrow will be hectic.'

'You'll be back to see Lockie, then?'

'Yeah, there's a lot to go through. It all looks cut and dried, but you can never make assumptions. There's the post-mortem tomorrow, and we'll need to get background and evidence of suicide before the case goes to the Coroner's Court. I should be home in an hour or so. If not, send out the search parties.'

I manoeuvred my way through the many patrons still at the bar, waved at and acknowledged those who said hi. It looked like a few of them were trying to deaden the night's memories with alcohol. Who could blame them? There were still a couple I wanted a quick word with, so I headed for the TV corner. Trevor Ray looked very much the worse for wear, slouched over the table and trying to look up at the wall-mounted TV screen at the same time. Can't have been comfortable. Bill and Craig Stevenson were with him.

'What's on the box?' I asked as I pulled up a spare seat.

'Just the late news,' Craig said. His hands rested around a glass of frothy amber liquid.

'I hope that's ginger ale in there, Craig,' I said in a mock stern voice. The blood rushed up his face as he mumbled something indecipherable.

His dad let out a snort. 'Of course.'

'Anything exciting?' I indicated towards the telly.

'Only if you like bad news,' Bill said. 'They're trying to scare us all stupid about the bird flu that's going to kill us, and to top it off they want to get us in a flap about the latest mad-cow outbreak in America. As if we haven't got enough to worry about.'

Trev giggled. 'Only mad cow you've got to worry about is your wife,' he mumbled, and I could tell by the glower from Bill that tonight he didn't see the funny side.

Trev's eyes were dozy and bloodshot, and I noted the tremor in his hands.

'OK, I can see you've had too much of a good thing tonight.' I addressed my next comment to Bill. 'He's not driving anywhere. Cole's at Lockie's; do you know if anyone's taking Trev home?'

'Already taken care of.' He pulled a set of car keys out of his pocket and jangled them around. I assumed them to be Trev's. 'Phillip Rawlings is out Trev's way. He'll do the honours.'

'Thank you,' I said. 'And thanks for everything tonight. I know you don't like the boat out in low light. You all did a great job.'

'Yeah, well I'm just glad we found her and poor Lockie isn't left wondering.'

'Yeah, me too.' I hauled myself to my feet and headed off towards the door. 'Night, guys.'

God, was I glad we'd found her. Alive would have been better, but at least Gaby wouldn't be a missing-persons file, to linger around for ages. Or worse – if we found her body two weeks down the track, only a couple of hundred metres from home or a few metres out of the search zone. That would have been my worst nightmare. My worst nightmare: bit of a selfish thought really. This was Lockie's worst nightmare. I shuddered. The sheer ferocity of Lockie's grief echoed in my head. Gaby was his wife and the mother of his child

– of course he would be upset – but some arrogant little child in the depths of my being was feeling a bit piqued that I'd never managed to evoke even a fraction of that kind of emotion out of him.

'You're a sick girl,' I murmured to myself as I stepped out into the dark.

4

Obscure dreams full of darkness and cloying dampness lingered at the edges of my consciousness, so even after two cups of coffee my mood was not good. It had been after one a.m. when I crawled into bed. I'd made a start on the requisite mountain of paperwork and compiled a 'to-do' list of scary proportions. It always amused me that on television shows police were never encumbered with such matters – bureaucracy- and paper-free zones. If only.

The first stop of the day would, of course, be Lockie's. Callous though it seemed, there were questions that needed to be asked, and many would not be palatable. I needed to establish a timeline of events and to delve into that question I knew would be ricocheting around Lockie's head – why?

I looked up from my half-eaten and now soggy bowl of cornflakes as Maggie breezed into the kitchen on her way to the door.

'Hi ho, hi ho, it's off to toil I go…' she sang, and lolled her head from side to side.

'If that's supposed to cheer me up, it's not working,' I said, giving her my very best forced smile.

'Great teeth.'

'Thanks.'

'What hour did you crawl in? I didn't hear you.'

'It was a bit on the late side, but I did make a good start on all the reports.'

She walked over to the table, leaned over and peered into my eyes.

'Yurgh, you might want to hide those haversacks under your eyes, unless you want to scare people into submission.'

I had noted their presence when I got brave and looked in the mirror this morning. Didn't need it pointed out, though.

'Oh ha-de ha-de ha. Bloody charming friend you turned out to be.'

I swatted at her like some pesky fly, but she dodged back out of the way. 'I wouldn't push it too far, Sunshine. I redefine the term grumpy.'

'You won't be the only one. I think there'll be a few people struggling this morning, judging by the amount of alcohol consumed last night. Due to demand, Pat stayed open a little longer than his liquor licence allowed. You're not going to arrest him, I hope?'

'I think the extenuating circumstances would allow for a bit of leeway,' I said, and smiled properly this time.

'My, that's a big word for this hour of the morning, even for you.'

'What? I?' I screwed up my nose at her and had the gesture repeated back as she headed for the door. 'Have a fun day,' I called after her.

'Yeah, yeah, yeah,' came the reply.

Maggie was a laboratory technician at the large meat-processing plant bang in the middle of town. It was by far the area's largest employer; in fact, the local economy was reliant on it. The closure of the pulp-and-paper mill in 2000, and the subsequent loss of around 150 jobs, were testament to the devastation of the loss of a core industry on a small community. Some people were absorbed by work available at the meat-processing plant and local factories, while others went on to boost the region's unemployment stats.

That reminded me. I called out just as she was about to close the door behind her. 'Hey Chook, have you heard anything more about work?'

She turned back to show me a slight grimace.

'Nothing official, only the same rumours doing the rounds about cost cutting. The money's on them centralising lab services to Invercargill, so let's just say I don't exactly feel secure in my world right now.'

The prospect of that had no appeal whatsoever.

'You do realise that even if they disestablish you and redundancy-alise your butt, you're not allowed to leave here, right? I thought I'd get in early and make myself quite clear.'

A smile ironed out her frown. 'How could I ever tear myself away from the bright lights and riveting nightlife? Nowhere else could compare. Your comments are noted, but, as in so many things in life, we shall see. Alas, I'm not calling the shots.'

'If worst comes to worst – which it's not allowed to, by the way – you could make your fortune here. Things are on the up in Mataura. You could start your own business doing…' I struggled for a suggestion before grasping at the sort of obvious. 'How's your trout fishing? There must be plenty of cash-laden tourists waiting to give some of it up for a Kiwi fly-fishing experience. It seems a popular business, so it must be a bit of a cash cow. You could handle that. Lure in a few American tourists, give them the sparkly clean-green-image thing, catch a few trout. How hard could it be?' I hoped I didn't sound too desperate, but the thought of life here without my good friend was not palatable.

'Well, the fish would be pretty safe, so I'd probably get myself sued. And anyway, I don't even like trout. Why anyone would want to eat something that tastes like the bottom of a river mystifies me. And on that cheery note, I must away.' She gave me a wave and exited stage left.

I looked up at the hideously cutesy Mickey Mouse clock on the wall – that thing really had to go. It was a little before nine a.m. As good a time as any to get on with it. I needed to pay a visit to a household in mourning. I slid the chair back from the table, picked up my dishes and after a detour via the kitchen sink, headed into the bathroom to brush my teeth. Not normally one for make-up anyway, I decided not to try to camouflage the telltale signs of a late night. I was sure to look better than those I was off to visit, and besides, my appearance was going to be the furthest thing from their minds. Any spruce-up would go unnoticed.

5

Once again, I pulled up outside the Knowes' house, and once again I parked on the grass verge, taking care not to end up in the ditch. I paused at the gate to take in the deceptively tranquil scene before me. Only the presence of several other vehicles in the driveway, including a rather impressive new Range Rover, signalled that all was not as normal. That vehicle had to belong to Gaby's mother – I'd heard Gaby's family were well-to-do. Her parents had moved to Queenstown from Auckland to be closer to her when she married Lockie. Her father was a company executive and flew back up north each week when needed. Nice for some.

Gravel crunched underfoot as I walked back up the driveway. This time, no one came out to meet me. I stepped up onto the veranda and rang the doorbell. It was only a moment before I could make out a distorted shape through the stained-glass panelled door. It was Colin Avery.

'Sam,' Cole said, swinging the door open wide to let me in.

I bent over to take off my boots. 'How's things this morning?'

'Much as can be expected.'

'That bad, huh?'

'Yup.'

'Thanks for staying with them. Lockie needed a mate around. What time did Gaby's mum get here?'

'Only quarter of an hour after you left.' He paused for a moment and waited until I was next to him. 'It was a very late night for us all.'

'What's her name, by the way?' I asked.

'Leonore. Leonore Watson.'

At the entrance to the lounge I stopped, aghast. I wouldn't have recognised it as the same room. Where last night there had been pandemonium, this morning there was pristine order. There was a small

pile of Angel's puzzle pieces, but otherwise the room – the whole
house – was lemon-scented spotless. Someone had been very indus-
trious. They still were, judging by the muffled sound of a distant
vacuum cleaner.

'Wow, who's been busy?' I asked Cole, who'd followed me into
the room.

'Leonore. She's been on the go, non-stop, since she got up.'

'I'm glad I took all those photos last night,' I said as I took in a scene
more *House & Garden* than family home. I had in fact toyed with the
idea of leaving it until the morning. That would have been a major
faux pas. Any trace of evidence looked like it would have been well
and truly sanitised. I made a mental note to self for future reference:
by the book, Sunshine, absolutely by the book. The higher echelons in
the district office were applying constant pressure to justify my exis-
tence here. Resources in the force were limited, and stretching the
budget by reducing the number of small stations was an obvious cost
cutter. Pencilling in more hours on traffic duty was another. I cringed.
It wouldn't do to make it easy for them by making basic errors.

I could understand where Leonore Watson was coming from;
I had witnessed exactly the same reaction in my mother in times
of high stress or tragedy. Busy, busy, busy. Clean, clean, clean. Do
anything other than accept the unfathomable had happened. Some
people just operated that way. My personal method for dealing with
stress involved dressing gowns, slippers, sofas and chocolate.

Involuntarily, I thought of my mother's response if I died. Despite
her well-constructed façade, her grief would be a yawning chasm,
inexhaustible. Mrs Watson would be no different. I could only
imagine what that family were experiencing – I'd been fortunate,
untouched by the death of anyone really close.

I walked through the living room to the kitchen, where Lockie
stared off into space while he fed something mushy into Angel. The
poor girl had her mouth agape as she tried to track and apprehend
the spoon. Lockie had a bristle of growth on his chin that only
emphasised the look of desolation.

'Lockie?' He looked up, startled by the intrusion on his thoughts. Once again, I was rocked by how hollowed out his eyes looked. The terror from last night had been replaced by a haunted numbness. He gave a brief jolt of recognition and then a brave smile at my greeting.

'Sam, back again so soon?'

'Afraid so. Had to see how you all were.'

'Bloody awful. Angel's the only one who slept. My wife's dead, it's all a bloody mess and it's nothing I can fix.' He raised his hand to his mouth; large tears rolled down his cheeks. His brutal honesty did nothing to ease my discomfort. I turned my eyes away towards Angel.

'God, Lockie, I'm sorry,' I said, and realised instantly how useless those words really were. 'I know this is not a good time, but I do have to ask you some more questions, and we need to do it while everything is fresh. I'm going to go and have another look around outside now it's daylight. I'll be fifteen minutes or so, then I'll come back and we'll go over things. You can do that?'

He drew my eyes with a look of resignation and weariness.

'Yeah, of course. Angel's almost finished.' He sighed and managed to get another spoonful into her mouth. 'Everything seems to take so long. She wants her mother, not me. She won't let me do hardly anything for her, not even brush her hair.'

I looked at her beautiful tousled curls. 'She'll be wondering where Mummy is, why she's not here. It's huge for you all.' Everything I said felt so inadequate. 'Look, I'll go and do what I have to do outside, then I'll be back soon to talk.'

'Do you want Gaby's mum there as well?'

'Please. We'll try and get through everything in one go, then we'll be able to leave you…' I didn't finish the sentence; I didn't know what to say. Leave you in peace, alone, leave you to grieve, leave you to wonder, blame, tear yourself apart? I left him with the best I could offer: a shrug and a gentle hand on his shoulder.

6

Early sunlight filtered through weathered summer leaves. The last tang of night chill lent an exhilarating freshness. In the still of the garden it seemed possible to forget, momentarily, the drama that was playing out inside. Remnants of dew clung to the grass. Excellent: that would emphasise any tracks in the grass that had survived the night.

I made my way, pace by deliberate pace, from the front door to the back door, and then the forty metres or so down to the back fence. The whole time I scanned for any sign of the path Gaby might have taken. The lawn was clipped short and the dew-coated grass was a uniform carpet of green. It revealed no evidence of her passage. Perhaps things would be more obvious in the longer grass over by the fence. I pushed my way through the wall of agapanthus; droplets of water kindly transferred themselves to my trousers again. Damp trousers had become a regular feature of this whole business.

From where I stood at the fence, I could still clearly make out my tracks down to the river from last night. It stood to reason that Gaby's would be evident too. I walked up and down the fence line several times and peered over at the other side, but there was no sign of Gaby's journey. I could only suppose that if she had crossed early in the day the grass would have had time to hide her path.

What I needed to establish was when she had decided to kill herself. I checked my thoughts right there. Do not make assumptions, Shephard. What was my father's mantra? Assume makes an ass out of you and me. Focus on the evidence to hand. The evidence to hand made it look as though Gaby hadn't climbed down to the river here at all. Despite the possible time explanation, the fact my own tracks looked as if they'd been created by a small herd of elephants made the absence of hers a concern. Why wouldn't she take the most direct route to the river? And if not here, where?

I turned around and leaned back on the fence to face the house. The view was unobstructed through to the laundry and back bedrooms. When I looked further afield, there was a clear line of sight to the neighbouring houses. They were distant, but easily visible.

Did she not want to be seen? Why would that matter?

The mindset of someone who had just undertaken to kill herself would be unpredictable, to say the least. You'd think she'd take the path of least resistance: that would be logical, drugs or not. I shook my head. Second-guessing Gaby Knowes made my brain ache.

'What were you playing at, Gaby?' I said aloud, and drummed a finger against my lips.

7

A mug of hot tea waited for me on the dining-room table; I felt fool-ishly pleased that Lockie had remembered my particular brew. The room looked set up for a conference. Angel sat near by on the lounge floor, surrounded by what looked like the better part of a toy store to keep her amused. Lockie and Leonore had seated themselves along one side of the table, and from the position of my drink it was appar-ent I was to sit on the other. I took my assigned place and reached into my satchel for a notebook and pen. A momentary flashback to Police College interviews hopped into my brain – sitting isolated on one side of the interrogation desk, intimidated by the panel on the other. It was rather different on this occasion; I was the one in control of the interview. Well, that was what I thought.

'She hasn't killed herself, you know. It's just not possible. There is no way Gaby would do that.' My butt had barely warmed the chair before Leonore launched straight in on the offensive with her elocu-tion-polished voice. 'She was murdered, I just know it. I don't care what you say, she was murdered. There, I've said it. I know Lockie thinks it too. My Gaby did not kill herself.'

My face must have registered surprise, because as if to drive home her point she looked me in the eye and folded her arms with a whumph.

'Lockie?' I asked.

'We need your help. I know how it looks, everything points to suicide, but I simply will not believe Gaby would do that. We're a happy family. Angel is her life, she'd die for her – she wouldn't leave us like that. She wouldn't.' His voice cracked and he reached for a tissue from the industrial-size box Cole had just placed on the table. With a slight cock of his head towards me, Cole pulled out a chair at the end of the table. I was grateful he hadn't joined the line-up opposite.

How to approach this? I hadn't anticipated their adamant denial of suicide. It was bloody naïve of me, really; I should have seen it coming. Be fair but firm, I told myself.

'This has been an enormous shock to you, and of course you don't want to imagine Gaby doing that.' I couldn't bring myself to say the word suicide in front of their broken faces. 'We can't make assumptions about anything at this stage. What we need now is to be logical and methodical and, as hard as it may seem, to keep emotion at bay. It will only cloud the issues and we can't afford to prejudice the investigation in any way. At the end of the day, we have to do what's right by Gaby, and—'

The doorbell sounded. We all flinched.

'Oh God,' Lockie said. 'I can't face visitors, not now.'

'It's alright, mate. I'll take care of it.' Cole stood up and pushed back his chair. I smiled my thanks at him.

We sat in dread silence, waiting to see who had intruded. Then the door closed and Cole reappeared with a large colourful bouquet of flowers. Leonore let out a strangled sob and Lockie leaned over to embrace her. It was a reality check via Teleflora. This was real, it had happened; Gaby's life, and death, were being acknowledged.

'To Lockie and family, our kindest thoughts at this time – the Stevenson family,' Cole read aloud. His Adam's apple bobbed up and down as he struggled to keep his voice even. An image of Gaby strewn on the riverbank flashed into my mind. After the work the Stevensons had done for us last night, they should have been the ones receiving bouquets.

'There will be a lot of this over the next few days,' I said, my voice betraying my emotion. 'This is a close-knit community and everyone will want to comfort you. It's overwhelming, yes, but you do need to be prepared for kindness.'

Lockie reached out for the flowers, and I thought for a moment he was going to throw them down. Instead, he cradled them and his shoulders shuddered with the effort of holding himself together.

'They're only trying to help,' I said.

'I know,' he said, 'it just makes it so real. She's really gone.'

We sat in an uncomfortable silence, punctuated by sniffs and nose blowing. I had always seen myself as a people person, charming and sociable, but in this charged emotional environment I felt completely inept. Anything I could think of to say sounded like a hollow platitude. So I reached out for my mug of tea and remained silent.

Cole, thank God, broke the impasse as he returned to his chair.

'Well, shall we get on with it, then?' It was all that was needed to focus us on the task at hand.

Lockie set the flowers on the table. 'OK, Sam, where do we start?' he said.

'I need to ask you some questions,' I said. 'Some of them may seem insensitive or downright hurtful. I don't intend to offend or harm, but I need you to answer honestly so we can get a picture of what happened.' Lockie gave a brief nod of acknowledgement, so I took a breath and ploughed ahead. 'We'll start with what time you went to work yesterday and when you last spoke to Gaby.'

He sat for a moment, elbows on table, chin in hands, as he contemplated his words. When he spoke it was in a quiet, measured tone.

'I left for work as usual at 5.30. Gaby was still in bed; she doesn't usually get up till seven or until Angel wakes up.' Lockie's eyes had slipped out of focus as he visualised the scene; a slight smile curled the edge of his mouth. 'It seemed just like any other ordinary day. I kissed her and said I'd see her tonight, then snuck into Angel's room to kiss her goodbye, and that was the last time I saw her.' The hint of a smile slumped.

'Did you speak with her at all during the day?' I asked.

'No, I don't normally come home for lunch.'

'Did you talk on the phone at all or text her?'

He shook his head slowly. 'They don't like us to use our phones at work.' Big plant, lots of workers – I wasn't surprised.

'What was her routine for a Tuesday?'

'Tuesday is usually a stay-at-home day – housework, gardening, stuff like that. Angel's just stopped her morning naps, so often sleeps for three hours in the afternoon. Gaby usually does a bit of study then. So if she goes out it's mostly in the morning.' He turned to look at Leonore, responding to the hand she had placed on his arm. 'Oh yeah, she always talks to her mum during the day.'

I looked up and enquired with a raised eyebrow. Leonore nodded. Yes, they'd spoken yesterday. I smiled at her and raised a hand to show I'd ask her about it later.

'You said last night Gaby didn't have any medical conditions. Had she given you any indication she wasn't well, or was stressed or unhappy about something?'

Lockie shook his head. 'No, that's the thing. She seemed happier; things were getting better, not worse. That's why I can't believe she'd do that. She's sleeping well, Angel hardly ever wakes in the night now, and with almost finishing the breast-feeding Gaby has more energy. She's great, great. We are even getting back to more, ah...' he paused, awkward, before he continued on, avoiding my eyes. 'You know, physically.'

It was just a bit more information than I wanted, and I thrust my hands in my lap to hide the telltale shakes. For God's sake, girl, grow up, I berated myself. Get a grip.

'Did you have any outside pressure or stress?' I asked. I had to change tack. 'Things OK financially?'

'Yeah, things are fine. If anything, we're starting to get ahead. We've even been planning a holiday to the Gold Coast in May.'

I felt a stab of pity for Lockie; he talked as if these things were still going to happen. I'd read that people often referred to their loved ones in the present tense, as though they were still here. Gaby wasn't ever going to come back. Poor guy still had to formally identify her: that would drive her death home. It would not be pretty. I knew protocol dictated I should be the accompanying officer, but there was no bloody way I was going to be around when that happened. I'd see to that.

I turned my attention to Gaby's mother, who had sat through my conversation with Lockie with her white-knuckled hands in front of her.

'Leonore – may I call you Leonore, or would you prefer Mrs Watson?' I didn't know if she was aware of the history between Lockie and me. Whether she was or not, I wanted her to know I would, with utmost respect, do my best for her daughter.

'Leonore. Leonore's fine, thank you.' She unclenched her hands and rested them on the edge of the table.

'You spoke to Gaby every day?' I asked. My mother and I talked once a week, if that, and that was quite enough. I found it odd someone would actually want to talk to their mother every day. What would you say?

'My day wasn't complete unless I'd talked with her.' She reached out for another tissue and delicately blew her nose.

'Is that a toll call from Queenstown, or is it classed as local?' I asked, curious.

'A toll call normally, although it's covered by the minutes in my phone plan at no extra charge. I rang Gaby mostly, so it wouldn't cost them anything.'

'So you talked to her yesterday?'

'Yes, we must have chatted for quarter of an hour or so in the morning. It would have been around ten o'clock. I'd just got home from doing the groceries.'

'And how did she sound?' I jotted down notes on my pad as I went.

'Fantastic. My usual chatty girl. She told me she was planning on getting out in the garden when Angel was asleep. Oh, and that Angel had taken her first steps – she was so proud of our little girl. She'd baked yesterday because it was her turn to take morning tea to playgroup today. Chocolate chip biscuits and a fruit cake.' Her voice rose as she got up a head of steam again. 'There is no way my girl killed herself. Something bad happened to her, I know it. Gaby would never do that.' Disquiet had edged its way into the pit of my stomach. To all intents and purposes it looked like a classic suicide: note, overdose – the out of choice for women. But the comment about the baking played in my mind. Why the hell would you bother to bake morning tea if you had no intention of delivering it? That would suggest she'd made a spur-of-the-moment decision. But those tablets had been acquired the day before she died. I shook my head. It almost added up, but not quite.

'Had Gaby mentioned any concerns about life in general? Did you have any cause to be worried about her?' I looked at Lockie, to openly acknowledge the question was about him. Leonore understood its tenor right away.

'No, she and Lockie had a wonderful relationship. She never said a bad thing about him.'

I doubted that. I was sure she would have mentioned some of his more irksome habits, especially those that concerned the use or lack of use of laundry hampers. I caught myself again and cursed my inability to let things go.

'I love my son-in-law, always have. He's a wonderful man. Gaby adored him.'

She wasn't telling me anything I didn't already know. My own glorious experience told me he had quite the charming effect on parents ... There I went again! I couldn't believe myself sometimes. If I wanted to be taken seriously and act professionally, self-control had to be the order of the day.

'Did Gaby mention plans to see anyone in particular yesterday? Friends? Any appointments?'

'No. As far as I'm aware it was just to be a normal day. She even said "Talk to you tomorrow", as always. Look,' she leaned over and gave me a direct stare, 'I know my daughter, Lockie knows his wife. Why won't you believe us? Gaby did not kill herself. This is foul play. Open your eyes.'

Part of me was irritated by such assertions, but again that sense of unease chipped away. And I had learned long ago to trust my gut instincts – they were generally accurate. I chose my words with care.

'We can't rule out anything this early in the investigation. We should have a preliminary report from the post-mortem tomorrow.' I saw Lockie wince. 'That may give us more information. In the meantime, we need to look at anything you think of as odd or peculiar.

Leonore, last night the house was a mess. As you were cleaning, did you notice anything out of the ordinary? We have the note from the table and the tablets in the sink. Did you see anything else?'

Leonore hesitated, and then spoke in a very small voice.

'May I see the note?'

I looked up. Her eyes were awash with fresh tears, her mouth pinched. I gave her a nod and retrieved the bagged page out of my satchel. I placed it on the table and pushed it over towards Leonore. She rustled around in her handbag for some reading glasses, then examined the note at length. I noted her frown of concentration.

'What are you thinking?' I asked.

'I don't know,' she said, brows still furrowed. She seemed genuinely puzzled.

'If something seems odd, don't be afraid to say so. You as much as anyone would know your daughter. It is her handwriting, isn't it?' I asked.

She looked up at me, and then tapped gently on the bag.

'Yes, it's her writing, but, well, it just seems very formal.'

Lockie, who had avoided looking at the note, leaned over to examine it. 'She never called me Lachlan, always Lockie. Same for Angel. See, we told you,' he said, and slapped his hand down on the table.

'Hey, we can't jump to conclusions, but thanks for that, Leonore. This is important. I'll have a closer look at the note later. Was there anything else?'

The silence from across the table indicated nothing else had aroused suspicion.

But they were right – the note was too measured, almost stilted. Had Gaby been trying to send an unspoken message? Or had a sense of occasion demanded a level of formality – her last written words recorded for posterity? It was yet another thing to bear in mind, at least until the post-mortem report. I contemplated a telephone call to voice my concerns – but then at what point did you have to be careful not to insult the skills of the pathologist in finding the truth? That jogged my memory. I looked at my watch.

'Lockie, you still need to formally identify her.' I looked at Cole, who had sat quietly throughout. 'Are you able to drive him down to Invercargill to do that? The sooner you do, then the sooner they can undertake a post-mortem and we'll get more information.'

Lockie's already ashen face took on a translucent quality; without thought, I reached across and touched his hand. He jerked up as if shocked.

'Look, Lockie, I know this is hard, but it is something that has to be done. If there is any question of foul play involved, the post-mortem could provide vital evidence. If it shows nothing sinister, then it will help you on the path to coming to terms with her death. It is important.'

He briefly grasped my hand, then flopped back in his chair, his gaze directed up at the ceiling. 'They'll cut her up, won't they?' he said. My chest tightened at the sight of him. I glanced at Cole, who had also blanched. Leonore shook, her shoulders racked by stifled sobs.

'Oh God, Lockie,' I said. I knew what he needed from me, and I did my best to provide that reassurance. 'They will have to open her, and I know you can't bear to think of it, but they'll do it with respect and with the knowledge Gaby was precious. When they've finished their work, and you get to see her, she won't be disfigured – she'll look peaceful and beautiful.'

Christ, this job sucked sometimes. Call it parental conditioning, call it stereotyping, but grown men were supposed to be stoic and they certainly didn't cry. To see a man I had loved – hell, still loved – openly weeping for his wife was more than I could stand. I'd managed it so far, but something was going to give, and soon. God, I had to get out of that house. I pushed the chair back and got to my feet. I had to avoid Lockie's eyes, so I directed my words at Cole as I gathered my notes and packed my satchel.

'I'll leave you for now. If there is anything else you think of, please call me. I'll get any results back to you as soon as possible.'

It was Cole who saw me out to the door, past Angel, who was still happily occupied with the pile on the lounge floor. That kid really suited her name.

The relief of being freed from the suffocation of that house was indescribable. I had to measure every step down the driveway to stop myself breaking into a run. But once within the sanctuary of the truck, I leaned hard back into the seat and allowed myself the luxury of a grown-up version of a tantrum.

After several deep breaths, a modicum of objectivity returned. Bad mood or not, there was work to do. While I was in the vicinity I'd call in on the neighbours and see if they'd noticed anything out of the ordinary. Then I'd follow up on any appointments Gaby may have had.

'Shit.'

In my headlong rush to get the hell out of Texas I'd forgotten to ask if Gaby had kept a diary. I knew I'd be going back to the house and could check it out later, but that wasn't the point. I had to focus, and fast. Mistakes were something I couldn't afford.

8

Dora McGann could finally be something other than a right royal pain in the arse. A town gossip of great renown, I often had the pleasure of her voice on the phone as she informed me of some piece of information that had come her way and demanded my immediate and undivided attention. Well, that's the way she saw it, anyway. Now it was me turning to her for information. Her face lit up as she opened her front door.

'Constable Shephard, Constable Shephard, I thought you might be around, I did. I said to myself you'd be around to see me. It's about that poor young woman next door, isn't it? A dreadful thing that. Oh that poor, lovely young man, left with a wee babe and all.'

I wondered if at any stage I'd actually be able to say hello.

'It's not right, is it? And people are saying she killed herself. Oh, that's just awful, a young woman like that. Everything to live for, she had. Dreadfully sad. I can't believe it, just can't believe it.'

Fortunately, she had to pause for breath, so I grabbed the opportunity to speak.

'Hello, Mrs McGann. I wanted to ask you a few questions relating to yesterday's events and Mrs Knowes—'

'Of course, of course, I'm only too happy to help. They were such a lovely young couple, you know, and that wee girl of theirs, she's such a wee angel.' She realised what she had said and gave a small chuckle. 'Well, of course she is, isn't she, Angel, but I shouldn't be laughing; this is no time for laughter, is it? No. Oh, but I'm being rude, aren't I? Come in, won't you come in? Of course, yes, if you've got any questions I'm only too happy to help.'

It was the first time I had been in Dora McGann's inner sanctum. I'm not quite sure what I expected, given her notoriety as a gossip and knower of all: binoculars, telescopes, listening devices? What I found was a rather dated but very welcoming home, festooned with photographs of children and grandchildren. The décor came right out of *House & Garden* magazine – a 1970s edition, complete with autumn-hued Axminster carpet, velvet drapes and three ceramic ducks flying their way across a rather busy wallpaper. I made my way over to the table she had indicated and tried to keep up with her constant stream of chatter. I recalled someone mentioning the late Mr McGann had been hard of hearing. Lucky bastard.

She must have had a pot of tea already brewed. I was only half settled into the seat when a tea tray appeared before me.

'How do you take your tea, love?'

I smiled despite myself. I was unaccustomed to being referred to as 'love' by anybody, particularly when on duty.

'Milk, no sugar, thanks.'

She was pouring what we referred to in our family as 'frilly tea'. Fine bone-china cups and saucers of a delicate floral design, milk jug covered with a crocheted, bead-edged doily, matching sugar bowl with delicate undersized teaspoons – silver, no doubt. She didn't have Devonshire scones or cream puffs, but served the next best thing – Toffee Pops biscuits, caramel filled, chocolate-coated goodness, on what even I recognised as Royal Doulton. I realised for the first time that day my heart rate felt somewhere about normal and the knot twisting my innards had begun to relax. She did have her uses, after all. And the tea was only slightly stewed.

From where I sat it was easy to make out the Knowes' house and part of the driveway. I couldn't see the back fence from here, but it would be visible from further into the room.

'Were you home yesterday, Mrs McGann?' I asked as I set my empty cup onto its saucer.

'Oh yes, dear, I was home all day. I had the girls around for bridge, so I had to make some scones and tidy the house. Tuesday is always bridge day. My turn yesterday, so the girls came here. Oh you know them all, there's Lola Bridges,' I worked hard not to laugh, 'she's very good, you know, and Jill Sanders. They always come in Lola's car. Jill hasn't got a driver's licence. Can you believe that? In this day and age. Lucky she's got Lola next door to run her around when Gordon's at work; it's about time he retired anyway. He's seventy-three now and still working. Mind you, a man like that would fade away and die if he stopped working. Anyway, Lola trots her everywhere. She's always trying to get Jill to take driving lessons, but she's not interested. And there's Beryl Rawlings – you know Beryl, she's president of the Country Women's Institute around here – boy, can she preserve. You'd have to be really good to beat her – at preserving, I mean, oh, and bridge too. She plays a mean hand. She was a wee bit late yesterday, some trouble with the cattle.'

Under normal circumstances, such drivel would bring out an urge to give the woman a good slapping, but today the chatter somehow comforted my frayed nerves.

'Did you notice anything unusual at the Knowes' house during the day? Different people or cars? Did you see Mrs Knowes at all?'

'Oh yes, dear, I saw Mrs Knowes. In the morning, early it would have been, nine o'clockish. She was hanging her first lot of washing out, as usual.'

That got my attention. Why the hell would you bother with the washing if you weren't planning to survive the day? I'd noticed it hanging up when I first searched the property, but what with the immediacy of Gaby's disappearance and Lockie's distress, I hadn't appreciated its significance.

'She was always out early with the washing – very good housekeeper, that girl. House always spotless, very organised. Fine girl, that one, fine girl.' She suddenly gave me a slightly abashed look. It was evident her local knowledge extended to my own personal history.

'Did she have any visitors during the day?' I asked.

She jumped at the opportunity to remove the foot from her mouth. 'I didn't see anyone, I was quite busy with the bridge. But the girls were here, they might have noticed something.'

'What time were they here?'

'Oh we always start at 10.30 with a cup of tea, then continue until lunchtime. So I suppose everyone was gone by, oh, two o'clock – some of the girls like to have a wee turn-up in the afternoon, especially after a couple of sherries.'

It sounded like a breath test or two could have interesting results after one of their bridge sessions.

'Could I grab their phone numbers from you, so I can follow up, please?'

'Of course you can, dear. I'm only pleased to be able to help.' She trotted over to the telephone and pulled out a battered-looking address file – the variety where you slid the marker up to the letter you wanted, then pushed the button and it flipped open to the page. 'I don't know the girls' numbers off by heart – well, other than speed-dial five, six and seven.' She chuckled as she handed it over. 'The only trouble with these modern phones. I had to get my Ben to put the numbers in for me; that was years ago, so I've well and truly forgotten them. I'm sure the girls will say if they saw something. Such a terrible shame all this, I just can't believe it.'

I was going to try to put the next question delicately, but thought, given her reputation, what the hell.

'Did Mr and Mrs Knowes seem to have a happy marriage?'

She blinked once or twice at my directness, and hesitated before answering.

'I thought they seemed very happy. I never saw them argue or anything and certainly didn't hear them – it's a bit far, you know. They were always off doing things, the three of them – playing with wee Angel, going out. I thought they were a very happy family.' She paused. Indecision tussled on her face.

'But?'

'I don't like to gossip, especially now that Mrs Knowes is gone.' She leaned forward and lowered her voice. 'I had heard … that someone thought … that Mrs Knowes might have been seeing someone else as well.'

My eyes narrowed. If anyone knew, it would be Dora, but even she had hesitated on that titbit.

'Did the rumour give you a name?' I asked.

'No. That's why I wasn't sure whether to mention it or not. I don't like to speak ill of the dead, and she was always such a lovely neighbour to me – even dropped in some baking at Christmas and all. I didn't believe it myself, but you never know. These ideas don't start by themselves, do they?' Actually there were plenty of those kinds of ideas that had started by themselves, snowballed out of all proportion and ruined lives along the way. She'd probably sparked a few to life herself over the years, but I thought I wouldn't mention that.

'Did you see Mrs Knowes at the back of their property at all yesterday? Near the fence?'

'No, love, I only saw her hanging out the washing – the last time I saw her alive, I suppose.'

'What about their dog? Did you hear it barking at all?'

'I can't remember. It's not a really barky dog, not like the Wheelers' on the other side. Theirs barks all the time, so I probably wouldn't notice if it did, sorry.'

'And no visitors or vehicles?'

'Not that I noticed. No one came to visit her, other than the van.'

'Van? What kind of a van?'

'Oh, a work van of some sort. It was white and had a ladder on the roof, but I couldn't see the sign on it from here. My eyes aren't as good as they used to be. I had my reading glasses on, not my looking glasses—'

'Why didn't you think to mention it earlier?'

Dora didn't notice the edge. 'Well, it wasn't really a visitor, was it? It was just a tradesman. Do you think that might be important?'

'Possibly. If we knew who it was, they might have been the last person to see Mrs Knowes alive. They might be able to give us a time, help us figure out the order of events. Did you see the tradesman?' My warm feelings towards Mrs McGann were evaporating fast.

'No, I only glanced really. We were in the middle of a hand.'

'So what time would that have been?'

'I suppose around eleven o'clock, maybe.'

'Did you notice how long the van stayed?'

'Not really, love. It was definitely gone when the girls were leaving. I'd have noticed it when I saw them out.'

That probably depended on how much sherry had accompanied lunch. I decided it was time for me to be seen out. My tolerance level for Dora McGann's prattle had just been exceeded. At least I had gleaned some useful information, even though she'd barely thought to mention it. You had to wonder what went on in some people's heads.

I didn't quite know what to think of the affair rumour. I didn't put it past Gaby to betray Lockie like that – a rebound relationship: did they ever last? – but it sounded like it was fourth-hand speculation. I couldn't let it cloud my mind.

The van sighting, however, was another matter altogether. The unease in my belly reasserted itself.

9

My brain had developed an awful habit of drifting into thoughts of Lockie rather than the investigation of his wife's death. The fact that I had to make a concerted effort to change my focus, to draw a clear line between my personal and professional involvement, annoyed the crap out of me. Maybe some people weren't cut out for divorcing the two. Maybe some things were too deep to ignore.

Direct action, however, might get me back in line, or at least improve my mood. With this thought I pulled up outside the Riverside Health Centre in Mataura, where I hoped Gaby's doctor might be able to shed some light on her supposedly precarious state of mind and I might learn how she got hold of those sleeping tablets.

I opened the door and was greeted by a large hexagonal tank containing several frilly goldfish. Bubbles of air drifted upwards and detoured around limbs of the artificially bright green seaweed. There was the obligatory blackboard and chalk and basket of wooden toys, currently being marauded upon by unmistakably twin boys. They matched even down to the trails of mucus working their way from nostril to mouth. I shuddered, smiled at them, and then at their mother, who reddened and ferreted around in her handbag – presumably, for some tissues. Apparently, I had been promoted to Sergeant of the Snot Police. With the efficiency gained from lots of practice, she dealt with the two faces before they could mount a protest.

Unusually for a rural-type practice, three doctors worked out of these rooms. That it was one of two medical centres in the town was even more remarkable. Perhaps the lifestyle was more attractive here than in other regions: usually, the low pay, long hours and being continuously on call made working as a rural GP an unattractive proposition. Hell, I'd even heard of some small towns throwing parties because their doctor had chosen to stay. Gaby Knowes' GP hailed originally from Britain. He and his wife had fallen victim to the charms of New Zealand while holidaying here and, like many smitten in the same way, had decided to make it their permanent home. I had been informed by many reliable sources that he was a charming and pleasant family man who fitted in well with the community.

Blessed as I am with the constitution of an ox, I hadn't seen Dr Tony Walden in a professional capacity before – or socially for that matter. My own GP, also in the practice, was hardly getting rich on the proceeds of my visits. The only thing I ever needed was a prescription for the Pill, and even that wasn't needed, strictly speaking.

Francine was at work behind the reception desk. She was always dependable as a sympathetic ear, and as circulation manager of the local rumour mill.

'You'll be here about Gaby Knowes, won't you?' she said. 'Is it right, what they're saying, that she killed herself?' She'd leaned forwards to prevent anyone overhearing, her expression almost eager.

'We're still investigating the case, so you know I can't comment on that. That is why I'm here, though. I need to talk to Dr Walden. Can you slot me in?'

'Course I can, Sam. I'll pop you in next. It's fairly quiet this morning. He shouldn't be too long.'

I sat down on a chair opposite the now clean-faced Symes twins. Adelle and John had decided to have a fourth child and had been rather surprised to find out there had been a buy-one-get-one-free special on that week and they'd be needing something akin to a bus to transport the expanded family. By now, the shock had worn off, but the twins did have a reputation for stretching their parents' patience, as well as their budget. They were a study in slow motion as they dragged their collective feet after their mother on the way to Dr Brightman's room.

After the emotional turmoil of the morning's visit with Lockie, I now felt sober and more together, but I was going to have to keep tempering my reactions and concentrate on doing my job – finding Gaby's killer. Interesting how the 'killer' word had snuck its way into my train of thought, how my mind had gone from having suspicions to deciding it was murder.

'Hmmmm,' I said. I hadn't intended for it to be out loud.

'Something else, Sam?' Francine asked.

'Ah, no … Actually, yes, there is something else you can help me with. I'll need to see Dr Arnold today as well. Can you get me in with him?' Dr Arnold, not Dr Walden, had written Gaby's prescription for Hypnovel. There could have been many reasons for that, but I wanted to see Dr Arnold regardless.

'He's not in until one o'clock. Do you want me to book a time?'

I was about to reply when Tony Walden emerged from the hallway, ushering along a rather frail-looking Mrs Ellison, who made painfully slow progress with the shuffle and lift required to animate her walking frame. I wished someone would upgrade her to one with wheels and a seat. Dr Walden was a slight man of medium height, with short, wavy brown hair and pleasant if not handsome features. He glanced up at me and paused a moment before resuming his conversation with Mrs Ellison and directing her to reception. The uniform often had that effect on people.

'Tony, Constable Shephard here would like to have a word,' Francine called.

'Yes, of course.' He clipped his soft British accent. 'Through this way.' He turned without further comment, headed down the hallway, then disappeared into a room off to the left.

I turned back to Francine. 'I'll pop by later and take my chances with Dr Arnold,' I said, then followed the doctor down to his room.

By the time I entered, Dr Walden was already seated behind his desk. I closed the door behind me, and as I turned back to face him, I caught him completing the kind of appraisal one would normally reserve for livestock. His eyes flicked quickly back to my face. At least he had the grace to look a little abashed. My so-called reliable informants had got it a tad wrong. Charming he might be, but having a doctor give you the once-over was akin to being eyed up by your priest. I shuddered.

'What can I do for you today, Constable?'

I dispensed with the usual social niceties and got straight to the point. 'No doubt you have heard about the death of Gabriella Knowes?'

His face registered an immediate expression of loss.

'I understand she was one of your patients, and I was wanting to ask you a few questions for our investigation.'

'Yes, Francine told us this morning. Everyone is shocked by the news. She was a very lovely lady. What happened?' He waved a hand in the direction of a chair, and I took the offer to sit down.

'We found her body on the Mataura riverbank last night. Mr Knowes had reported her missing when she wasn't at home when he'd returned from work. It was very out of character for her. You've no doubt heard the speculation of suicide. She'd left a note, and also an empty box of Hypnovel tablets.'

I noticed a slight frown at the mention of the Hypnovel.

'The tablets weren't prescribed by you, but by Dr Arnold. Had you given her sleeping tablets on other occasions?'

He sat there, elbows on desk, hands clasped. Index fingers drummed on his mouth. Then he leaned back in his chair, folded his arms across his chest and looked at me.

'No, I don't think I've given Mrs Knowes sleeping tablets before. I'd have to check her notes to make certain. She would normally see me, though, not Dr Arnold.' He paused. 'I must have been away that day.'

'I'll be seeing Dr Arnold later on, when he gets in,' I said. 'He'll be able to clarify that for us. But can you tell me if she'd ever mentioned feeling suicidal or had a history of depression?'

'Sorry, I wish I could, but I can't,' he said.

'And why not?'

'I'm limited in the information I can give you because of the Privacy Act. We have to be very careful, you know.'

I resisted the urge to do a massive eye roll.

'Mr Knowes is aware of my visit and I have his permission to ask about his family's medical history,' I said. I knew for a fact that under these circumstances Dr Walden could answer questions relating to Gaby's death. 'He wants to understand why this has happened. Anything you can tell us to explain it would go a long way to helping Gaby's family cope with her death. As you can imagine, they're in a state of shock.'

'I understand how awful this must be for him, but what passed between Mrs Knowes and me is covered by doctor-patient privilege. I really can't give out her personal information,' he said, and he leaned forward onto the desk.

'Would it help if I had Mr Knowes' permission in writing?' I asked, although I already suspected what the answer would be.

'That wouldn't matter. The only one who can give permission is Mrs Knowes,' he said, and shrugged his shoulders as if he didn't have any say in the matter.

'I had hoped that your concern for your patient and her family would prompt you to help us in our inquiries,' I said, emphasising the word 'concern'.

'Don't get me wrong, I think this is an awful thing to have happened and I would help you if I could, but I'm afraid the Privacy Act precludes me from divulging that kind of information to you.'

I was very tempted to go and find the relevant bit in the Act, blow it up on the photocopier five hundred percent and staple it to his desk, or elsewhere. But I could see I was going to get nowhere on this one.

'Well,' I said, and rose to my feet. 'Your reluctance is noted. If you think of anything you can divulge which may be helpful, please call me.'

He gave me a look that tried to convey it was all beyond his control.

'Good day, Officer.'

I somehow managed to exit the room without acting on the urge to slam the door. I knew he was an import, that I should give him the benefit of the doubt on his understanding of our laws, but his choice to hide behind the Privacy Act did not exactly endear him to me. I didn't know what he thought he was going to achieve, other than seriously pissing me off. It wasn't as if Lockie was going to turn around and sue him for revealing family secrets. Most people actually liked being able to assist the police in an investigation, especially in such tragic circumstances – young family, baby losing a mother. Lockie would be disappointed at the doctor's reticence.

'What an idiot,' I whispered under my breath.

'What was that?'

A voice startled the hell out of me. I was relieved to see it was Chrissie, the practice nurse.

'Shit, you gave me a fright,' I said, and grinned at her. Chrissie and I couldn't be described as friends, but we did get on very well. 'You heard about Gaby Knowes?' She nodded. 'I was just talking to Dr Walden about her.'

'Yeah, that was awful. I assume he was helpful?'

'Yeah, right.' I was unable to hide the sarcasm in my voice.

'I'm surprised,' she said as we walked back to the front door. 'I'd have thought he'd be able to give you some information.'

'I thought so too, but he quoted the Privacy Act at me and that was the end of the conversation. I suppose that's his right, but it doesn't aid the investigation and it sure as hell doesn't help her family.'

'Well, if there's anything I can do to help,' she said, accent on the 'I', and quietly so only I could hear. I looked at her, curious, but she just smiled and returned to the practice rooms.

An invitation?

I waved farewell to Francine and headed out the door. I'd visit people who might actually be cooperative.

10

I brushed the remnants of pastry crumbs off my trousers, swung the truck door open and jumped down to the road. I had just troughed down a steak and cheese pie, and succeeded in both burning the roof of my mouth and getting indigestion. Served me right for being in such a rush. I glanced sideways at the gelatinous-looking slab of custard square that sat on the passenger seat and thought better of it.

The morning hadn't been a complete and utter write-off. I had tried to contact the remainder of Dora McGann's bridge group, but none was home. Chances were they were out together, enjoying lunch, drinking too much sherry and talking about Gaby and the van. The exact thing I didn't want them doing. Witness by committee was not the best. But during the wait until I could see Dr Arnold, I'd followed up on Gaby's script at the pharmacy in Gore that had dispensed it. I thought it odd that she'd have her family doctor in Mataura and then travel over to Gore to have scripts filled when there was a pharmacy here. Convenience would have been my choice, but I suppose everyone had their favourites. My chat had been most productive and had only strengthened my apprehensions about Gaby's death. The Gore pharmacy had never dispensed sleeping tablets for her before this, nor had she been given any medicines that would suggest a problem with depression. The staff had been stunned at the news of Gaby's death and had been very keen to help in any way possible – no quoting law at me there. Unfortunately, no one could tell me who had picked up the Hypnovel script, although they were unanimous it wasn't Gaby. Definitely wasn't Lockie either, but they were pretty sure it was a man. They had assumed it was a brother, or one of Lockie's relatives.

I'd have given anything for some video tape, but here at the back of nowhere surveillance cameras weren't high on anyone's must-have list. Bugger it. I really wanted to know who'd gone in and collected that script.

I glanced once more at my watch. One o'clock.

'Here we go again.'

As I strode across the road to the medical centre, I hoped like hell I wouldn't meet up with Dr Walden in the waiting room. Mercifully, he was elsewhere.

'Sam, go straight through,' Francine said as I walked into the reception area. 'Dr Arnold's expecting you.'

'But I didn't make an appointment.'

'Saw the truck parked across the road. Did you enjoy the pie, by the way?'

'It was pretty damned average, but it filled a gap.'

'You should have come in and eaten in the staffroom. We wouldn't have minded. We'd have even given you a cuppa.'

It was lovely of her to say, but the thought of trying to eat with Dr Walden staring at my breasts would have given me worse indigestion than I already had. Either that, or he'd have worn the pie.

'Maybe next time,' I said.

'You know where to go,' Francine said, and she pointed her pen towards the rooms. I wandered down the hallway, past Creep-Face's closed door.

'Hello,' I said as I pushed open the door to Dr Arnold's room. 'Anybody home?'

'Sam, always a pleasure. Come in.'

Ranjit Arnold was a fifty-something of obvious Indian extraction. I was dying to know how the hell he managed to get a surname like Arnold, but was far too well brought up to ask. He carried an air of quiet strength and serenity normally reserved for royalty or the clergy. He was also a jovial character who could put anyone at ease; you could see humour dance a jig in the creases around his eyes as he spoke. His easy manner and caring nature had endeared him very quickly to a community normally wary of anyone of foreign descent.

Word of mouth from rapt patients had meant his client list filled up quickly. He sure as hell got my tick of approval.

'Ranjit, how are you?'

'Damned fine, damned fine. Patients keep coming and paying their money, despite my not being able to cure them; children still think I'm God with a lollipop; and occasionally I get to play surgeon and stitch something up. What more could a guy ask for?' Mischief was painted all over his face. 'How are you, Sam? Go on, give me something exciting to do. Nasty skin rash? Growing an extra limb somewhere? Something I can get the scalpels out for? Please, please.' He flexed his fingers in mock anticipation.

'Ahhh, hate to disappoint you.' Then I put on my best serious voice and assumed my best constabulary pose. 'I'm afraid I'm here on official business today, Dr Arnold. I would like you to assist me in my investigations.'

'Ah, that serious, is it?'

'Well, actually it is,' I said quietly, back in sombre mood. 'Have you caught up with Gaby Knowes' death?'

'Francine mentioned it when I came in. Suicide, she said.'

'That's what it seems but, to be honest, I have my doubts.' As well as valuing his medical advice, I valued Dr Arnold's opinions as a man. He was a good sounding board for all manner of complaints, physical and emotional.

'How so?' he asked.

I shrugged.

'Nothing concrete I can put my finger on, just lots of things that don't quite add up. Call it a gut feeling.'

'Doesn't hurt to listen to that gut, my girl,' he said, monstrous brows knitted together. 'What is it I can help you with?'

I fossicked around in my satchel and produced a copy of the prescription for Hypnovel. The pharmacist, God bless her, had been very helpful.

'I was wanting to ask you about the script Gaby had for Hypnovel.'

'I think Tony was her GP. Have you spoken to him?'

'Dr Walden was not particularly forthcoming. In fact, he was quite obsessed with quoting the Privacy Act at me.' I didn't really like to play tattle-tales, but after this morning's episode: stuff him. 'I didn't learn anything that could help with the investigation.'

'Well, Sam, to be fair, we do have to tread very carefully around privacy issues, and if he couldn't help you, then I really can't undermine him and give you personal information about Mrs Knowes.'

'I realise that,' I said quickly, 'and I'd never put you in that position. No, I just wanted to ask you about the script you wrote her for Hypnovel.'

'Pardon?'

A puzzled frown crossed his face, so I passed over the copy I'd acquired from the pharmacy. He examined it closely, and then tapped it with his finger.

'Well, Sam, you've found your smoking gun,' he said, grim. 'I didn't write this script.'

'What? That's your letterhead, isn't it?'

'Yes, it looks like it, but I didn't write this script. I've never had a consultation with Mrs Knowes. This script is a forgery.'

'Shit,' I said, and then clapped my hand over my mouth. 'I'm sorry, I didn't mean to swear. That just slipped out.'

'That's OK. Quite OK, considering. See, that's not my signature or writing.' He cocked his head to the side to peer at it from a different perspective. 'It's kind of like it, so I can see how you'd be fooled, but it's definitely not mine.'

'Can you do me a comparison?' I asked, getting up to move around behind him.

He pulled out a blank piece of paper, copied out the details of the script and then signed it. With the two documents side by side, we compared the writing. Presented like this, Gaby's prescription was clearly not from the same hand.

'Surely the pharmacy should have noticed the difference,' I said. 'They see your writing every day. They should have picked this up.'

I must have sounded a tad accusing, as he looked up at me sharply.

'Not necessarily. The last thing they'd expect is a forged script, and it is on my script pad, after all.' He tapped on the document. 'Superficially, it could appear to be mine.'

'Have you had any pads go missing recently?' I asked.

'No, no break-ins or anything odd.'

'How would someone get hold of one of your script forms then?'

We sat in silence for a moment and pondered the paper in front of us. Then I saw it.

'It's got a serial number. Do all your scripts have serial numbers?'

'Yes, they come printed on the pad, see.' He reached into a drawer and pulled out an unused pad. In the bottom corner of each page, printed in red, were consecutive serial numbers.

'Do you record the serial number for each script you write?'

He laughed. 'No, firstly, it has never occurred to me to do that. And, secondly, who has the time?'

I smiled back at him. True, there was enough paperwork in this world without creating more for yourself on the off chance someone would play forger.

'Who else has access to things like prescription pads?' I asked.

'Well, any of the staff, really. I don't lock them away. But I don't believe any of them would do that. You know them, they're good people.'

He was right there. I couldn't imagine Francine, Chrissie or any of them forging a script for anything, let alone sleeping tablets to kill someone off. Perhaps Gaby could have done this, after all? No, she'd have waited around to pick up the script if she'd gone to that much trouble to bump herself off. And the pharmacy staff had said it was a guy who picked it up. It was definitely the killer's work. But how?

'How would I do it?' I thought out loud.

'Pardon?' Ranjit asked.

'How would I forge a script, and have enough faith in it to give it to a pharmacy that sees the doctor's writing pretty often? That was pretty ballsy.'

'Yes, you'd think they'd go somewhere miles away to have it filled.'

'Come to think of it, they must have done enough research into Gaby to know that her regular pharmacy was in Gore. It was dispensed at Cleveland's, by the way; and not the most convenient one near by in Mataura. She'd used that one too, I checked this morning, but she had a preference for Gore, for whatever reason.' My mind was racing through the possibilities. 'Maybe it was a fluke. Maybe the killer thought the forged script was more likely to be detected at the Mataura Pharmacy so tried Gore, as it was far enough away to improve the odds, but not so far off the beaten track to arouse suspicion. Other than Gore, the nearest pharmacy would be where? Wyndham, or Invercargill? That's forty minutes away. They must be local.'

We looked at each other, and I shuddered. The thought of the town harbouring a murderer was unnerving. The area hadn't seen a murder for – well, I couldn't recall any. It was a pretty bloody safe place to live, until now.

'Scanned,' I said suddenly.

'What?'

'Scanned. You get hold of a genuine script, scan it into your computer, and not only have you got a nice sample of the doctor's writing and a signature; delete out the writing and you've got a blank script. Print it off, write what you want, away you go.'

'Do you always do that?'

'Do what?' I asked.

'Come up with stuff like that out of left field? We were talking about other towns.'

'It's a gift,' I said, and laughed. 'Years of cryptic crosswords and associated lateral thinking. According to my flatmate, you do get used to it.'

'Lucky flatmate. You're probably right, though. With the technology around, it doesn't sound that difficult. In fact, most households would probably have a scanner nowadays. I've had one for two years. Haven't plugged it in yet, but I've got one.'

Couldn't help but smile at that one.

'So, if they did that,' I said, straightening up and pacing the short distance across the room, words drummed out with each measured step, 'they had to get a script through normal means to copy. If they scanned an existing script, they would have scanned and repeated the serial number. We know the serial number of the forgery, so if they were stupid enough to present the original script to the pharmacy, and we can get them to search through the serial numbers, they might find a match. If they are really, truly stupid, they will have used their name and address and voilà.'

I didn't believe for a second that anyone who had gone to that amount of trouble would be so thick, but hey, you never knew. Stranger things had happened. We had all laughed at reports of hapless crooks who'd left wallets behind at the scene of the crime, or balaclavas with their names carefully sewn in by Mummy.

'It's worth a try. Never underestimate basic stupidity,' Ranjit said. Then he peered intently at the two pieces of paper again. 'If you were going to scan it, a script for, say, athlete's foot cream or ABT tablets would do.'

'ABT tablets?'

'Any Bloody Thing,' he said.

I laughed. 'That original script would have been handled by every-one under the sun, but we might get a useful print from it. I'll have to fingerprint all the pharmacy staff, and quick before any possible traces are obliterated. Oh, they're gonna love that.'

'Just one little thing,' Ranjit said, and looked up at me.

I came back over beside him, and looked at the spot his finger tapped on the forged script.

'Whoever wrote this knows their drugs – they've stated the strength. Anyone could get the name right, but they'd have to know this drug specifically to know the strength. Hell, half the time, I don't even write the strength down on something like this – there is only one tablet available.'

The image of Dr Walden immediately leaped into my head. I shook it. He had been fairly hostile during my inquiries and he was definitely a sleaze, but that hardly qualified him as a murderer. It did bring him up on my radar though.

'Thanks, Ranjit,' I said, picking up the script copy and the comparison he had written. 'This certainly changes things. Now we have a strong suspicion of foul play, it's time to call in the heavies.'

'The heavies?'

'Yes, this is a murder inquiry now. We'll be inundated with police and CIB. The circus is coming to town.'

11

Now that this was a full-blown murder investigation I had the undesirable task of kicking Lockie out of his own home. It was now considered a crime scene and, as such, had to be secured. Somehow, I didn't think he'd take the news well.

I parked on the roadside, well back from the driveway, which would have to be cordoned off. The household wheelie bin was out at the road. I lifted the lid – damn it, it had already been emptied. I wondered if I could get the truck stopped before any potential evidence got emptied at the dump. A truckload would be a hell of a lot less unpleasant to search through than a dump full.

My footsteps crackled on the driveway. God knows how many cars had been up here in the last few days; I didn't rate the chances of finding any trace of Dora McGann's white van. My gut told me that it had everything to do with this case.

I stepped up onto the veranda, smoothed down my uniform, drew a big breath and rang the doorbell. After what seemed an age, the door opened.

'Oh. Ah, hello, Mrs Watson.' It hadn't occurred to me someone else might answer. 'I was wondering if Lockie was in?' Leonore opened the door fully when she saw it was me.

'Well, actually, he's out at the moment. He took Angel to the doctor; she's been grizzly and rubbing at her ear. We wondered if she had an ear infection and, considering everything that's happening, thought we'd better get it checked out. Is there something I can help you with? Do you want to come in?'

Shit, that was the last thing I wanted to do. But this couldn't wait until Lockie got back. There was no way around it: I would have to take the direct approach.

'I can't come in, but there are a few things I need to discuss with you. If you could come out here it would be helpful.'

Leonore looked puzzled, but obediently stepped out onto the veranda. She was a tall woman, like her daughter, and I was eye level with her chin.

'Has something happened?' she asked.

'Yes.' I had to force myself to look her in the eye. 'There's been a major development in the case.' I couldn't think of a gentle way to put it, so spoke the words with care. 'Gaby's death is now being treated as murder.'

She stared at me for a moment, then said 'Murder', as though testing the word out for size. She then stepped back and leaned hard against the door jamb. Her face had paled and tears trickled down her cheeks. She reached into her pocket, pulled out a perfectly pressed handkerchief and dabbed at the tears. I waited to see if she would say something more, but no words came, so I fumbled for something comforting to say.

'I'm sorry, I know it must be a huge shock, but yes, it now appears that Gaby was murdered.' There was no good time for the next bit of news, so I pressed on. 'It also means that the case is now a murder investigation so—'

'But that means we were right all along,' she said, still wiping her eyes. 'I told you from the beginning that Gaby would never kill herself.' Leonore stood upright; her pallor had begun to infuse with blotches of pink. The more she said, the higher her voice rose. 'You're sorry, you say you're sorry. I said there was no way, no way she would kill herself, but you wouldn't listen.' Her index finger now waggled near my nose. Her anger blew in like a storm. I had to take a step back.

'Mrs Watson, I know that is what you said, and I know you are very upset, but whoever killed Gaby went to a lot of effort to make it look like she killed herself. To all intents the evidence pointed to a classic suicide.'

'Oh, you have classic suicides now, do you? Is that how you justify not doing your job properly. It looked like a classic suicide?'

This was not quite how I'd imagined this conversation would go and I certainly hadn't expected to have the finger pointed at me. It was difficult to think under her accusing glare.

'Mrs Watson, initially it looked like suicide, but new evidence leads me to believe Gaby was murdered. What that means—' Leonore went to interrupt again, but I put up my hand to stop her. Her face looked like thunder and I knew I would pay for the gesture. 'What that means is that this is a murder investigation now and that the house is a crime scene. I'm going to have to ask you to quickly pack what you need for yourself, Lockie and Angel, and to leave the house.'

'Oh, bloody hell.' Somehow the expletive sounded shocking coming from her. 'You're going to throw them out of their home, after everything they've been through? How can you be so heartless? Is this your way at getting back at him? Your petty jealousy? I don't believe this. Who is your superior?'

I concentrated hard to keep my voice measured and calm.

'We need to secure the house, so the forensics team can search for any evidence that might lead us to the killer.'

'In the time you've fiddle-faddled around, the murderer is probably at the other end of the country. What evidence could they find now? Tell me that? If you'd done this right at the beginning they might have found something, but for heaven's sake, everyone's been through the house, it's been cleaned top to bottom. Whatever do you expect to find? If the murderer gets away, it will be entirely your fault. You didn't believe us. You didn't act straight away. It will be on your head.'

I had to push my hands into my pockets.

'Mrs Watson, I had to make a judgement call based on the evidence to hand. I followed procedure, and it is in the follow-up investigations that evidence of foul play has become apparent. I know you are upset, but right now the most important thing to do is secure the house to give the forensics team the best chance of finding any remaining evidence. So I am going to have to ask you to get what you need immediately, to touch as little as possible and leave the house.' My mouth crackled as I spoke, saliva nowhere to be found. God, I wished this conversation was over.

'I don't believe this. Where am I supposed to go? Tell me that. Where are we all supposed to go? What about Lockie and Angel when they get home?'

'I've made arrangements for you all at the Angler's Lodge Motel. The police will pay for the expenses. You can go straight there. I'll wait here for Lockie and explain the situation to him. He won't be able to enter the house, so I need you to get whatever he and Angel will need.'

'What they need is to be left in peace, not to be thrown out of their own home. I can't believe you'd do that to them. I'll do what you ask, but you mark my words, I will be talking to your superiors about this.' She pointedly turned her back on me, went into the house and slammed the door.

I flinched, then let out a breath that came from my boots, right about where my heart lay.

She had every right to be upset and angry, and I knew I'd just copped a lot of her pent-up frustrations. But it still didn't stop me from feeling foolish as I wiped away the tears that rolled down my face.

I turned and crunched down the driveway, feeling the imaginary daggers Leonore Watson was likely firing into my back. I would wait in my truck until Lockie and Angel got home, then I would have to gather up the strength to endure a replay of the whole conversation.

12

Thank God for coffee and the relative sanctuary of the station. Lockie's reaction hadn't been vehement like Leonore's. I would have preferred it though if he'd yelled or argued or sworn. The sullen silence and hurt-laden eyes were far harder to stomach.

'Fine,' he'd said.

I'd told him his wife had been murdered, and I had kicked him and Angel out of their home, and all he said was 'Fine'.

The only good news was that I'd managed to track down the rubbish truck before it offloaded at the tip. It would be an unpleasant job for some poor sucker, and chances were they wouldn't find anything of interest, but it was a job that needed to be done. You never knew what got put out in the trash.

I'd also made another phone call, hoping I wouldn't be stepping on any toes, but the person I wanted to speak to was out, so while I waited for him to return my call I'd been entertained by the trainee fire-truck driver having to make a second attempt at backing the fire engine into the station next door. He'd get heaps about that at smoko. The last call-out the volunteer brigade had attended was a fire caused by a poled possum. The dumb bugger had fried itself on some over-head power lines and set fire to the grass when its blazing carcass hit the ground. That happened a bit around here.

I snatched up the phone on just the second ring.

'Shephard.'

'Sam,' the voice drawled, 'that's a very officious greeting.'

'Alistair, nice to hear your dulcet tones. Is the old boy away on one of his trips again?'

Alistair Gibb was the junior pathologist at Invercargill's Southland Hospital. He was also a close family friend. Way back in my youth, he would come and spend school holidays with our family on the farm, before being shipped back to boarding school. His parents were both professional folk without the time or inclination to spend the vacations with their son. He was in the same class as my older brother, Mike, so came home with us every holiday – kind of like looking after the class goldfish.

'The boss went to Rarotonga and left me in charge of the kingdom. Silly him, eh?' he said, with just a hint of a gloat in his voice.

'Tut, tut, some people never learn.'

'Tut, tut, yourself, sunshine. By the way, interesting little case you sent me. Lucky for you we were quiet. I was able to get on to it straight away.'

'I wanted to talk to you about that. I have strong reason to believe this was not a suicide.' OK, my reasons were not that strong, but I wasn't going to let him know that.

'Well, I'd have to agree with you there.'

It probably sounds crass to say, but I was delighted to hear my instincts had been proven correct, especially now the CIB juggernaut had rolled into action on my call.

'You got my attention. What's your verdict?'

'Official cause of death is drowning, which you would expect considering you found her body in the river. She was alive when she went in. We've sent a blood sample away to ESR for an urgent Midazolam level – that's Hypnovel – but it will be another twelve hours before it's back. I would be prepared to put money on its being ridiculously high.'

'Define ridiculous?'

'Higher than what you'd expect from the number of tablets she swallowed.'

I didn't say anything, so he continued.

'Well, her stomach contents show she had swallowed perhaps five or six tablets.'

'But there were thirty tablets missing from that new box. Why would there be so few in her stomach?'

'That's where it gets interesting. Granted, she could have vomited.

Then she wouldn't have been as sedated, and anyway, that's not what I think happened.'

'Get on with it, Sherlock.'

'Seeing as she didn't have many tablets in her stomach, and they weren't that well dissolved, I paid really close attention to her skin. Sure enough, there was a puncture mark on her right buttock.'

'Puncture mark? A needle?'

'Needle. There was a tiny bruise. She must have moved when it went in. So, my theory is that someone made her swallow enough tablets to make it look the part, then injected her with a huge dose to knock her out. Given in higher doses, Midazolam is used as a general anaesthetic. She would have been out in five minutes, tops. There were no other signs of bruising, so she didn't struggle. A few scrapes, which you'd expect from someone bumping along a river bottom, but that was it. She would have been completely unconscious. If, by chance, she was semi-conscious, she wouldn't have remembered a thing.'

Well, she wasn't remembering anything now.

'You, sir, have been watching far too much Discovery Channel,' I said, grateful for the fact my friend was a first-class nerd.

'I know, but do I get full points?' The gloat was very evident now. Deservedly so.

'Abso-bella-lutely. If you're right, which given what you've described, I have no doubt about, someone has gone to an awful lot of trouble to make this look like a suicide.' I thought through the implications. 'Why would they only make her swallow a few tablets?'

'Have you ever tried taking more than two? Firstly, it would take too much time, and secondly, you'd get pretty bloated and horrible on all that water needed to wash them down before you got enough into you. Quite clever of them really. I have no doubt the drug they injected would have been the same as the oral tablets. They appear to have been quite determined to make it look like a suicide, even to the extent of trying to fool a post-mortem.'

'The swallowed tablets, for the stomach contents?' I asked.

'Exactly.'

'Who would be able to get hold of Mizadolam?'

'Midazolam.'

'Midazolam.' I corrected the word on the notes I'd been jotting down. 'Who would be able to get hold of it in an injectable form? The tablets were from a forged prescription. Is the injection available on prescription too?'

There was a bit of a pause while he ruminated on that one.

'Yes, but it's not straightforward. They have to get special dispensation. I suppose it's used in veterinary medicine. I wouldn't know offhand, you'd have to check with a vet. It can't be that easy to access. Then again, you can buy anything on the internet now – no prescription required, a credit card is all the authority you need.'

I made a mental note to do a search and see what websites came up.

'What did you estimate as the time of death?'

'Given the water temperature and conditions, my guess would be between ten a.m. and midday on the Tuesday. I'll send you the full report as soon as it's written up.'

'Well, Alistair.' He was quite particular about being called Alistair, not Al. 'You've been a marvel. The boss better watch out; his job might be in jeopardy when he gets back from the sunshine.'

'Of course you'll put a good word in for me when I try to usurp him?'

'Naturally,' I laughed.

'I'll be in touch when that blood level comes through. I did mark it urgent, but you can't expect miracles. You must keep me posted on any developments. I'm really curious. This kind of thing doesn't happen around here.'

'You're right. It's provided our bit of excitement for the month. Thanks.'

'Oh, one last thing.'

Please, not another invitation for a date.

'She was pregnant, three months.'

'Jesus,' was all I could manage.

13

Once again I had to pay a visit to Lockie, although this time it was at the less than homely Angler's Lodge. There was no sign of Leonore's vehicle, but it was only a small consolation. I thought my heart couldn't feel any heavier after having to tell him of Gaby's death. I had been wrong. It took several moments to work up the courage to knock. A brief reprieve – it was Cole who answered the door.

'Sam.'

'Cole. Is Lockie in?'

'No. They've gone to the funeral director's.'

Relief was immediate, and breathing a lot more comfortable.

'You're holding the fort?'

He nodded. 'Angel's asleep, so I'm babysitting – kind of.' He didn't seem entirely comfortable with the idea, and no doubt desperately hoped Angel stayed asleep. Still, he occupied the doorway and showed no sign of vacating it. I was unsure as to my next move.

'Something wrong?' he asked.

What wasn't wrong? 'No. Well, yes actually.'

How much did I tell him? I figured he was the family's advocate, so to speak; he was certainly Lockie's rock. Unlike a few others in the town, I didn't really give a toss about privacy issues. As far as I was concerned, a bit of freedom of information, within reason, was to everyone's benefit.

'Well, you know how Lockie and Leonore have always maintained this was not of Gaby's doing?'

A slow nod was as far as his response went.

'And I'm sure they told you why they've been moved to a motel. Well, there's more now I've had the interim post-mortem report.'

'You'd better come in then,' he said.

I'd chosen the Angler's Lodge because it was a little more spacious than most. The luxury stopped there. Its eighties' décor and mass-produced pastel artworks would have been welcoming once. Now, it just looked tired. There was an abundance of floral tributes occupying every available surface, a sure sign of a household in mourning. It always seemed a bit absurd to me – killing flowers to acknowledge a death – but to some it was a form of comfort. Leonore must have thought so: she'd rescued them from the house.

'Cuppa?'

'Thanks, that'd be great.' I pulled out a chair and plonked myself down at the Formica-topped table.

'Tea, isn't it. Milk, no sugar?'

'That's right, thanks.' I was very impressed he too remembered.

I thought back to earlier conversations, particularly my unfortunate talk with Leonore. Somehow that one affected me more than the others. The thought that she viewed me as jealous and incompetent bothered me. But how could you explain to someone so aggrieved that you'd done everything right? I'd replayed the order of events over and over, and there wasn't any other way I could have called it. The murderer had gone to great lengths to make Gaby's death look like suicide. This investigation was far from over and I'd be seeing Leonore again, and often. So how could I repair the damage? I needed to.

'Here you go.' Cole pushed across a coaster and sat the tea down on it. 'So, what's happened?'

I was just about to launch into a summary of Alistair's report when a hearty wail erupted from one of the bedrooms. A look of abject panic crossed Cole's face. Who would have thought ten kilograms of baby could cause such terror in what must have been one hundred kilograms of male?

'Shit,' he muttered, leaping up from his chair as if stung on the arse by a bee. I doubted the child had a chance to draw a second breath before Cole had dived into her room.

'Shit,' I heard him say again. I couldn't help but let out a snort, and then realised that he did mean shit, and plenty of it, judging by the aroma that wafted in my direction. He came out with a very grumpy-looking Angel, dangling her by the armpits, held out at arm's length. I didn't even bother trying to disguise my mirth now, and erupted into laughter at the sight of his obvious discomfort.

'You couldn't, could you?' he begged.

I love the way men assume women know how to deal with babies. And although I generally enjoy the sight of a grovelling male, compassion kicked in – for Angel. It must have been hard on her armpits.

'Hand her over,' I said, and stood up to take her. Cole thrust her into my arms as if she was an unexploded mortar. The fact she had already 'gone off' was lost on him.

'Where do they keep the doings?' I had attended to the business end of my nieces on occasion, so at least I knew what was required.

He inclined his head towards a nappy bag in the corner of the lounge area, next to the sofa. This wasn't in my job description, though I did have a vague recollection of a clause concerning chemical and biological contamination in the health-and-safety section. I pulled out the changing mat and accoutrements and spread them out on the floor. Thankfully, Angel decided to cooperate and lay pretty much still for me. As I dealt with what could only be described as DEFCON 1, I outlined the day's events and my conversations with Dr Arnold and Alistair. I left out Gaby's pregnancy – that was a bit too sensitive to share with a third party and I still didn't know exactly how I'd broach that one with Lockie.

Cole stood at a discreet distance, his face unreadable as I related what I knew. He didn't offer any comment or question; only an occasional twitch and a severely glum expression gave any sense of the depth of his feelings.

I fastened the last dome on Angel's pants and let her loose on the world. She immediately crawled over and pulled herself up against Cole's legs. The sheepish expression that crossed his face was rather endearing. He picked her up by the armpits again and took her over to some toys in the corner.

'Why would someone want to kill Gaby?' he finally asked.

'Well, that is the million-dollar question. If we could answer that, we'd find her killer.'

I was about to find a place to dispose of the nappy bomb when a vehicle pulled up outside the motel room. My innards gripped. The little interlude with Angel's nether regions had momentarily eased my trepidation. It came back with a vengeance. I looked up at Cole; it was my turn to plead.

'Cole, I need you to stick around. I've got something bloody awful to tell Lockie, and it's not going to be good.'

14

The sound of chair legs screeching across the wooden floor grazed my eardrums and did nothing for my already jangled nerves as I watched the procession of officers enter and settle into place. The Mataura Elderly Citizens Centre had been promoted from sometime housie venue to official command centre. There was more rank here than a dung heap, and I was acutely aware they were soon going to have their collective attention focused on me. It was incredible how quickly the police behemoth could shuffle into action when it had to.

It was now 6pm, only four hours after I'd called the District Commander, and here they were, illuminated under a flicker of fluorescent light: a collection of CIB detectives and officers from as far afield as Invercargill and even Dunedin.

Time is of the essence in any murder investigation as evidence has a nasty habit of being cleaned away and even the hottest of trails chills with time. The first twenty-four hours are vital. In this case, because of the efforts of the killer to disguise the crime, we'd already lost that window. But the hours couldn't be wound back. We'd have to make do with a cool trail. This lot would be out this evening, door-knocking and poring over the crime scenes.

Lockie and what was left of his family were now involved in a murder investigation, and their home was under the microscope that was the ESR forensics team flown down from Christchurch. I didn't fancy their chances of finding new evidence – Leonore's cleaning frenzy would have seen to that.

The Gore station commander, Senior Sergeant Ron Thomson, tapped me on the shoulder and whispered into my ear. 'Show time.' He smiled, with what he probably thought was reassurance, and nodded towards the hordes. 'They don't bite. Just give them the rundown, you'll be fine.'

Ron Thomson cut an imposing presence: tall, solid and with a face that in its resting state looked bloody mean. The powers that be were probably relieved he worked for us and was not on the other side of the ledger. We always referred to him as the Boss. Despite his exterior, he was quite approachable and had a hard-earned reputation for being firm but fair. He also had more hair on his chin than the top of his head, but no one was brave enough to make light of the fact.

I rubbed damp hands down my trouser legs and hovered behind him as he moved towards the lectern, ready to address the troops. Normally, I considered this room to be spacious, but with the number of bodies crammed in on chairs and desks and lining the walls, any glimpse of the wallpaper was obscured by a sea of blue. It felt uncomfortable, stuffy, and smelled heavily of male, even with the windows thrown open.

As Senior Sergeant Thomson began the formalities, welcoming everyone present, and thanking them for gathering so promptly, I took the opportunity to examine the array of faces while their attention was elsewhere. Some were familiar, and there were plenty I had never seen before. The majority of the district staff had been called in for the meeting; local knowledge was a valuable tool.

Paul Frost, a Gore detective, gave me a wink. I wrinkled my nose at him: God, he was a trier. He'd asked me out on a date a few times, and didn't seem to be deterred by the fact he was consistently refused. Persistent? Oh yes. Thick-skinned? Definitely. Too egotistical to accept a woman might not be interested? Absolutely.

The mention of my name pulled my attention back into focus. The Boss had wrapped up his introductory spiel; I was next in the hot seat. I wiped my hands again and, with a here-we-go glance at him, exchanged places.

If the Senior Sergeant dwarfed the lectern, I struggled to see the front-row faces over the top of it. The fact was not lost on some of the more obnoxious local chaps in the audience.

'Stand up, Shep! We can't see you.' That was Paul sodding Frost.

'Oh, sorry mate, she *is* standing.' His partner in crime, Darren McKenzie, this time.

I gave them my very best 'may-your-private-parts-wither-and-die' look, as a wave of laughter washed around the room. Apparently, the others thought it was funny too. I wasn't particularly amused, especially in light of the fact they were right. But I tried to look casual as I stepped around the lectern to address the room from the side of the rotten bloody thing. At least the laughter had broken the tension.

'Thank you very much for your astute observation,' I said, 'although I liked the view better when I couldn't see the front row.'

Another ripple flowed around the room, so I used the moment to regroup. My voice was fragile and high-pitched; it took a conscious effort to lower it to something that at least sounded informed and confident.

As I related the information we had, which was precious little, the vague nausea that had been touring its way around my innards began to ease. We would, I said, have to start out with very little in the way of clues. We knew the first scene in this distasteful crime took place in Lockie's home, but we needed to locate where Gaby was assisted or dumped into the river. We knew the script for the Hypnovel was forged, though unfortunately the perpetrator hadn't had an attack of the stupids and presented the original script. All of the region's pharmacies had been notified to keep on the lookout for it. As it turned out, the tablets were just a prop. We would have to wait another twelve hours for the interim blood-level results from ESR.

I reported that no suspects immediately jumped to attention. Naturally, the first person looked to was the victim's spouse, and Lockie had been eliminated easily. A quick phone call to the works had confirmed he'd been on site all day. He'd eaten lunch in the canteen with his shift supervisor, so had a solid alibi.

I'd never considered him a possibility. Statistics might tell us the spouse is often the most likely candidate, but in this case they'd be wrong. Besides the alibi, and the fact that his performance as grief-stricken husband would have been worthy of the highest accolades had he killed Gaby, I didn't think I could have been such a bad judge of character. I'd lived with the man for two years; I was pretty bloody sure I knew him. He didn't have the stomach for a good argument, so I couldn't picture him having the wherewithal to kill off his wife. He was Mr Peace-at-all-costs.

I didn't mention to the assembly my unease about Dr Walden. I had nothing concrete on him, but he'd hovered on the fringe of my attention after our meeting. His mother couldn't have stressed upon him the importance of a first impression quite the way mine had; as a result, it had made me think about his access to prescription pads and his drug knowledge.

Of course, the other question that screamed to be asked was why? Gaby Knowes was a young mum in a small town. God knows I didn't particularly like her, but it was difficult to imagine she could have made enemies desperate enough to kill. Angel had been spared. A killer with a conscience? Or a killer lacking the guts to kill a child? Perhaps Angel was alive by grace of the fact she was too young to talk.

God, if only she could.

15

It was close to ten o'clock when I finally crawled home.

Maggie greeted me from the sofa. She looked extremely comfortable in her pyjamas, and nursed what I assumed was a good book.

I shut the door and slumped back against it. 'There are days, and then there are days.'

'I take it you've had a day,' she said, a smile spread across her face. 'Put your feet up. I'll make you a Milo, then you can tell Mummy all about it.'

It was by far the best offer I'd heard in a long time.

'Weet-Bix for dinner, I see.' Maggie was a firm believer in breakfast cereal as the perfect meal substitute at any time of day.

'Breakfast of champions,' she said. 'So that must make me…'

'Too lazy to cook!' I chipped in.

I laughed at the rude gesture fired my way and headed for my bedroom to change. I was sick to death of the sight of constabulary blue. When I re-emerged sporting my sexy flannelette pyjamas – passion killers, as my mother labelled them – and Ugg boots, an industrial-sized mug of hot, steaming Milo was waiting for me. It sat next to that other big girl's comfort-food essential – a packet of Toffee Pops. 'You are just too good to me, my friend,' I said, and gratefully collapsed into the other sofa.

'I'm sure you'd do the same for me.'

'Damned right.' I raised my Milo. 'To any excuse for a Toffee Pop. Cheers.'

'Any excuse for a *packet* of Toffee Pops,' Maggie said. It would prove to be an accurate toast.

'So,' Maggie said, having given a couple of the biscuits a new home, 'what's going on? I see the reinforcements have come to town; there were a hell of a lot of cars with matching uniforms. Rumours are rife. Mrs McGann is just about having apoplexy – she rang, by the way, along with half a dozen others trying to find out what the story is.'

'God, where do I start?' I was polite enough to swallow before I continued. 'As you've probably guessed, we're picking Gaby was murdered. Poor Lockie, how the hell do you live with that? He's not a suspect, by the way.'

'Good alibi?' Maggie spoke with just a hint of mockery.

I shot her a look. 'He was at work all day. Anyway, we don't have any suspects really – well, maybe a vague one. In a nutshell, we know sweet stuff all. Someone has gone out of his or her way to make it look like a suicide. There were no signs of struggle, so she was persuaded to write a note and must have cooperated with everything. I'd hazard a guess Angel was used for leverage there. She was made to swallow some sleeping tablets, then injected with a dose of sedative big enough to stop an elephant, then popped into the river to drown. That's all we know, really.'

Most officers had wives, husbands or partners to offload their day on. I had neither the luxury nor benefits of pillow talk, but Maggie was the next best thing, and I knew whatever I discussed with her would not be repeated. Chatting with her about cases always helped to clarify my thought processes. She was an unpaid team member, really; I was lucky to have her.

'Why on earth would someone want to kill Gaby?' Maggie asked the obvious.

'Exactly.'

'And they made it look like suicide?'

'Did a good job too. A fair bit of planning must have gone into it. The tablets were from a forged script in her name and the injection isn't the easiest of stuff to get hold of, so initially we'll be looking at who can source it. We know doctors can; pharmacists and possibly vets – oh, I must check out if the vets—'

I was interrupted by the sound of Maggie doing her best to choke on a biscuit – the last one, I might add.

'You OK?' I hopped up, ready to administer some emergency first aid.

She waved me off and, when she could finally get the word out, said hoarsely, 'Doctors?'

'Yes, but it's a bit of a rigmarole apparently. Why?'

'Well…' She hesitated a bit. 'I'm not one to gossip, but – Christ, I sound like an agony aunt from a B-grade TV show. Anyway, this is only second- or third- or fourth-hand information, and I have no idea if it is actually true.'

'For God's sake, girl, get on with it.'

'Gaby was having an affair.'

This was the second time I'd heard that rumour. Somehow it carried more weight coming from Maggie.

'An affair? Who the hell with?'

'Her doctor.'

It was my turn to spit and choke.

'Walden?'

'Yup.'

'That supercilious bastard! Gaby … she … but, Lockie. That bloody tart! How the hell could she betray Lockie like that? My God, how dare she…' Then another point dawned on me. 'How long have you known about this? Weeks? Months? Why didn't you say anything before?'

'What were you going to do? Go down and arrest her for adultery? You know as well as I do that the freezing works is Grand Gossip Central, and everything gets embellished. I wasn't going to give credence to a rumour by spreading it. All it would have succeeded in doing was upsetting you.' She gestured her hand towards me. 'Look at your reaction now.'

She did have a point, but I wasn't going to concede it.

'I am not upset. Well, yes, I am upset. Of course I am. I thought I knew you better than that.'

I knew I shouldn't go off at Maggie, but I couldn't help myself. I was too tired and too strung out to stop it. My rational self was MIA.

'Don't you think Lockie had the right to know that something was going on under his nose? If he knew that I knew, he'd be mortified. And if I had known, I should have been able to tell him. Don't you think I owed him that? You should have told me. How could you have hidden that from me?'

My voice was laden with hurt, but Maggie's face showed little sign of sympathy.

'Whoa, back off, sunshine. Get down off your high horse. God, I knew this would happen.' She threw her hands up in the air. 'If you would stop feeling miffed long enough to get back to what we were talking about. Firstly, the rumour is just that: rumour. Secondly, you're missing the point here.' Her voice was getting as loud as mine.

'And what point would that be?'

'Do I have to spell it out? Gaby was having an affair with her *doctor*?'

She was about to get a 'who-bloody-well-cares-who-it-was-with' lecture when the red murk cleared and realisation whacked me in the guts with a baseball bat. I whumphed back into the sofa.

'Shit.' The shot of perspective had pushed my petty feelings of betrayal back to where they belonged.

Our voices descended to a more conversational level.

'Perhaps she became too high maintenance for a bit on the side. Who knows? Walden knew she was pregnant, decided that was too much bother and arranged to take care of the baggage.'

Maggie's face reflected her incredulity. 'Oh God, she wasn't, was she?'

'Oh yes, she was.'

'Well, that could certainly be classed as motive for murder.'

'Yeah, but it's too easy, too straightforward. It's a small town, everyone would find out. That would be too risky, even for him.' I half believed it myself.

'Have you met his wife?' Maggie asked.

I hadn't had the pleasure. The Waldens chose to live in Gore, rather than in the kind of accommodation Mataura had to offer. It might have only been fifteen minutes up the road, but Gore was a different world.

'Bit of a battleaxe?'

'She is one scary chick, and I can't imagine her lying down and letting herself be trodden over. She would take him for every cent she could lay her well-manicured hands on. He wouldn't have a chance.'

'Perhaps she did it, then?' I mused. 'Found out through the grapevine that some cheap troll had the audacity to screw her slimy bastard husband and decided to take matters into her own hands?'

'Maybe, maybe not.' Maggie shrugged her shoulders.

Call me old-fashioned, but I just couldn't picture women being ruthless enough to be killers. Psychological warfare? Yes. Manipulation? Yes. Cold-hearted killing? No. It was really a bit naïve, considering how many murderers were busy rotting away in our women's prisons, but it was something I just couldn't get my head around. Murder was too personal, too ... messy.

'You know, this was very well organised and executed – excuse my choice of words there. Perhaps he, she, they paid someone to do it,' I said, thinking out loud.

That was a very real possibility. Discreet, and you didn't have to look the victim in the eye: an excellent solution for someone with a surplus hanger-on.

'Who would do that kind of thing?' Maggie asked. 'You can't exactly look up "Killer for hire" in the Yellow Pages.'

'Good point, but it must be possible. Policing doesn't pay that well. Maybe *I* could take it up, you know, part-time – still keep my day job.'

'Hon', you get squeamish popping your own zits, let alone popping off a customer.'

Somehow, that seemed absurdly funny, and we laughed a lot longer than was strictly necessary before we tailed off to an almost awkward silence. I did feel better about things after a good guffaw, but still resented Gaby for betraying my Lockie. Perhaps some people just got what they deserved.

I hauled myself out of the sofa. 'Time to crash. Thanks for telling me about Walden. And I'm sorry, you know, I shouldn't have jumped down your throat. It's been a long few days.' But curiosity still had a hold of me, so I posed the question that nagged.

'How long have you known, by the way?' I tried to sound casual.

'I think I'm damned no matter how I answer that question,' Maggie said. Quite a clever response really – it avoided a definitive reply.

I grinned at her. 'Any other interesting rumours or bright ideas, please fire them my way.'

She gave me a salute and called out 'Night' as I headed to my bed.

I was going to have to take Chrissie, the practice nurse, up on her hint and figure out how to see her tomorrow without arousing suspicion. Some digging into Dr Walden's history was in order. Meantime, what I needed was the oblivion of sleep, and lots of it.

16

My much-anticipated oblivion never eventuated. Despite an over-whelming need for sleep, I couldn't turn off my bloody brain. It kept rerunning conversations in the hope of picking up missed clues, flashing back to the more unpleasant moments of the previous thirty-six hours or so.

Of course, wakeful in the dark, I indulged in some mental mud-slinging too. I couldn't keep my mind from Lockie, and how he would feel on discovering his wife was a two-timing bitch. I just couldn't understand where she was coming from. Lockie was a won-derful man, a fine father, I was sure – and, come to think of it, no slouch in the sack either. Why the hell would that daft cow risk throwing it all away on a sleazoid piece of shit like Tony Walden? Especially a piece of potentially homicidal sleazoid shit.

And then there was the whole pregnancy thing. Whose baby was it, anyway?

I wrenched my mind away from what could only turn into a downward-spiralling string of blame and obscenities to focus on the task at hand. At some ungodly hour of the morning, a germ of an idea crept into my head. There was one sure-fire way of talking to Chrissie in private without drawing any suspicion from the other staff at the medical centre. So here I was, in the full glare of day, parked outside the surgery, yet again, like some sick playback of *Groundhog Day*. I garnered up the courage to go through with my plan. A shot of Dutch courage would probably have helped, but this wasn't really the time or place.

'Get on with it, Shep.' I jumped down out of the truck and headed towards the medical centre before I could change my mind. Then I marched straight up to the reception desk.

'Can I see Chrissie, please?' I whispered to Francine.

'Is this about that poor young woman again? I can't stop thinking about it, such a waste…'

'Actually, it's something more personal today. I'm due for my cervical smear test. Can't put it off for ever, I suppose.' I could feel my nose wrinkling up, unbidden.

'Oh, that. Lucky you. Take a seat. Chrissie won't be long.'

I couldn't believe I was about to carry out a police interview from the business end of a speculum. I would place bets that no male officer in the country had ever conducted police work with a finger poked up his arse, while his doctor checked his prostate. Of course, I could just have requested that Chrissie come down to the station for a wee chat, but firstly, I didn't want Dr Walden getting a jump on us and ditching any potentially damning evidence and, secondly, the whole affair thing was just hearsay. I thought it wise to be sure of my facts before I made a fool of myself in front of my superiors.

Smear tests are just like car maintenance, I told myself. You might not like it at the time, but it could improve your overall mileage. Besides, I'd always thought it funny that most of us were squeamish about the damned things, considering what else got poked up there in our lifetimes.

'Sam, you want to see me?' Chrissie came over.

'I don't know if "want" is the right word. Let's just say I'm being a good girl.' I got up and followed her down to one of the nurses' rooms.

'So, what can I help you with? Are you here on business or pleasure?'

I toyed with the idea of direct questions, but thought better of it. Want it or not, I did need to do this.

'I wouldn't exactly call it pleasure. I need a smear test.'

'When was your last one?'

'Five years, give or take a few.'

She gave me a tut-tut look and smiled. 'You're not afraid of them, are you, Sam? Was the last one normal?'

'Perfectly, and I'm not ashamed to say these things make me nervous.'

'Don't be silly, they're a doddle. Just undress from the waist down, hop up on the bed and I'll be back in a moment. Use that sheet to cover yourself.'

She left the room and closed the door behind her, so I stripped down, folding my trousers and underpants over the chair. I shoved my socks into their respective shoes and lamented the poor state of my toenails – I'd forgotten they'd be on public display, otherwise I'd have removed the chipped remnants of 'lunar' nail enamel still clinging to the top half of each one. Thank God I'd shaved my legs.

Perched up on the bed, sheet strategically placed, I looked around the room like someone surveying the crowd before their execution. Along with the usual array of posters displaying alarming-looking skin conditions, there were rows of shelves full of medical paraphernalia – oxygen cylinders, nebulisers, scales – as well as a sharps container, and a worrying-looking light and magnifying glass on the end of an articulated arm clamped to the end of the bed. I started at a knock on the door, and patted the sheet more firmly as Chrissie came back into the room. She donned a pair of latex gloves with an efficient snap.

'Don't look so worried. This won't take long. You've had smear tests before.'

'Yes, but it's never something you can say you enjoy, is it?'

'No, that's true, but it is a necessary evil. Now, I'll get you to lie on your side and face the wall, then bring your knees up to your chest.'

This was new. Last time I had this done I'd had to lie on my back, feet up, knees down, splayed like a spatchcock chicken. I rolled obediently onto my side, examined the paintwork closely and listened to the chinks and clunks as Chrissie arranged her implements of torture on a tray.

'Right, I'm just going to slide it in now. This may be a little uncomfortable.'

Just what I wanted to hear.

Anything that could clench, clenched.

'Just take a deep breath, let it out slowly and relax,' she said in her beautifully soothing voice.

It seemed to work, because with no discomfort at all I felt the speculum slide in and felt the small clicks reverberate through my innards as she spread the blades apart. Now was as good a time as any to be direct, considering how exposed I was.

'Were Tony Walden and Gaby Knowes having an affair?'

'You've chosen an interesting time to ask that question,' she said, without missing a beat.

I felt a slight scraping sensation somewhere entirely unnatural.

'Well, you seemed to want to talk to me, and this was the only way I could figure to do it discreetly, and in private.'

'You got that right; I can guarantee no one will walk in on us.' She chuckled. 'Hang on a moment, I've finished here.' She slid the speculum out and draped the sheet back over my bare bits.

That really had been a much better way of doing it, I decided. Looking at the wall was much less personal than trying not to look at someone as they peered at your privates.

I sat up and swung my legs around to face her.

'I wouldn't exactly call it an affair,' she said. 'They were having sex, but it was fairly one-sided, I imagine.'

'What do you mean?'

'To be blunt and concise, that revolting prick was blackmailing her. I overheard her one day, telling him she wouldn't do it any longer, and you know what he said?' Her eyes flickered above my head as she groped for the right words. 'He told her – no, reminded her, I should say – that all it would take would be one phone call to Child, Youth and Family and he could have Angel taken away from her.'

For one of the few moments in my life, I was speechless. No one could be that bloody rotten, surely? When I finally found my tongue, I was hardly pithy.

'He was what?'

'Blackmailing her.'

'That dirt-bag, opportunist bastard! But he wouldn't have any grounds to call them, would he?'

'No, but he could just make the details up. He could add a little here and there in her notes to create a bit of a history. No one would even consider the doctor could be lying. They're God, you know. And we all know what CYFs is like. Take the kid first, ask questions later. He could have ruined her life – well, actually he did. It was probably the prospect of losing Angel that drove her to take her life – and I didn't do a bloody thing about it.'

Chrissie looked away, tears misting her eyes. Only then did I notice how deeply ringed they were. She must have been beating herself up all night.

I reached out and touched her shoulder. 'Gaby didn't kill herself,' I said. 'She was murdered.'

Shock streaked across Chrissie's face.

'Murdered?'

'It was just made to look like a suicide. That's why I wanted to talk to you without anyone getting curious. The…' I was going to use the word 'affair', but that wasn't right. 'The blackmail makes Dr Walden a suspect, so if there is anything else you can tell me, I need to know.'

Chrissie did a very rattly sounding sniff and shook her head. 'I only overheard that one conversation. I kept my eyes out for signs he was doing it to any other poor women, but no, I think it was only Gaby. Do you really think he could have killed her?'

'I don't know, but I can't discount it. He was capable of blackmail, so who knows what else he could do. But, I have to ask you, Chrissie. Why didn't you say something about it earlier?'

She blew out a big breath and looked up at the ceiling. 'I should have, and God knows I regret not saying anything now, but things are kind of tight money-wise and I didn't want to risk losing my job. It would come down to my word against his, and I didn't think anyone would believe me.'

'When did you overhear the conversation?'

'It would have been a few weeks ago. It will be in the appointments diary when she was in.'

'Then tell me, how would he get hold of injections such as Midazolam?'

'An order form through the pharmacy is the usual way,' she said, then reached over for a tissue and blew her nose.

'I'd better get out there again. We've been a while.'

'I know this will be hard, but you must carry on like it's business as usual. We'll be bringing him in for questioning later. In the meantime, just keep your eye on him. I'll need you to make a statement later too. You can do that?'

She nodded, then turned and headed for the door.

'Thanks, Chrissie.'

She didn't look back. She would be battling her conscience for quite some time to come.

Blackmail. That placed quite a different complexion on everything. But it seemed so unlikely. The more I thought about it, the more it seemed like a pretty high-risk move for Walden. All Gaby needed to do was make one squeak and his career would be in tatters. There must have been something more to it for him to feel confident blackmail would work. Perhaps Gaby did have a bit of history – some of the most normal people you could meet have experienced drug addictions in their past or mental illness – any number of things. Maybe there had been some accident or incident with Angel that could easily be misconstrued to look like abuse. Why else would she feel he had the power to have Angel removed? How did the situation arise in the first place? I thought about the extent to which a woman would go to protect her child, and felt a pang of guilt of my own. I'd said and thought some nasty things about Gaby Knowes that had proven to be completely unwarranted.

It wasn't as if I could apologise to her in person, so I mumbled a 'Sorry, Gaby' in the general direction of the ceiling and jumped down off the bed.

It was only then that I realised I was still half naked. Chrissie's revelations had completely distracted me from self-consciousness. I hurriedly donned my clothing and exited the building as fast as I could. I had a ripe piece of information to take back to the Boss now. At last we had a solid suspect.

17

I took a slight detour on my way back to the command centre. In the wee hours of the morning another thought had come to me – one concerning the site where Gaby had been dumped into the river. I was by now absolutely certain she had not gone into the river from the back of the Knowes property, and the absence of her footprints made sense now. She would have been moved in a vehicle of some sort – the white van the most likely candidate. CIB were following up Dora McGann's sighting, but thus far had no idea as to who the mystery tradesman could have been or why he was there. Lockie knew nothing about him either. The TV hadn't blown up or the fridge conked out, as far as he knew. He said they always discussed things like repairs before calling anybody in.

Did Tony Walden have a van, or access to one?

I drove slowly along Wyndham Road. It was pretty quiet at this time of day. The only traffic I met was a couple of cars and a milk tanker. There weren't too many places where you could access the river between Gaby's house and the spot she had washed up. She must have gone in somewhere south of the house. The murderer would not have risked her coming to ground upstream. Even my grasp of physics told me bodies didn't travel against the current. I drove along, following the path of the Mataura, and pulled into the first river access. It was, I suppose, a good half a kilometre downstream from Lockie's, and was visually isolated from the road. I had to drive fifty metres or so along the track, the dips and hollows rocking me violently from side to side, before my truck disappeared down into the mantle of willows. Someone had the bright idea of introducing the willows along the riverbed for erosion control a hundred years ago. Like many introduced species, both flora and fauna, they were thriving in their new environment, to the detriment of the natives.

Here, they provided perfect cover from any observers passing by on the road.

I parked the truck on the last of the gravel and hopped out to make my way to the river on foot. There were several tyre imprints in the mud, which I carefully skirted. You'd need a four-wheel drive to get any further down this rutted, poor excuse for a track, unless you wanted to be towed out by a tractor. The chances had to be good that one of those sets belonged to the vehicle that transported Gaby. It was a wonder it hadn't got stuck.

The soundscape was almost deafening, with a mixture of the wind rustling the willow leaves, the low roar of the river and the throaty call of some tui. I moved on and negotiated the drop down the grassed bank to the shingle riverbed and walked across to the water. The river flowed fast, deep and relatively straight from this point, and with the higher than usual water level, there were no places a body could get snagged and be found too quickly. Its surface glittered fresh and lively in the morning light, and while there was no visible taint of its recent deathly cargo, to me it would never seem clean again.

I turned around and scanned for any glimpse of the nearby houses or the road. The belt of willow and poplar trees obscured them all. It was pretty much a perfect spot to slip someone into the river without attracting unwanted attention.

I wandered back towards the truck and took a closer look at the tyre prints. There were some beer-bottle caps pressed into the mud and grit, but judging by the rust, they weren't recent arrivals. It was impossible to know how many vehicles had been down here since Gaby's death. Some of the searchers had probably parked here. But anything was worth a crack: I'd get the forensics crew down here straight away. The sky was overcast to the south and threatening rain though. So just to be sure, I got out the camera and ruler and photographed the impressions. I would have covered them with my tarpaulins, but they hadn't been replaced after being used to cover Gaby's body.

The last thing I did as I left the access way was to block off the entrance with tape. It now sported a nice 'Police Scene, Do Not Cross' banner. It would have to do for now; there was no lockable gate. I was sure people would get the hint and stay the hell out.

Further down the road it was evident from a fair distance that the next access way was far too exposed. The river was clearly visible from the road, as was the car park. No one in their right mind would attempt anything nefarious in full view of the neighbourhood. I didn't even bother to stop, and instead turned around and headed back to see the Boss.

It was only nine-thirty a.m. and I thought I'd achieved a lot. I hadn't seen any of the other boys and girls in blue out and about this morning. The day's briefing wasn't due till 10, so perhaps they were having a late start or just busy setting up the command centre.

I looked forward to telling the Boss what I'd uncovered.

18

The Elderly Citizens Centre had undergone an amazing transformation overnight. Desks and computer terminals were congregated in the middle of the main room, their tendrils of cables radiating outwards, anchored periodically by blue duct tape. Sad to say, the effect was an improvement on the foul over-patterned carpet. Maps and photos adorned the walls, along with depressingly blank whiteboards. The room was abuzz with activity, and the phrase 'busy as a blue-arsed fly' jumped to mind. I smiled at the aptness. A few heads looked up as I entered; some of them continued to stare as I walked past. I acknowledged them with a quick hello and kept my eyes open for any sign of the Boss.

'Shep, the Boss is looking for you.' A voice I immediately recognised as Paul Frost's spoke from behind me. I turned and was about to give him some stick about the previous night's comments when I saw his face and thought better of it.

'What's wrong?' I asked. 'Is he in a bad mood?'

'Just slightly. He's over there.' Paul pointed towards the corner and a conglomeration of small rooms.

I headed over, taking care not to trip over any of the cabling. People were still staring, so I wiped at my face, in case anything was stuck to it.

'Constable Shephard, so nice of you to join us this morning.' The Boss was leaning against the doorway, clutching a large mug of coffee. He did look rather grumpy, but given his normal demeanour, that might not signify anything. The slight sarcasm in his voice wasn't lost on me, though.

'I have had a very productive morning and have uncovered some things you'll be very interested in.'

'Well, you'd better step into my office then,' he said, and moved out of the way to let me pass.

They must have set this up as an interview room. As well as a table with several chairs, the room had a video camera set up on a tripod, and sound-recording equipment. I plonked myself down at one end and waited.

When the Boss came in a moment or two later, he was with the District Commander and another man I recognised from the previous night's briefing. I stood up as they entered.

'This is District Commander Ian Frederickson.'

'Sir.' I reached across and shook his hand.

'And this is Detective Inspector Greg Johns.' I reached over and repeated the ritual. The Boss was being very formal. 'Constable Shephard is the Mataura station officer. It's a sole charge, so she is probably the most knowledgeable person when it comes to the local population. Take a seat, Constable. We're videoing this, by the way.'

There was a pause while we took our seats. Then the Boss got things under way.

'So what's the interesting information you uncovered this morning?' he asked.

I took a deep breath. 'Last night I heard a rumour that Gaby Knowes was romantically involved with Dr Tony Walden. Dr Walden is her GP, one of the doctors here in Mataura,' I added for the benefit of the out-of-towners. 'I thought it best to clarify the information, so this morning I went to the surgery and talked to Chrissie Andrews, his practice nurse. She was able to confirm that yes, Dr Walden and Gaby Knowes did have a relationship, but here is the major catch. Dr Walden was blackmailing her for sex.'

Three sets of eyebrows simultaneously shot up to the ceiling.

'That is quite an allegation to make,' DI Johns said. 'Why did she think that?'

'Ms Andrews overheard a conversation in which Mrs Knowes said she wanted them to stop meeting, but Dr Walden said he'd report her to CYFs and have her daughter removed from her unless she continued giving him sex.' The frowns that shot across the faces of such seasoned officers showed this was a new low, even for them.

The Boss shook his head. 'That certainly makes the doctor a viable suspect.'

'He would have access to the Midazolam injection and to Dr Arnold's prescription pads, and know how to write a script correctly for the tablets. With Mrs Knowes being pregnant, he may have had the impetus to remove a possible major complication in his life. He'd also know how post-mortems work, and therefore how to fool them.'

'You didn't question him at all, did you?' the DI asked, concern creasing his forehead.

'No, of course not, and I was very discreet. No one would have known I was questioning Ms Andrews.'

'How on earth did you manage that?' the Boss asked.

'Believe me, you do not want to know,' I said, and smiled.

'Well, actually, Constable, we would very much like to know.' This time it was the District Commander who spoke, and it was quite apparent he expected an answer.

I looked at him, hesitated, and then glanced at the Boss, who gave me a questioning look. There was no way out of this one. 'Well, I talked to her while she was giving me a cervical smear test.'

That really was more information than any of them wanted, judging by the 'ahems' and sudden fascination with the walls and ceiling.

'Well, that's an original way of conducting an interview,' the Boss said.

I laughed, a little too loudly, and felt the odd need to justify my actions. 'It was the only way I could think of to talk to her without arousing suspicion, and also to gain her trust.'

The DI took charge of the conversation again. 'Was she able to give you any other information?'

'Not specifically about the blackmailing. She did say it would be easy enough for Dr Walden to change the family's medical records to back his lie. Who would question his integrity? Also, she was able to clarify how the doctor would get hold of a drug like Midazolam in an injectable form, through a pharmacy order. We would be able to check the pharmacy's records to see the last time they received any.'

'The practice nurse is prepared to put this on record?'

'Yes,' I said. 'She feels badly about not speaking up earlier, so she'll make a formal statement.'

They looked at each other before the Boss asked, 'Was there something else you uncovered this morning?'

'Yes. I was thinking about where the killer would have dumped Mrs Knowes into the river. They would have had to use a vehicle to transport her, probably the van described by Mrs McGann, so I had a look at the access ways. One of them was far too exposed; it would be visible to the road and several neighbouring properties. But the entrance just south of the Knowes' house would be ideal. Once you turn off, it travels a distance towards the river, then trees obscure any view from traffic on the road and surrounding houses. There were a few tyre tracks down there, so I've taped off the entrance way till the forensics guys get down there.'

'Anything else?'

'No, I came straight here after the river.'

They did another round of eyeball and eyebrow conferring, before the Boss gave a nod and DI Johns cleared his throat.

'Constable Shephard, can you verify your whereabouts on Tuesday.'

'Pardon?'

'Can you verify your whereabouts on Tuesday?'

I became acutely aware of the fact we were in an interview room and there were three high-powered officers opposite me.

'I was on duty and have a record of visits in my notebook. It was a busy day – I saw quite a few people.' I cast my mind back: it had been full on. 'Fred Phillips reported a farm-bike theft. I went out to George Porter's – some of his sheep had been mauled by dogs; that took a while. I returned a recovered car stereo to Trevor Ray … there were several others. Why?'

'Do you have your notebook with you?'

'Yes, of course.' I fished around in my satchel and pulled out my work record.

'We will be taking your notebook into evidence, Constable Shephard.'

The sinking sensation that had been working its way through my chest finally hit my boots.

'Am I a suspect?' I asked, very quietly.

'Why didn't you inform me of your previous relationship with Lockie Knowes?'

This time the scrutiny was coming from the Boss. I was so flummoxed I couldn't even bring myself to reply.

'Constable, why didn't you inform me you used to live with Lockie Knowes?'

Like my private life was any of their bloody business.

'You have the right to have a lawyer present if you wish.' This time it was the District Commander.

Unbelievable. I had been running around all morning, going to great lengths to find leads and a bloody strong suspect, and here they were treating me like one?

I finally found my voice, and I'm afraid it was a little strident.

'I don't want a bloody lawyer present. I haven't got anything to hide.'

'You might like to watch the language, Constable. As I said, we are recording this interview.'

I swung my head around and registered the accusing glare of the video camera's red LED. The significance of his earlier comment about videoing the interview hit home. My legs thrust downwards and I was on my feet before I realised it.

'I am not a bloody suspect, I'm the bloody police.' I banged my hands on the table, and then pointed my finger directly at the Boss. 'You cannot possibly believe this crap. How the hell can I be a suspect?'

The Boss hauled himself to his feet and, in a voice that gave no room for discussion, roared, 'Sit yourself down right now. I will not have that kind of disrespect from my officers. You will answer the questions and you will do it now. Am I clear?'

I suddenly felt very small and very hot.

'Am I making myself clear?' The roar left no room for doubt.

'Yes, sir.'

Like a possum caught in headlights.

'Now sit!'

I felt like a chastened schoolgirl and, by God, I resented him for it. The silence in the room was intensified by the deafening silence on the other side of the door. Everyone within a ten-kilometre radius would have heard that outburst. How the hell would I be able to face any of my colleagues again? Slowly, the muffled sounds of work resumed.

The three sets of eyes opposite shot bullets and I cursed myself for my impulsiveness. I could see I would gain no quarter from these men.

'I'm sorry, sirs, you took me by surprise. I didn't mean any offence.' It was the best I could do at arse-licking for now; anger was too busy wrestling under my skin for me to be truly repentant.

'Now, will you answer the Senior Sergeant's question?' DI Johns took over the interview. 'Why did you not inform him of your past relationship with Lockie Knowes?'

'It didn't occur to me I'd need to. It was so long ago, it didn't seem relevant.' Of course, with the luxury of hindsight it was obvious I should have told the Boss. Of course, I would be a suspect. But it was all a bit late now. 'And I thought it was common knowledge. Everyone knew Lockie and I had been together. I assumed you knew.'

That sounded pretty feeble, even to my ears.

'How did you know to look for Mrs Knowes' body in the river?'

With that question I became uncomfortably aware of my predicament. What could I say? It seemed the obvious place to look. How the hell do you describe women's intuition? I suppose the men would call it a hunch. I decided on the educated-guess approach.

'Both Mr Knowes and I' – I tripped back into formal speak – 'had searched the house and surrounds. It was getting late and there was a possibility that Mrs Knowes was still alive. I needed to make a decision quickly about a search, so I thought the river would be the most obvious place for her to go if she didn't want to die in the house with the baby present. It was the place of greatest risk to her life; if she was determined, it would almost certainly result in death.'

That seemed to satisfy them, and I desperately hoped that was going to be the end of the matter. The room was feeling very close.

'It seems very convenient that you would be the one called out to the Knowes situation and could therefore be selective about the evidence, or contaminate it.'

It was an accusation that froze my blood. They were actually serious – it wasn't just going through the motions. They thought I killed her. I looked to the Boss for help, but was met by cold, dispassionate eyes. I began to wonder if a lawyer might be a good idea; but then this was not my doing; the guilt-free had nothing to fear. Why then did my bowels feel uncomfortably twitchy? I was going to have to choose my words carefully.

'I called in assistance from the Gore station immediately it became apparent a life was at risk. I collected the evidence at the Knowes house by the book.' Thank God. 'I photographed and quarantined evidence for removal and fingerprinting. Mr Knowes and Colin Avery were present at the time. All evidence pointed to a suicide at that stage, so I proceeded accordingly. As soon as it was apparent there could have been a homicide, I called in the CIB.'

'Don't you also think it's convenient your tyre tracks are now at the crime scene after your visit to the river this morning? A nice justification for their presence if the forensics team identifies them?'

How was it the innocent could dig themselves into a hole without even realising it? Here I was, thinking I was doing my job well, when in fact I was just incriminating myself. The pressure in my innards was building rapidly. God, I needed to go to the toilet. The last thing I wanted to do was crap myself in front of them. I took a deep breath, tried to ignore the cramps and squeezed my sphincter tight.

'I didn't take the truck onto the dirt. I parked it on the gravel, out of the way, to preserve any possible tracks.'

'But you then walked out to the river?'

Holy shit. I hadn't even considered footprints.

'Yes.'

The cramps got too much for me.

'May I be excused to go to the bathroom?' I was awash with sweat, my stomach seethed and I must have looked the part, because the Boss stood up immediately to escort me out.

A sea of faces turned and stared as we went out the door. They had a distinctly grey tinge to them and wavered in a most disturbing way. A large hand grasped my elbow and pushed me in towards the amenities.

'Oh Christ,' I said, and lunged towards the cubicle. I fumbled with my button and zip and didn't even bother to shut the door before I sat down. I didn't realise the Boss had followed me in until I looked up and saw a pair of blue legs – just before I vomited all over his shoes.

It took a while for me to get myself into some semblance of humanity again. I only just managed to keep it together enough to wipe my arse, get dressed and get out of the cubicle without fainting or slipping in the vomit. I had expected a tirade from the Boss, but he was uncharacteristically quiet as he handed me a damp cloth to clean myself up. He'd kicked off his shoes and they sat at the edge of the puke, a reminder of my moment of glory. My arms still tingling, I leaned against the basin and looked at myself in the mirror. It was not good. Unrecognisable, bloodshot, watering eyes returned my stare. My normally olive skin had taken on a transparent quality: I'd seen corpses with more colour. The hair around my face had glued itself to my forehead, and unfortunately some strands had picked up a few chunky bits. The unmistakable waft of vomit…

'Oh, Christ.' This time I made it to the other cubicle before I threw up.

Strong hands helped me back up and sat me on the toilet lid.

'I'm sorry,' I said, croakiness tingeing my voice. I blew my nose on some toilet paper. 'And I'm really sorry about your shoes. I'll buy you some new ones.'

'That won't be necessary,' he said as he passed me a glass of water. Then he looked at me contemplatively. 'You've made life very difficult for me, Sam. Why didn't you report in this morning? It didn't look good having you arrive late. You should have rung.'

'I didn't even think to. I'm so used to working by myself. I had this idea about interviewing the practice nurse and I just wanted to get it done.' Once again, hindsight told me he was right. But then: 'I had my cellphone; nobody rang me.'

He had to concede that point.

'I wish you'd told me about Lockie,' he said. 'Because you might be seen as having compromised the evidence. Any defence lawyer is going to have a field day.'

I looked up at him, but his face was, as usual, unreadable.

'The interview is unpleasant, I know, but necessary. Best you get it over with now.' That was not a request.

'Do you want me to clean that up?' I said, and leaned my head against the cubicle wall, tilting in the direction of my impressive miss.

'No, I'll find someone to do that.' I pitied the poor bugger.

The faces at the table did not seem any friendlier when I returned to the interview room. I had walked back through the main hall with my head down to avoid meeting anyone's eyes. It was almost a relief to hear the door close after me. Almost.

DI Johns started straight in.

'For how long did you have a relationship with Lockie Knowes?'

'Two and a half years.'

'You lived with him for all of this time?'

'No, we lived together for two years.'

'Who ended the relationship?'

I really didn't want to go into all that.

'He did,' I said quietly, knowing what was going to come next.

'Why?'

I looked up at the ceiling and tried very hard to prevent any tears betraying my emotions. I'd fail dismally if I was tortured. I wouldn't be heroic. I'd tell them anything they wanted straight away to put an end to the scrutiny. This was torture. Not only was my integrity being called into question but they also wanted me to bare my personal life for public record. My colleagues would see that video. I could already hear their sniggers and feel their derision. Oh Christ – and they would all find out how I questioned Chrissie. I could just imagine the quips I'd have to endure at work: jokes about smear tactics, running a smear campaign. That's assuming I still had a job. That's assuming I wasn't in jail.

'Constable Shephard, I asked you why?' The voice was very insistent.

'Lockie really wanted to settle down and have a family. He talked about marriage all the time, about having babies. I was very wrapped up in my job. I love policing; I wanted to advance my career, sit my exams. Ultimately, I want to become a detective. I felt too young to have children. I didn't want to postpone or give up my career prospects just to have kids. Lockie believed I could have both. I knew that was all he wanted, and I thought he understood my position and was prepared to wait a bit. I never realised how important it was to him.' My mind played back the awful night it all turned to custard, and I cringed at my stupidity. 'He proposed. He got down on bended knee with a beautiful ring, and he proposed. He asked me to marry him, to have his children…' I hesitated, still cursing my decision. 'And I said I wasn't ready. I chose my job. He chose to leave.'

There was silence in the room; I looked over towards the door. I couldn't meet their gaze.

'When did Mr Knowes start seeing Mrs Knowes?'

That question brought with it the taste of bitter acid. I closed my eyes, then opened them again with a sigh.

'Lockie started seeing Gaby within a month. They were married three months later. Angel was born within a year of their wedding.'

Please, I thought, don't ask me how I felt about it.

'How did that make you feel?'

I couldn't disguise the sarcasm in my reply. 'How do you think that made me feel?'

'Constable,' came the warning growl.

'Upset, disappointed, angry.' Words like nails in a coffin.

'Did you think Mr Knowes started seeing Mrs Knowes while you were still together?'

'No, no. They weren't introduced until after he left me. They met at the Middlemarch Singles Ball, of all places.' The event designed to match up lovelorn farmers with eligible women – the ultimate rebound fixture. 'No, Lockie was a good man. He would never have betrayed me like that.' I still defended him, even here. But I knew, deep down, my losing Lockie was one hundred percent my own damned fault. I had been blind to the warning signs, and too selfish to notice his unhappiness. It shouldn't have shocked me that he latched on to the first pretty face to come along.

I suspected what would come next. They had seemed pretty unsurprised by the order of events thus far.

'We have been told that you harassed Mr Knowes when he became engaged to Mrs Knowes.'

My misery was complete.

'I didn't harass him. I had one irrational moment when I had had a bit too much to drink and threw a beer bottle through his window. It is something I am very ashamed of, and I shall probably regret for the rest of my life. Lockie threatened to take a trespass order out on me. I fully realised my stupidity and the impact that it could have on my career. It was a real wake-up call. He knew it was just one drunken moment, and that I didn't want to hurt him or Gaby. He didn't lay charges or take out the order.'

I hung my head.

It was the Boss who summarised the situation for me.

'From our perspective, you had the motive to kill Gaby Knowes. You had the means to doctor the evidence to cover your tracks. You haven't adequately explained why you came to search the river so quickly, unless you already knew the body was there. You came up with an explanation for the forged script very quickly. You went to the river site this morning to create a viable reason for your vehicle tyre prints and your footprints to be there. Likewise, by being the first officer inside the Knowes house, you created a justification for your fingerprints and any possible DNA evidence to be there. Either you are very good at your job but very naïve, or you are culpable.'

What could I say to that? Argument was pointless.

'Am I under arrest?'

'Not at this time. We have your notebook in evidence and will examine it closely. We will be checking to verify your whereabouts. When that is completed, we will require you to come back in for further questions. You have given us another positive line of inquiry with Dr Walden, which we will have to verify was not fabricated.'

I was astonished. It was the only viable lead, and they could potentially stuff it up by questioning its authenticity. But from now on, I knew, they would question everything about me.

DI Johns continued on with more bad tidings. 'We require you to stay in the district and we require your passport.'

'I don't have one,' I said, numb.

'As of this moment you are suspended from duty. You may be called upon at any time to give further evidence. You are dismissed.'

I heaved myself to my feet and, with what felt like a mammoth effort, moved towards the door.

'Your keys.'

'Pardon?'

'The keys to your police vehicle and the station.' I dug into my trouser pocket and tossed the keys unceremoniously onto the table. Then with as much dignity as I could muster given the circumstances, I opened the door and then closed it gently behind me. Leaning back against the door jamb, I silently mouthed a very rude word, before I realised I had an audience. With great effort, I looked straight ahead, squared my shoulders and crossed the silent and watchful room.

It was a very long walk home.

'Thank God for small mercies.'

There was some tonic water in the cupboard to dilute the contents of the bottle of gin I clutched to my chest. Too bad if it was an improper time of the day to start drinking. I'd make an exception on this occasion – lunchtime was as good a time as any to start anaesthetising my woes. I would, however, make some nod towards decency and pour my G & T into a glass rather than a beer jug.

I took a sip that ended at the bottom of the glass, then poured myself another. Then I stripped off my uniform and tossed it behind the sofa where I didn't have to see it. It had suddenly made me feel very dirty. I couldn't be stuffed putting on anything else, so plonked down on the sofa in my underwear and settled in for an afternoon of wallowing in misery. I wondered how much alcohol it would take to slip into a coma.

The sound of a key in the door disrupted my pity party.

'Oh shit.'

'Sam?' Maggie's voice filtered through the murk in my head.

'Over here,' I said, and held my glass up by way of showing her where I was ensconced. She took one look at me draped across the sofa, looking ever so elegant in my red undies and matching eyeballs, then came around and gave me an enormous hug.

'So, it's as bad as they said?'

'It's worse,' I said before the question really registered. 'Who said?'

'I was rung at work and told you'd been thrown off the case and it might be a good idea if I came home.'

Who, I wondered, gave enough of a toss to ring Maggie? It certainly wouldn't have been the Boss. But the fact that someone showed at least some level of concern for my welfare made me start snivelling again.

'Who rang?'

'They really didn't want me to say.'

'If you don't tell me, I'll just keep asking and pouting and whining until you do.' I gave her my best doleful look and she shrugged her shoulders.

'OK, OK, enough with the Bambi eyes, it was Paul Frost. He didn't give me any details, just said he really thought you shouldn't be alone.'

Paul Frost. That was unexpected. For all of his badgering, pig-headed rudeness, he must actually care.

'So are you going to tell me what happened?' But before I could open my mouth in reply she interrupted. 'Hold that thought.' She grabbed the gin bottle and confiscated it, taking it out to the kitchen. 'How many of those have you had?'

'You came home too early. I only got two into me.'

'It's too bloody early for that and it won't help matters. I'm going to make a pot of coffee. Have you had lunch?' I shook my head. 'I'll make you a toasted sandwich. Go get some clothes on, then we can sit down and talk about it.'

God, I loved my flatmate.

><

Once attired in jeans and a long-sleeved T-shirt, I sat at the table and picked at the cheese and Vegemite toasted sandwich while Maggie poured very strong coffee into my mug.

'They think I killed Gaby.'

The pouring stopped abruptly, then resumed. 'Well, they must be mad.'

I managed a smile at the immediate vote of confidence.

'I'm serious. I'm a suspect. They interrogated me. Oh God, Maggie, it was awful.' Tears seeped out again.

'Why would they think you a suspect?'

'Oh, apparently I have motive. I was jealous enough of my ex's wife to knock her off.'

Maggie reached out her hand and grabbed the teaspoon I was ting-ting-tinging against the tabletop. 'Oh, I get it, because that would win him back, and all.'

'Yeah, men love being fought over. Seriously, though, they truly believe I could have done this.'

Maggie pushed the coffee towards me, and then sat down with her own.

'They must be clutching at straws. Did you tell them about Gaby having an affair with her doctor?'

'Yes, and they're going to check it out because they don't really believe me.' God, the thought of that irked. 'I talked to Chrissie, and did you know that bastard of a doctor was blackmailing Gaby for sex? She didn't want it, so he threatened to have Angel taken off her if she didn't comply.'

A slosh of Maggie's coffee hit the table. 'He was doing what?'

'You heard, blackmailing her.'

'And they think *you've* got motive? That poor bloody woman.'

I thought about that statement and realised that I felt something other than resentment towards Gaby Knowes. I did feel sorry for her, for what she had endured in life and probably in death. Her world was not quite the fairy tale I'd envisioned.

'What are you going to do?' Maggie asked, mopping up the spill with some of my tissues.

'What do you mean, what am I going to do?'

She gave me 'the look'.

'I'm going to get horribly drunk, cry some more, drink more, then, if I can walk that far, I'll go to bed.'

'Well, that's a very grown-up approach.'

I didn't appreciate the tone. 'That's easy for you to say. My career's up the pole, people think I'm a killer and, at the end of the day, I could very well end up in jail. How the bloody hell am I supposed to take it?'

'Well, that's better, anyway.'

'What's bloody better?'

'A bit of fight left in the old girl somewhere. Good to see.'

Maggie could always do that. Say the right flaming thing to get me focused again.

'Bitch,' I said, by way of compliment.

She flashed me her best smile.

'You can make light of it all you want, but you know I'm in serious trouble.'

Maggie shook her head at my words. 'No, Sam, you would be in serious trouble if you were guilty. Sure, you're suspended, but they have to do that – it's protocol. If they truly believed you were guilty, you wouldn't be sitting here at home drinking coffee. You'd be warming a cell down at the station.'

Maggie was right. They'd have me under lock and key if they were that convinced. The gauge on my pity-o-meter clicked down a cog or two.

'Even if they suspect you, it's only until they can rule you out of the equation. No one at the station would want to believe you could be guilty of murder. I think they'd work pretty damned hard to prove it wasn't you.'

I thought about Paul Frost phoning Maggie. Perhaps there were some people on my side. The coffee and company must have been working their magic: I was starting to feel a little more rational.

'At least they've got a real suspect now – or two. They would have to seriously look at Dr Walden's wife too. The microscope isn't focused on just me any more.'

'They have you to thank for that information, and they've kicked you off the case. That's gratitude for you.' Maggie reached over and pulled my plate away before I could mutilate the sandwich any further.

'It wouldn't be so bad if I was just off the case. I'm off the job. What the hell am I supposed to do?'

'Can you go home to the farm for a few days, till this blows over?'

'I'm not allowed to leave the area.'

Come to think of it, they hadn't defined the word 'area'. Mum and Dad weren't that far away – only an hour. A bit of home comfort and TLC would be nice, though the inevitable parental interrogations wouldn't be. Besides, it probably wouldn't be wise to piss off the Boss over semantics at this delicate time.

'I think it best I stay here. I'd rather be close to the powers that are deciding on my fate.'

20

Maggie was mean enough to confiscate the gin, but not to ban me from the pub. In fact, she insisted on playing chaperone, but only at a respectable hour. I managed to fill in the afternoon with an obscene amount of housework. Maybe I was more like my mother than I liked to admit.

Another more difficult chore involved the telephone. There was something I had to do and I wasn't at all sure how it would go down. I picked up the handset and tapped in the number I'd written down, then, as the phone started to ring, I had to stop the urge to hang up. My innards felt like they were about to betray me again. I was seriously considering a trip to the loo when someone picked up.

'Hello.' The voice was quiet and familiar.

'Lockie. Hi, it's Sam.'

'Sam, what's happening? Do you have some news?' He sounded almost eager, and I felt even worse about what I was going to tell him.

'No, nothing like that. It's just, well … I wanted you to hear it from me first.'

'Hear what?'

I took a very deep breath. 'They've thrown me off the case and suspended me.' I spat the words out quickly before my nerve deserted me. 'I'm a suspect, Lockie.'

There was deathly silence from the other end of the phone.

'I promise you, Lockie, I had nothing to do with Gaby's death. I'm only a suspect because of our past … you know, relationship.' It sounded so awkward, but I had to try to explain. I was going to say something more when he interrupted.

'Is that it?'

'Well, yes, I just wanted you to hear it from me.'

'You shouldn't be talking to me, then.'

I flinched at the click, and then listened for a while to the series of regular beeps before I hung up.

I decided I did need that trip to the toilet, after all.

21

I turned my head aside to discreetly stifle the beer belch. It didn't work: the damned thing escaped anyway, as did the accompanying guilty giggle. It was echoed from the other side of the table.

'Oh, you're just class, girl,' Maggie said with a slightly exaggerated wave in my direction.

'At least I tried.'

As soon as it was a socially acceptable hour, we'd shifted camp to The Arms. There were, thankfully, only a handful of patrons, most of whom barely registered our arrival. Perfect by me, though I did take the care to turn my back to the rest of the pub. If people did happen to talk about me, I preferred to stay ignorant.

Two hours later, the place had filled up considerably and so had I. Maggie and I had carefully avoided any conversation about the whole Lockie business; instead, we had busied ourselves with the consumption of impressive quantities of beer while talking utter drivel. Beer – the choice of chumpions. I generally got too bloated to want another drop before I got to the hideously pissed stage; nonetheless, I had quite a sway on when I finally had to get up to pay my respects to the ladies' room. I wove my way over to the small hallway, and thought I had made it to sanctuary without being accosted when a large hand slapped my shoulder.

'Sam, Sam, Sam.' The slur in those three words told me Trevor Ray had put quite an effort into his drinking tonight too. 'Who's been a naughty little girl, then?'

Oh Christ, just what I needed right now – a pissed old geezer in a confined space. I looked over his shoulder, desperate to catch anybody's eye.

'Your friends in the Fuzz have been checking up on you. Wanted to know if you'd been out to see me? Think you've been popping off the opposition, do they?'

Man, living in a small town was a pain in the arse sometimes. I leaned against the wall for support, knocking a stuffed trout trophy askew in the process, and removed his hand from my shoulder.

'Mind your own business, Trev. It's nothing to do with you.'

'Hah, that's right. This is bloody brilliant: the Fuzz versus the Fuzz.' His chuckle was positively girlish. 'You do my heart good, girl. It's bloody hilarious.' The offending hand had found its way back onto my shoulder.

'Well, I don't find it bloody funny at all.' I had an overwhelming urge to wipe that childish grin right off of his face and was about to forcibly remove his hand from my shoulder when someone else did it for me.

'Off you go, leave the lady alone.'

Trev looked indignant for a second and then, when he saw who it was, grinned again and obligingly shuffled off, prattling on to himself about police suspecting police.

'Thanks, Cole.'

Cole worked for Trev, which probably explained why Trev was willing to take the hint.

'Lockie told me.' It was brief but direct and, considering how much I'd had to drink, so was my response.

'Well, it's a crock of shit. Did they tell him about the doctor?'

Cole's brows clashed together. 'The bastard.'

'How's Lockie taking it?'

'Not well.'

'You make sure he doesn't do anything stupid, you hear?' To emphasise the point I leaned forwards and jabbed him in the chest. He grabbed the offending hand and bent down to give me a good look.

'You've had too much to drink.' It was a statement, not a question, and no defence I could mount to the contrary would have had a leg to stand on.

'Just enough to take my mind off it all.'

'Did you drive here?'

'No, no, no, no, no,' I said, shaking my head. Oddly, Cole kept shaking long after my head had stopped moving. 'The bastards took my truck off me. I'm wheel-less.'

'I'll give you a ride home.'

I was going to protest, then thought better of it. It had been a shit of a day, and bed was an alluring prospect.

'Where's Maggie?' he asked, assuming, correctly, we would have come here together.

'Over by the sofas. But I gotta pee first.' I lurched into the bathroom.

When I finally got out of the ladies' room, Cole was still leaning against the wall, ready to escort me over to Maggie. She looked up at our approach and waved cheerily.

'I was wondering where you'd got to. I was just considering sending out a search party.'

'I was accosted by the toilets, but thank God Sir Lancelot here came to my rescue. We've got a ride home.' I patted Cole on the arm.

'Hallelujah,' she said, and then gathered up her bag. She wobbled over to Cole, stood up on tiptoes, soundly kissed him on the cheek and proclaimed, 'My hero.'

I believe the hero blushed.

22

My hair hurt.

I didn't even know that was possible. My head hurt too, but my hair, being attached to my head, made me feel like Medusa with a snake ache. Blinking made matters worse; it invited my eyelids to join in the torture party.

Gawd, if only we'd stuck to the beer. But Maggie and I had made the ill-conceived decision to polish off an open bottle of port scavenged from the back of a cupboard after we got home. It had an unsophisticated nose with a hint of currants and old sock, but we didn't care – it had an alcohol content. Cole, quite understandably, had declined our invitation to join us. Probably thought he'd get far more sensible company back at the pub.

When I heard a fumbling from the direction of the kitchen, I briefly toyed with the idea of getting up to join Maggie, but then snapped myself out of it. I took the long- distance approach.

'Coooooofffffffffffeeeeeeeeeee,' I called, as quietly as I could.

A moment later there was a tap at my bedroom door and an apparition appeared around the corner. 'You rang?'

'Need coffee, give it to me.'

'Yes, but only if you promise to give me a head transplant. Whose bloody stupid idea was it to hit the port?'

'Committee decision.'

'For God's sake, sack the committee.' Maggie turned to head back to the kitchen, and then turned around for a parting shot. 'I told you alcohol wouldn't make you feel better.'

I poked my tongue out at her. Nobody liked a know-it-all.

Somehow, I managed to get myself into a vertical position and into the kitchen. Even under normal conditions neither of us was at our best in the mornings; today, we were barely functional. We made another committee decision to keep the curtains closed.

'One thing about being suspended – at least I don't have to go to work this morning.'

Maggie grimaced. 'Life's a bitch like that. Ugh, I need drugs.' She fossicked around in the top cupboard and fished out a box of paracetamol. She popped two out of the strip, gingerly chugged them down with some water and offered the box my way, but I declined the invitation. For some absurd reason, I didn't want to dull the pain.

'What are you going to do with yourself today?' she asked.

'Believe it or not,' I said, and cringed at the thought, 'I might go for a run. Try to clear my head.'

'If it doesn't explode. I didn't realise you had a thing for sadomasochism.'

'You'd think I did. OK, maybe it will be a walk. I really need some fresh air and sunshine. OK, sunshine probably isn't too good right now, either, but you know what I mean.' I tried to stifle what turned into a yawn. 'Meanwhile, I think I'll go back to bed, just for a few minutes…'

23

At first, the knocking at the door went unnoticed over the generalised thumping in my head. It finally registered through the murk on the second barrage. I could make out the sound of the shower running, presumably with Maggie in it. Guessing that put me on door duties, in one swift movement I heaved myself into an upright position and swung my legs over the side of the bed to wait for the inevitable head rush. Its ferocity didn't disappoint. I breathed into my hands to test the air quality and wished I hadn't. If it was someone I didn't want to see, I could huff on them and send them packing. Either that or the sight of my Tweety Pie flannelette pyjamas would put them off – why did I buy those again?

By the time I made it to the door, the person was knocking again. Insistent and impatient. I turned the handle and pulled, with no effect whatsoever, then realised unlocking it would help. I got the door open, and at about the same time as I opened my mouth to yawn, it dawned on me that the grey fuzzy thing in front of my face was not some mutant soft toy but a microphone, and it came with a companion in the form of a television camera.

'Shit.'

Of course, all this equipment came with human accompaniments too, one of whom I recognised from the news.

'Samantha Shephard?'

'Huh?'

'Rachel Longman, *One News*. Sources tell us you have been suspended from your duties with the police while an investigation is undertaken into the death of Mataura woman Gabriella Knowes. Do you have any comments to make?'

I looked at the camera, looked at her, looked down at my pyjamas, looked at her again and, with one smooth movement, swung the door shut. Once I heard that blessed click, I leaned my head forwards against the cool wooden surface.

'Shit, shit, shit.'

Oh, I was good. Definite future in media liaisons there.

Stupid as it seemed, the encounter had sent my heart rate through the roof, and my head was not coping with the altitude. I swallowed back a surge of nausea and tried to think. Surely there were rules about that sort of thing. My house was private property, so they were trespassing. Then again, I had opened the door. It was definitely time to badger the landlord about getting that peephole put in; I'd only asked him twice already and it could have proven very useful this morning. Bugger it all, what was I going to do?

Another knock at the door.

I thought it fairly obvious I didn't have any comment to make; these people were slow learners. I retreated back to my bedroom to hide from the noise and to resist the temptation to yell at them to bugger off. I didn't think that would do my media image any good. Not that my pyjamas and cutting repartee would. Jesus, imagine it if they put that to air. Imagine if my mother saw it. My hands came up to my face as I slumped onto my bed and tried to push that idea back into my head.

'Was that someone at the door? Should I get it?' Maggie called out from the direction of the bathroom.

I leaped to my feet yelling, 'No', as I ran to intercept her. The panic in my voice stopped her in her tracks.

'OK, OK, you don't need to tackle me. Calm down. Who was it?'

'Shit, sorry, God, it was the media.'

'The media? What media?'

I had to lean over, hands on knees, and breathe deeply several times to avoid throwing up.

'The variety that comes with video cameras and microphones.'

'Oh,' she said. 'You didn't open the door, did you?'

'Yes.'

'Looking like that?'

'Yes.'

Her expression said it all.

'Crap.'

'Exactly. What the hell am I going to do?'

'Well, what did you say to them?' Maggie came around and rubbed my back. The gesture made me want to burst into tears, and it took considerable effort not to.

'Oh, it was something really profound like "Shit", and that was just before I slammed the door on them. I was impressive.'

'Sounds it. And what were they wanting to know, exactly?'

'If I had any comment on being suspended from the investigation into Gaby's death. I didn't give them a chance to ask anything else.' I was still stunned by being confronted by the media at all. It hadn't occurred to me that I might become the centre of attention. 'I'd like to know how the hell they found out about my apparent involvement in all this. And how did they get my address? I'm not even in the phone book.'

'Small town, Sam. Everyone knows you. There'll be someone, or ones, out there who wouldn't be able to wait to dob in the local police officer. No matter how popular you think you are, there are those who get a kick out of blabbing. Getting their five minutes of fame. Makes them feel important.'

Not a comforting thought, but she was right. And it was a more palatable prospect than the other possibility: that the information had come from the police force itself. With one notable exception, I didn't seem to have too many friends there right now.

'Maybe they won't show it. I didn't have anything important to say. They might decide it's not worth it. It wasn't good television.'

Maggie gave a derisive laugh.

'Don't hold your breath, sunshine.'

24

It was an hour before I was in any fit state to attempt exercise, physically or psychologically. After the departure of the news crew, I flinched at any sound that could have signalled another intrusion. It was tempting to hole up inside for the day and try to stay invisible, but the fact was that the thought of hanging around home doing nothing was worse than that of being accosted by journalists, or anyone else for that matter. Anyway, I had prepared a kind of statement if the chance came up again.

Despite my own assurances, I looked up and down the street several times before being satisfied I was not under surveillance. I'm sure I looked the part – running shoes, bike pants, sports top, cap, sunglasses. OK, the sunglasses weren't standard-issue running gear, but you had to make allowances. At least I was mobile. I started out at a light jog, which lasted all of thirty seconds before I realised pounding the pavement was going to be reciprocated by pounding in another rather tender part of my anatomy. I'd settle for a brisk walk.

To give myself some credit, I did make the effort to walk up a hill. Part of that was to throw off any imagined followers; I figured they'd decide it wasn't worth it if it involved huffing and puffing. The Terrace walkway proved to be a bit of a trap for the unwary. It had been an age since I'd walked through it, and I'd never seen it this overgrown before. The wooden walkway was as slick as soap from the heavy dew – I almost came a greaser a couple of times – and the only reprieve was on the odd areas that had been overlaid with chicken-wire to afford some kind of grip. I thought I'd cheat and have a rest on the park bench and take in the view, but the overgrowth had blocked out any sight of the town. The self-seeding pittosporums – the opportunist sods – had taken advantage of nobody ripping them out. They created a lush, green wall. Consequently, the only thing of interest to ponder was the graffiti on the bench. Every one of my senses was in overdrive. The light was too glary, even through the sunglasses, the damp scent of earth and rotting leaves overwhelmed to the point where I could taste it and I wished the over-exuberant grey warblers would shut the hell up. Did they have to be so bloody cheerful? The whole idea of exercise under adverse conditions suddenly lost its charm. Stuff this, I thought, and headed back down to town.

I decided to cut across the river at Bridge Street and walk casually by the police command centre, just on the off chance I'd run into someone I knew. I was dying to find out if anything new had happened in the investigation. There was also the issue of where the reporter had got her information from. If it had come from the police, I would be not only highly pissed off, but also rather nervous, as it would mean I hadn't been ruled out as a suspect yet. The water beneath the bridge had a repugnant yellowy frothed scum drifting along its surface. It seemed an oddly appropriate adornment, considering the Mataura's recent cargo. My eyes followed the scum's trail upstream to the back of the meat works. Not the most picturesque of vistas today. The smell wasn't too flash either and my stomach threatened to protest.

My thoughts were disturbed by loud voices, and as I reached the other side of the bridge I saw two men gesticulating angrily.

'Oh shit.' I ignored the pain and broke into a sprint for the Riverside Medical Centre. One of the voices belonged to Dr Tony Walden and the other to Lockie Knowes. Those two in close proximity was not a good thing. In fact, they had got to the point of shoving and I was pretty sure blows were about to rain down if someone didn't intervene.

'Lockie, you stop it right there!' I hollered.

Both men looked up, startled, and when they saw it was me gave me looks best described as unwelcoming.

'What the hell is going on?'

I finally made it to where they were having it out and stepped into the narrow gap between them. Francine stood in the doorway, clutching the phone, as if ready to call the police. Christ, that would be all we needed. I waved her away.

'What are you doing, Lockie? It's not a good idea for you to be here, you know.'

'I was just going to show this filthy piece of scum what I thought of him and his treatment of my wife.' Lockie leaned over me to have another go at Walden, who looked like he'd be quite happy to shove back. I pushed Lockie away to get some room between them, but the idiot of a doctor moved towards us again, so this time I turned my attention to him.

'Just step back and get out of the way.' I was in no mood for taking any crap from either of them.

'What's it to you?' The doctor's voice spat with venom. 'You've done enough damage already with your groundless accusations.'

That was a bit more than I was capable of shouldering right now, so I jumped astride my high horse and charged.

'Me? You're blaming me for your problems? Me? You were the one who couldn't keep your puny little dick in your pants. You were the one who could only get someone to sleep with you by bloody well blackmailing her. I bet your own bloody wife won't sleep with you and, Christ, I hope she leaves you and takes you for everything you've got. You bloody deserve it. How dare you blame me for your pathetic little troubles. You should be ashamed of yourself. People trust you. You're a doctor, for God's sake. You were the one who chose to destroy a life just so you could get your rocks off. You. You make me sick.'

Walden had moved several steps backwards. But I sure as hell wasn't going to let him escape until I had finished my lecture: I was just getting warmed up. I pressed on forwards, right in his face, my finger levelled millimetres before his nose.

'If it turns out you didn't kill Gaby, I will still personally make sure you never practise medicine ever again. You blackmailed your patient! Christ Almighty, you threatened to take her baby away. What were you bloody thinking?' By this stage he was backed up against a railing with nowhere else to go. And I hadn't finished yet.

'You won't be able to show your face around here by the time I'm done with you. Your name will be crap. People will look upon you like something cheaper than roadkill. By God, I will make sure you suffer just as much as Gaby did.'

I would have spat at him if I had been that way inclined; as it was, it was bad enough manners for me to swear and yell. I don't know what my blood pressure was doing, but judging by the heat in my face and supernova in my head it was probably getting dangerously high. I thought perhaps it was time to retreat. I looked around, and there were several others as well as Walden now looking pretty startled. I turned to Lockie, grabbed him by the arm and guided him, stupefied, back to his car.

'He's just not worth it, Lockie. If you hit him, the bastard would just have you charged with assault. Angel's already lost one parent, don't let her lose another.' I said it loudly enough so everyone present could hear.

I think they were all clear about my opinion on the matter.

25

A few streets over, Lockie pulled off to the side of the road and stopped the car. He leaned forward and rested his head on the steering wheel. I wanted to reach over and touch him, comfort him, but something stopped me. He finally leaned back, turned and looked directly into my eyes. Even now, after all that had happened, I felt uneasy under his gaze and extremely aware of his proximity.

'Thank you,' he said.

'You don't have anything to thank me for, Lockie. I don't seem to be doing any good for anyone at the moment.'

'You saved me from making a big mistake.' He was damned right there.

'Hitting him might have felt good for a moment, but it wouldn't have solved anything for you.'

We lapsed into our own thoughts for a moment. When I did go to say something, Lockie spoke at the same instant. We both laughed like a case of first-date nerves.

'You go first,' Lockie said.

I took a deep breath. 'Look, I'm really sorry about the way I behaved towards you and Gaby. I won't make any bones about the fact I was jealous, and I did some stupid things that I really regret. But I would never have wished any harm on Gaby, and I'm so truly sorry that you've lost her.'

'I know you wouldn't have harmed her,' he said. A mantle of tiredness fell across his features. 'I can't understand why anyone would have.'

Neither could I. That was the problem.

'Walden is the only person who could possibly have motive to kill Gaby, but I simply can't picture him having the guts to do anything like that.' Lockie gave me a sideways look, so I explained myself.

tisfied with the testimony of the people you called on.'
n with the intoxicated Mr Ray at the pub had already
'd followed up on my activities. 'So you don't want me
uestioning?'
is time, no.'
s he stepped into the trap. 'So I am no longer a suspect?'
rrowed his eyes at that. 'Have you ever considered going
ation?' he asked dryly.
swer the question, please.' I never did know when to

pegged up a notch or two. 'Constable, that is enough.
e dismissed. Leave, or I will have you escorted off the
d if I get wind of you doing any poking around, there
linary action. Am I understood?'
o, and couldn't help but smile.
e, sir,' I said, and walked out of the room. I strode across
barely registered the stares. I might not have succeeded
y job back, but I sure as hell felt better. That round went

'Well, the whole way he blackmailed Gaby was just so … cowardly. He's too obvious a suspect. I feel there's something else.'

'It's a bugger you're off the case,' he said. 'I know the others will do their best, but I think you would have gone that extra bit further.'

I was startled, and oddly pleased. All I'd copped lately was criticism, and his approval gave me the resolve I needed for my next move. There were a few more things I needed to tell him first.

'Lockie, please don't be angry at Gaby for what happened with Walden. He is the most despicable kind of monster, a predator. He was the one who held all the power – he had all the credibility. Who would have believed Gaby if she'd told? You can't hold her responsible in any way.' Christ, my attitude had taken a check. At some point in the last few days Gaby had made the transition from being the enemy disguised as a rebound dolly-bird to an actual person. Lockie's grief no longer hit me like a stab in the chest. It was a dull ache.

'I know that,' he said. 'I'm not angry with her. I just wish I'd noticed something, anything. She had this bloody awful thing happening in her life, and I didn't even know. She seemed OK, perhaps a little down sometimes. I thought she was tired.' He brushed aside an errant tear. 'Why didn't she feel she could talk to me about it?'

I had no answer to that, so sat quietly and waited for him to speak.

When he did, it was in a voice charged with revulsion.

'My wife is dead, my child motherless and all I can think about is whether the baby she was carrying was mine or his. I am such a bloody louse.'

What could I say? One thing was certain. I could no longer sit around and watch while others took over the investigation. It was all too close to home.

'Why don't you drop me off at the command centre?' I said.

'I didn't think you were working.'

'Yeah, well, I'm going to see what I can do about that.' I wasn't exactly dressed for business, but right now I didn't care. I had never been one for sitting around with my finger up my arse.

The pity party was officially over.

26

Bold and brash was the approach to take here, I decided, as I marched through the command centre. Numerous pairs of eyes bugged out of their heads as I walked past. No androgynous, figure-hiding police blues today. Lycra and quite a lot of bare skin left no question as to the good shape I was in. Let them drool.

'Where's the Boss?' I asked Darren McKenzie, noting that his offsider, Paul Frost, wasn't about. That was a pity. Darren stood dumbfounded, and pointed in the general direction of the side rooms without taking his eyes off my chest.

The door was partly ajar, and I could see that the Boss was alone. I knocked and walked straight on in. After a momentary flash of surprise, his face was a study of control.

'Constable, what are you doing here?'

Not the cheeriest of welcomes, but I wasn't really expecting hugs and kisses. I thought I'd follow his tack of easing in first before going for the jugular.

'I thought you should know I stopped a wee altercation between Lockie Knowes and Tony Walden this morning.'

That got his attention.

'What the hell were they doing together?'

'Lockie had gone down to the Medical Centre to give the doctor a piece of his mind. Fortunately, I got to them before any punches were thrown, so if Walden comes in to make a complaint, nothing actually happened.' I chose not to enlighten him on my contribution to the fracas.

'And why were you there?'

I gestured down towards my running gear. 'I was just passing by.'

I stood there while he pointedly turned to resume his work. After

a few moments he sighed and turne[d]
placed his pen down on the desk.

'No.'

'I thought not. Well?'

'When do I get my job back?'

His jugular twitched. 'You are still
crime, Constable. You may get you
satisfied you are no longer a suspect.'

I leaned forwards, my hands on th[e]

'You know damned well I have no[t]
best knowledge of anyone about the
be out there helping with the invest
useless at home.'

'Well *you* know damned well that
anyway. There's too big a conflict of i

'Well, put me back on normal d[uty]
be doing the everyday stuff while yo[u]
murder.'

'Sorry, Constable, you are still und[er]
to, I don't have the authority to reinsta[te]
of the internal investigation by Profe[ssor]
out of my hands.' That was most defi[nitely]
barked case closed.

I stood up straight, ready to sulk o[ff]
it. Damned if I was going to give in th[at]

'What about if I poked around in [a]

'No. Now out – you shouldn't eve[n]

I could see I had managed to wind h[im]
that. 'Well, while I'm here, did you hav[e]
I pulled up a chair and sat down, lean[ing]

'What kind of questions?'

'Last time I was here I was being ac[cused]
notebook into evidence and said I wou[ld]
of any time unaccounted for during th[e]

'We are
My run
told me th
for further
'Not at
I smile[d]
He just
into inter[r]
'Well, [
stop.
His voi
Now you
premises.
will be dis
I stood
'Of cou
the hall a[nd]
in getting
to me.

27

My exit from the command centre wasn't as easy as waltzing out the door and walking off down the road. The presence of yet another media crew out front forced a quick swerve to the right and a detour via the back car park where, fortunately, no one either expected or recognised me.

By the time I'd walked home, I'd hatched a plan. Even the hangover had been relegated to the back of my mind. I could not sit by and be a spectator: I was far too involved for that. The Boss had expressly ordered me not to snoop but, bugger it, it was time I undertook a little civil disobedience in my otherwise law-abiding life. The first thing I needed was information, and I knew just where to get it.

Once again I picked up the phone. I made a truly lame attempt to disguise my voice to the officer on reception duties, and was soon transferred through to my intended target.

'Paul Frost speaking.'

'Paul, it's Sam. Can you talk?' I felt a bit like Secret Squirrel.

'What do you mean, can I talk?'

'Will you be overheard?'

'Why?'

God, he could be infuriating. 'Because I need information,' I said a little tersely. 'I need to know what's happening with the case.'

There was a pause. 'I heard you've been in to see the Boss. Didn't he tell you everything you needed to know?'

Rotten bugger was not going to make this easy for me.

'Do you think I would need to ring you if he'd told me anything?' The pitch of my voice was rapidly climbing.

'Aren't you still under suspension?'

'God, Paul, do you always have to answer a question with another question?'

'Well, you just did, didn't you?'

If I could have reached down the phone line and ripped out his throat, I would have. He thought he was funny.

'But seriously, Sam, why would I give you details about the case?' The humour had gone from his voice. 'I could get into a lot of trouble for that.'

'You know this whole thing of my being a suspect is a crock of shit. I just want to know if I'm still under suspicion and how things went with questioning Walden. When are they going to arrest him? Is he still a suspect?'

There was silence from the other end of the phone, and I began to wonder if Paul was such a good bet, after all. But I pressed on.

'I still think I'm the best one to talk to the locals. I know them all and live among them. I think they trust me. I may be able to bring to light information they might not share with outsiders.'

Another pause.

'What's in it for me?'

The bloody creep!

'I'm not going to sleep with you, if that's what you mean.'

Paul choked down the other end of the phone. 'No, no, no, that's not what I meant.'

I could just about hear the blush. 'I mean, if I help you out, will you send any information you find my way?'

I considered for a moment, enjoying the tables turned.

'That sounds fair and reasonable,' I said.

'OK, then. For the record, I thought they were bloody stupid pinning you as a suspect. They treated you like shit. You didn't deserve that.'

That reminded me. 'Thanks for ringing Maggie yesterday. I needed the company.'

'That's OK.' He sounded vaguely embarrassed. 'She wasn't supposed to tell.'

'Just goes to show, you have to be careful who you trust, Paul. So what can you tell me about the case? Oh, and who dobbed me in to the press?'

'For a start, you are pretty much off the suspect list, although they won't take you off completely. To cover their arses, just in case.'

'Yeah, cause I'm the psychopathic killer type.'

'I wouldn't joke about it. Statements like that could come back and bite you.' He was right, of course. I let him continue. 'Have you had trouble with the press?' he asked. 'No one here would have said anything, unless it was one of the out-of-town big brass. But I doubt it. There is still some code of honour.'

'Thanks for that. Let's just say I had a wee run-in this morning and am hoping nothing comes of it. But what else can you tell me?'

'The Knowes house has just been released back to the family.'

'That was quick. Did the forensics team find anything?'

'Nothing of significance. You were right about the mother-in-law's cleaning; she was thorough. They realised fairly early that any obvious evidence would have been obliterated or thrown out. The important thing, though, is they found no blood evidence, no fingerprints, no sign at all. The killer was very careful. Bloody TV teaches them how.' He wavered before he added the next bit. 'There was a bit of muttering from ESR about not getting to the scene early enough.'

I could guess who they were muttering about.

'Well, there's a familiar complaint. Jesus, how many times do I have to state I had to make a judgement call?' The last seven words were fairly emphatic.

'Hey, I'd have called it the same. Don't beat yourself up over it.'

'I'm not,' I said, though I didn't even convince myself with that one. 'Did they go through the rubbish truck, or did poor Adam get pulled off the road for nothing? He was a bit shitty about not being able to finish his run.'

'They've quarantined the contents, but haven't sorted them yet. I don't know what the delay there is – probably can't find some mug to volunteer. Ugh, I hate that job.'

'You and me both.' Sifting through rotten garbage rated up there with traffic duty and sewer searches. 'So, what's the story with the doc?'

'The doc and his wife. Interesting couple.'

'What do you mean?'

'Well, they both have a reasonable but convenient alibi – each other – so unless they were in it together, they are out of the picture. It was Dr Walden's morning off on Tuesday and they claim to have spent the morning at home.' He hesitated so I filled in the gap for him.

'But?'

'But, I dunno – apart from the fact he was blackmailing a woman for sex, which he categorically denies, by the way, I feel there was something he was trying to hide. That they were both trying to hide. The blackmail is a given. Chrissie Andrews came in and signed a statement about overhearing the conversation between Mrs Knowes and Dr Walden, so I don't think she'd perjure herself by making it up. To me it seems so unlikely for Mrs Knowes to let herself get into that situation in the first place. I can't figure out the dynamics there. Maybe he's very slick. I don't know. I'll have to do some digging into his work in Britain. There's something about him I don't trust.'

He wasn't the only one there.

'I've heard that Angela Walden is a scary lady.'

He laughed. 'Scary? She was downright hostile.'

'You'd be a bit put out too, if you were in her situation.'

'Which is another reason I don't think the doctor is our murderer. He's got a highly pissed-off wife who, I imagine, would be the first to line up and point the finger at him if she thought he'd done it, or even if he hadn't done it, just to punish him. But she hasn't. Tell you one thing, though. Can't picture that marriage lasting out the year, or the day for that matter.'

'It would be damned hard to stand by your man in those circumstances. He'd have to be pretty special or be in for a huge inheritance.'

Paul laughed again. But I had to agree with his opinion of the doctor.

'I guess I didn't really believe Walden had enough spine to kill. Pity, it would have made it very neat and tidy. He certainly had a good motive, specially with Gaby being pregnant and all.'

'Yeah, well, he vows and declares he knew nothing about the pregnancy, and anyway, the child couldn't have been his because he's had the snip.'

Finally, there was one piece of good news I could take back to Lockie. A little something to ease his pain.

'There're no new leads?' I asked.

'Not a one. Have you got any ideas?'

I wished I did. 'Not offhand,' I said, 'but I've only been thinking about the case in terms of Walden's involvement. I hope the police are sending an official complaint about him to the Medical Council.'

'It's already done. Everyone wants that bastard to fry.' A picture of Angel playing happily jumped into my mind. Having that monster using her for leverage must have ripped Gaby apart. I pulled my thoughts back to the present.

'Did the blood results come back from ESR?' I asked.

'Yes, and the Midazolam level in her blood was much higher than what you'd expect from the number of tablets she'd taken – as predicted by the pathologist.'

'One thing I've considered about the case,' I said, 'is that it may have been a professional hit.'

'That's been bandied around here too, which is another reason why Walden – and you – haven't been ruled out as suspects.' He hesitated a bit, and went on. 'Don't be surprised if your bank accounts get checked out soon. You haven't made any large cash withdrawals recently, have you?'

'Oh ha ha. I barely make the rent.'

The thought of them going through my bank accounts really pissed me off. I've always viewed my finances as extremely personal, and didn't want all and sundry knowing how much I spent each month on junk food or HPs. Still, my chat with Paul had gone better than expected; he could prove to be quite an ally.

'Thanks for your help, Paul. Keep me posted of any developments.'

'And don't forget to call me if you come up with anything interesting.'

'Of course,' I said, 'if you're lucky.'

28

The next part of my plan, if you could call it a plan, involved Lockie. I needed to look through Gaby's things, and now that the house had been released back to the family, all I had to do was persuade him of that. After our wee chat in the car, I felt I was in with a decent chance.

I could think of no reason why someone would kill a young mother in a small town in the back of beyond, and why they would go to such lengths to hide it. The crime scene hadn't yielded any clues. Perhaps Gaby could. I needed to learn more about her. Actually, that was wrong. I needed to learn *anything* about her. I'd never before looked past her pretty face and the fact she'd married someone I saw as rightfully mine. It was unfortunate that I'd waited till now to bother getting to know her.

The odd vehicle passed me by on my walk down Wyndham Road and interrupted the tranquillity of the countryside. A few tooted, blasting the quiet. I wasn't quite sure whether to wave or give them the finger, so instead, I ignored them. One or two shaved by a little too close for comfort. The verge wasn't that wide here with a drainage ditch on one side and the road on the other. I had to weave around the white reflectorised PVC traffic markers every 20 metres or so on the curves. Someone had got a bit too carried away with the weed spray around the base of the things, judging by the expanse of dead grass around each one. Toetoe and flax bushes lined the far side of the ditch, interspersed with the odd spindly looking cabbage tree. The *wardle wardle* cry of a magpie coming from a stand of pines made me look up warily. Those buggers could be quite vicious if they were protecting their territory. Plenty of unsuspecting passers-by had the scars to prove it.

As I approached Lockie's house on foot, I got a new appreciation of how isolated it really was. The road wasn't that busy and it was a reasonable trot to the neighbours. It must have made things a lot easier for the killer. No one driving by would notice a nondescript work van. Even the grand spymaster next door, Dora McGann, almost missed it. I bet she noticed my walk past though.

After trudging all this way, it had only just occurred to me that Lockie might not be home, so I was relieved to see his ute was out front – and even more relieved to see that Leonore's Range Rover wasn't. I crunched up the driveway and, with my heart racing – and not just from the exercise – I knocked at the door.

Surprise and some discomfort drenched his face as he saw me there on his porch.

'Sam, what are you doing here?'

'I need to ask you something. Can I come in?'

I went to move closer, but Lockie didn't budge from the doorway, forcing me to back-pedal.

'Did they give you your job back?' he said.

I was afraid he'd ask me that.

'Look, I have to be honest with you, Lockie. No, I'm still on suspension and still officially on their suspect list.' I took a deep breath, not quite sure how to word my request. 'The thing is, I want to help find Gaby's killer. I can't sit back and not get involved. It's too personal.'

'You think it's personal? What do you think I feel?' He looked away, but not before I noticed his eyes welling up with tears.

'I can't even imagine what you're going through. You and Angel. That's why I have to help. The police don't seem to have any strong leads – there's so little physical evidence. I think if we knew more of what Gaby was doing before she died – I mean in her life in general – we could get some clues as to why it happened.' He still couldn't look at me, so I kept on. 'What I need is for you to let me look through Gaby's things. I know the forensics team and God knows how many other officers have been through your house and through her belongings. You're probably sick to death of people poking around, but I think I'd see things from a different perspective. Will you give me a chance?'

I'd laid the cards on the table; now all I could do was wait.

It seemed an insufferable length of time before Lockie finally sighed and moved out of the doorway.

'You'd better come in, then,' he said quietly.

It felt very strange to be standing alone in Lockie's and Gaby's bedroom. Lockie had left me to it, and gone to hang out some washing. Leonore was still at the park with Angel.

It was an orderly room, sparse but comfortably furnished. The piles of 'worn-once-but-don't-know-whether-to-wash-them-yet' clothes, that had decorated Lockie's and my bedroom, were non-existent here. A large cane laundry hamper in the corner must actually have had some use. I seemed to recall Lockie was very good at putting dirty clothes *on* the hamper, on the floor in front of it, but never actually in it. Times had changed.

I sat down at Gaby's dressing table. Again, everything was orderly. Wooden jewellery box in the corner, an attractive cane basket containing hairspray, moisturisers, fragrance. I picked up her bottle of Coco Chanel and inhaled the remnants of scent around its neck. Warm, spicy, exotic. It brought to mind richly decorated pavilions draped with exquisite tapestries: Gaby had sophisticated taste in perfume. I supposed it was a small consolation for moving from the city to the back of beyond. She maintained some standards. Her silver-handled mirror in the middle of the dressing table looked out of place without a matching hairbrush. I assumed she'd had one and the police had kept hold of it for fingerprints and DNA. I hoped they would return it soon, the table looked incomplete without it. It was quaintly old-fashioned for a city girl.

My eyes were drawn to a silver-framed photograph of the family in happier days, Angel held between her adoring parents. I looked at Gaby's features and couldn't help but compare them with my own. I looked at my reflection, turning my head slightly to catch the profile. We both had dark blonde hair, although Gaby had been blessed with curls, whereas mine only carried a wave. With hair like that I'd have kept it long, not cropped short as she had. Both of us had brown eyes and full mouths, but that's where the similarities ended. Gaby had a strong angular nose, whereas mine was nothing of note. She had classically arching eyebrows framing almond-shaped eyes that sat atop highly defined cheekbones. It was a face that turned heads and loved the camera. I'd always considered myself to be attractive enough, but no one feature of mine stood out. Perhaps my eyes, which were large, but I certainly didn't have 'bone structure'.

I had to admit to feeling diminished by this woman, but that was probably dictated by circumstance, as well as her appearance.

I pulled open her top drawer. This one contained an assortment of make-up and jewellery. I scanned its contents, not wanting to disturb anything, and closed it again quickly. Other drawers contained clothes and underwear. I didn't examine them too closely; it seemed too intrusive.

I sensed rather than saw Lockie enter the room, and felt the tension in his body. The sight of me sitting at his wife's dresser must have been disconcerting.

'Did the police take many of Gaby's personal things?' I asked. I tried to sound professional, even though I felt like I'd just been caught with my hand in the till.

'No, not really. A couple of blokes came and told me what they'd removed. I didn't recognise them. I assumed they were the out-of-towners.'

That was odd; I'd have thought they'd send a local detective, someone familiar.

'Who have they got liaising with you now?'

'Actually, it's your boss, Ron Thomson.'

'Oh.' That could potentially make life difficult. 'You realise that he would not be very pleased to find me here, and he would be very upset if he found out I was doing any investigating.'

He sort of smiled. 'Don't worry, he won't find out from me. As far as I'm concerned, I don't care who gets to the bottom of all this, as long as someone does. I just want to know what happened and make sure the bastard who did it rots in hell.'

'I presume you mean jail, Lockie.' Having seen him in action with Walden, it was apparent he wouldn't shy away from a bit of personal retribution.

He just shrugged.

I was going to change the subject, but there was still the news I'd stored away from my conversation with Paul Frost. I tried to be casual.

'Did you know that Dr Walden has had a vasectomy?'

'Really?' Lockie's face lit up immediately, and then just as quickly darkened. I could see the full realisation of his loss hitting home once again. He turned away, his chin quivering and headed towards the door.

It seemed to be my function in life to reopen his wounds.

'One more thing, Lockie,' I said, and followed him into the hall. 'The other day you mentioned Gaby had been doing some study. What course was she doing?'

'Journalism,' he said. 'She was doing a correspondence course, something to keep her sane, she said. She was really enjoying it and seemed to be getting good reports from her tutor.'

It was as good a place as any to get a feel for what made Gaby tick: what she was interested in and cared about.

'Do you mind if I have a look at her course material?' I was curious to see what she had found to write about in these quiet parts. 'It is still here, isn't it, or did the detectives take it?'

'They didn't mention taking it. Come and have a look for yourself. She worked down here in the spare room – all her notes and things are in here.'

We walked into a beautifully sunny bedroom. As well as housing a double bed, with what I guessed was Leonore's suitcase placed on it, it had a large desk, bookshelf and the trappings of an office – notepads, pen holder, cork board with clippings, notes and pictures attached with colourful pins. Again, there was a framed picture of the perfect family in the corner.

'Where did she keep her course material?' I asked, still a bit loath to ferret it out myself.

'She had a big folder and a file box she kept everything in,' Lockie said, opening a few drawers. 'They should be in … ah, here they are.'

The bottom drawer held a large silver-coloured ring binder with Journalism Course emblazoned across the front, as well as several clear pocket files. Lockie pulled them out and placed them on the desk, then pulled out a file box from another drawer. There looked to be quite a bit of material there – more than a five-minute casual glance would cover. 'Would you mind if I took these things away, to have a really good look through?'

He hesitated a bit.

'I'll be very careful with them. I want to get a feel for what Gaby was doing. There may be something useful or relevant to our understanding of the case.'

'You think it had something to do with her studying?' he asked.

'I don't know. There just seems to be no apparent reason why she was killed. It was highly organised; in fact, it makes me think it might have been a professional job.'

The other officers had clearly not mentioned that suspicion.

'A hit?' When he could finally spit the words out, his face was a study in incredulity. Life had been a continuous series of shocks for Lockie these last few days; repetition hadn't dulled his sensitivity to them at all.

'A hit. So I have to ask myself why? The only thing I can think of, besides drugs – and to be honest Lockie, you don't have the trappings of wealth I'd associate with a good income from drug money – the only thing I can think of is that she stumbled onto something accidentally and was seen as a risk.' I let that sink in for a few seconds, then continued. 'If I could find out what she was doing in the weeks leading up to her death, and followed her trail, I might find something. This seems like a logical place to start looking.' I indicated the pile on the desk.

'I would also need to look at her computer.' Come to think of it, where was the computer? I didn't recall seeing one in the lounge, or anywhere else in the house, and there were no telltale cables or even a printer in here. 'Did the detectives take Gaby's computer? I assume she had one?' I asked.

'Computer? Oh, I'd forgotten about that. Gaby had a laptop, but Angel knocked a cup of coffee over the keyboard, so it's been in getting fixed, over in Gore.'

'So the detectives don't know about it?'

'No, I guess they don't. Should I have told them?' He looked concerned, as if he'd done something wrong. How could I reassure him and yet get him to do something not strictly legal?

'It may have been helpful to their investigation, but then, they didn't ask about one, did they?'

'No, they didn't.'

'So you weren't withholding anything. You overlooked it, which is perfectly understandable considering what you've been through. And they overlooked the possibility too.' I was rather surprised about that. I would have thought they would assume everyone nowadays owned a computer. But then, the rather sudden and awkward transition of my being in charge and then turfed off the case and the lack of official handover may have caused that one to slip by for the moment. I was certain someone would think of it soon.

'I suppose you're right,' he said. 'So what should I do about it?'

I tried to play it cool. 'How would you feel if I went and picked up the computer, had a look at it first, and then brought it back, so you could hand it over to the police?'

His eyes widened. 'I could get into a lot of trouble doing that, couldn't I?'

'I'd be the one who'd get into trouble, but they don't need to find out. If they do, I'll say I collected it without your knowledge. It wouldn't reflect on you.'

He didn't seem convinced.

'Look, Lockie. Gaby's computer could hold the one piece of information we need to understand all this. It could be the key.' I was overplaying it a bit, but it was for a good cause.

He heaved a sigh of resignation. 'Take what you want – take the computer, take it all. I don't care any more. Just find out who did this.'

I smiled at him, trying to be reassuring, and couldn't help but reach out and touch him on the arm.

'Thanks. I'll be careful. Do you know if Gaby used passwords? Did you use the computer much?'

'Hate the things. I don't use it at all – wouldn't know how to.' He always had been a bit of a technophobe. The only piece of gadgetry I knew him to be fully conversant with was the TV remote control. He had a complete grasp of how that worked.

'OK. I'll get everything back to you as soon as I can.'

I leaned closer to Gaby's noticeboard and had a last look across the desk for anything else that could be of use. The sun had reached the corner of the desk, bathing the pens and notepad in light; its slanting rays cast shadows into tiny indentations on the pad. I scanned the smiling faces of the real-estate agents printed on it – then it hit me.

'Lockie, is that the same pad the note was written on?'

'The note?'

'You know, Gaby's note.'

My meaning finally dawned on him. 'Yes, I think it is.'

'Is it usually kept in this room?'

'No, it's normally by the phone in the dining room. Leonore must have tidied it away here.'

The page on which the suicide note was written had been ripped off when we found it. The pad must have been near by but I hadn't noticed it – I'd have to look through the scene photographs later. Oh Christ, no I wouldn't; I wasn't on the case any more. I wouldn't be allowed anywhere near the photographs. I decided to conduct a little experiment.

'Lockie, could you get me a crayon, please?' He looked at me as if I'd lost the plot. 'I just want to try something. If you haven't got a crayon, a pencil will do.'

'There'll be a crayon somewhere around,' he said, and wandered off to hunt.

The Boss's words about contamination of evidence came to mind. Using a pen so that I didn't actually touch the notepad, I folded over the top page and looked at the one beneath. There appeared to be an impression still there.

Lockie came back in clutching a green crayon. He handed it over, then hovered behind me as I carefully ran the crayon diagonally back and forth across the entire page. It wasn't a sophisticated way to try and bring to light what had been printed, and it was a far cry from the methods used by the forensic-documents folk, but it worked. Even though this page would have been at least three down, the message that was embedded into its surface was loud and clear. The gasp behind my shoulder told me Lockie could see it too. Standing out in white lettering against the waxy green background were the words 'The Telemax man is killing me'.

Goosebumps erupted across my skin. 'Is that Gaby's hand-writing?'

'Yes.' The word sounded choked.

'I wonder where the original page went? Perhaps the killer found it?' I said, my thoughts thrown out loud. But the words looked hurriedly scrawled, and she must have pressed down pretty damned hard. No, if she'd gone to the trouble of writing it, she'd probably hidden it. Nothing had been discovered on her body, so the note would have been left in the house.

Poor Gaby must have invited her killer in, thought he was a tradesman. That might explain why Radar was shut in the bedroom. She'd probably put him there to keep him out of the way. The suicide note had been found on the table. I rushed back to the dining room, got down on my hands and knees and had a good look at the underside of it. There was nothing there. I did notice the table had a small hidden drawer at the end, so clambered out and opened it. All it contained were place mats, coasters and crumbs. No note.

Lockie watched on, curious.

'The original note has to be somewhere,' I said. My eyes scanned around the area. Everything was so spick and span. For all we knew,

Leonore could have cleaned away her daughter's last desperate plea. 'It could have gone out in the trash and no one even noticed.'

'Are you going to show that to the police?' Lockie asked, his voice a mix of concern and accusation.

What kind of person did he think I was?

'Don't be bloody stupid. Of course I am. This is solid evidence. I'm here to help the case, not hinder it. I've got a friend at the station I can tell about this. They'll probably want to get on to the rubbish search immediately. At least it will give them a decent lead to follow. They're at a bit of a loss. This ties in with Mrs McGann's sighting of a work van in your driveway too.'

The blank expression on Lockie's face told me he wasn't being kept informed.

'I'll collect Gaby's computer and I'll take away her study materials to look at this afternoon and see if they bring anything into context. Let's see what she was into. I'll need a car, though – they took the police truck off me. Can I use one of yours?' When in doubt, take the direct approach.

Lockie looked towards the garage where Gaby's car was parked. As if my sitting at her dresser was bad enough, my using her car was apparently too much for him to entertain.

His voice was steely. 'You can take my truck. You're not having Gaby's car.'

I was grateful for anything, so Lockie's old Toyota Surf would do me just fine. 'I promise I'll look after it. I might even wash it for you.'

I tried to make light of it, but I could see by his dark look that Lockie had had his fill of the ex. Gaby's funeral was the next day – I could forgive him for a bit of animosity.

I took the keys and beat a hasty retreat.

29

I'd just lifted Gaby's documents onto the passenger seat when the crackle of gravel under rubber announced the arrival of another vehicle. I looked up in time to see Cole pull alongside. He wound down his window and leaned out with his elbow over the side. He had a strange expression on his face.

'Sam,' he said, his usual spartan salutation.

'Hi Cole.' I tugged the bottom of my T-shirt down over the top of my jeans. 'I'm just borrowing Lockie's truck for a while, until I get a work one back again.' Why did I always feel the need to explain myself?

He looked at the pile of papers and folders I'd arranged on the seat. 'What's all that for?' he asked.

'Just some of Gaby's things. Lockie said I could take them to have a look through, see if I can find some new leads on the case. There haven't been many so far.'

He looked at me for several moments, and I could feel the heat gradually work its way up my face. 'Should you be doing that?' he asked. It was a perfectly valid question, but I couldn't help but feel chastised.

'Officially, no, but unofficially I think I'm more in a position of trust with Lockie and the locals than any of the flash detectives they've brought into town. I might find some scrap of significant information where they wouldn't – local knowledge and all. Anyway, if they thought it was of any consequence, I'm sure they would have taken it all away for examination by now.'

My, how I jumped on the defensive, and I felt damned annoyed with myself for it. I didn't have to justify myself to Cole. Lockie was the one who counted.

'Fair enough,' he said. 'Good luck, then.'

'Yeah, thanks, Cole.'

I shut the door and slunk around to the driver's side, face still aglow. Bugger it. Why should I feel like the criminal? I could be a stupid cow sometimes.

30

Cross-legged, I sat on my bed and settled in for an afternoon of research with Gaby's course material spread about me, smorgasbord style. It didn't take long before I had to make the grudging admission that this woman was really good. Her writing style was concise, flowed easily and was very readable. Her tutor seemed to agree with me – all of her assignments had great assessments.

Gaby appeared to have been highly organised and capable, so I was still puzzled that she didn't seem to keep an appointment diary. When I'd asked Lockie about it, he'd directed me to a little diary near the phone, a giveaway from the local pharmacy. Now, of course, even that diary was admitted as evidence and out of my reach. I had flicked through it briefly on the night she went missing, but didn't see anything that could be of interest. It had a few coffee dates and birth dates written in it, but that was about all. Perhaps she had a great memory for times and dates. Me, I had to write everything down, otherwise I knew damned well I'd forget something. My world ran off to-do lists. The other alternative was she kept an electronic diary on her phone, but likewise, that was held in evidence and out of my reach for now. If she did, I might be able to access it from her laptop later.

Notebooks were another favourite tool of mine. God only knew I had enough of them. My long-term goals notebook, short-term goals, computer stuff, police stuff, ideas notebook, things-I-couldn't-find-any-other-place-to-put-them notebook. My mother laughed at my seemingly obsessive need for them, but they were better than having lots of loose bits of paper floating around to get lost. I considered my notebooks an essential organisational tool. I wondered if Gaby did too.

'Here we go.' I pulled a large black spiral-bound volume out of her filing box. Under it were hidden a couple of small 3B1 school-type notebooks. 'A woman after my own heart.'

In more ways than one, when it came down to it.

I started with the smaller ones. The first contained websites and email addresses; I had one of those too. The other seemed to be an ideas notebook, quick jottings about potential stories. The Volunteer Fire Brigade's reaction to having to undergo unit standards training; Bill Ward's Matchbox car collection – an idea that had made it into an assignment I had just finished reading; tourism opportunities in Mataura; fundraising for the new town library. Mostly human-interest stuff. Nothing I deemed worthy of a murder. Not that I deemed anything worth killing over.

The little notebook was obviously the hatchery; the big black book was the incubation chamber for ideas to grow into fully fledged stories. A photograph of Bill Ward grinning proudly in front of his beloved cars. We all knew never to bring them up as a topic of conversation at the pub unless we had a few hours to spare. Jotted around his photo were numerous notes and thoughts on the subject, including information about the value of such vehicles, especially in their original boxes. Frankly, I was surprised by their worth. Made me wish I'd looked after my toys better when I was a kid. She'd written down the dates and times she'd rung Bill. She'd even logged a call to an antiques dealer in Dunedin to ask about saleability. So I'd been right: Gaby was a very organised kind of a girl. This was her diary; it was just not in the form you would have expected.

The skeletons of several other stories were recorded there too – including, in clear blue biro, the story she must have been at work on when she died.

'Eureka. Thank you, Gaby.'

My elation was short-lived. Her pending article on bovine tuberculosis was not exactly earth-shattering, and most certainly not worth a murder. She can't have been very far into her research, as she hadn't logged many calls – just an email to the Ministry for Primary Industries, which covered all matters agricultural, and a call to Darryl

Fletcher – a local vet. There was a bit of paperwork, though. Tucked in between the pages were a couple of newspaper advertisements cut out of the *Southland Times*. 'Cattle farmers, for your next pre-movement TB test', blah, blah, blah, and another: 'Stop before you go', again outlining the procedures to be undertaken before moving cattle. I scanned down the pages and suppressed a yawn. Oh yeah, this was riveting stuff. There was a web address at the bottom of the page. If I had any difficulty getting to sleep, I'd look it up.

Also tucked in was a sample Animal Status Declaration from P. K. Rawlings Ltd, Phillip Rawlings' stock-carrying firm. There was another name to add to my follow-up list. But meantime, I'd start by calling our friendly vet Darryl – see what sort of things Gaby had been asking him about. Her log recorded that she'd questioned him about national protocols on TB testing and that he'd referred her to MPI. Gaby was nothing if not thorough.

Then I'd check out Gaby's computer. I'd driven straight over to Gore to collect it when I'd left Lockie's; there was no way I was going to risk the police beating me to it. But it felt odd – thinking of the police as competition, or even the enemy. One unforeseen hitch had been the demand for payment on pick-up, and for the printer that had been in for repair too. I couldn't understand why you'd get a printer repaired – it was probably cheaper just to buy a new one. However, she had and it would have looked a bit suspicious to leave the printer behind, so I'd had to fork out for both of them. Thank God for plastic. Pity it had maxed out my credit card, though.

I closed the notebook and was just about to throw it back into the box when I noticed a corner of paper poking out between some pages near the back. I opened the book to where it was marked, and was disappointed to find only a blank page and an old Telemax envelope. The irony of that find wasn't lost on me. I turned it over and – 'Bloody brilliant.'

Gaby must have been a bit of a recycler, for there on the back of the envelope she had written a to-do list, and presumably a current one, as a couple of items had been crossed off – ring the vet, worm

Radar. So she would have visited the vet, killed two birds with one stone. This was more like it. She'd also written her intention to call my favourite lush, Trevor Ray, as well as Phillip Rawlings – she had one of his documents so had been there already – and John Fellows, a manager at the local freezing works.

I blinked hard and had to reread the last name on her calling list to make sure I had seen correctly. But there it was: Sam Shephard, with a question mark.

Why the hell would she want to call me? I would have thought she'd rather have an anaesthetic-free arm amputation than a private conversation with me. As I recalled our last one-on-one hadn't gone that well. Could have been something to do with the fact I was rather drunk at the time and the lack of inhibitions meant I had got a little offensive. Not my proudest moment. I sat the note down on my crossed legs and contemplated it some more. If it had been a policing matter, I was sure she would have bypassed me and called the Gore station direct. I couldn't imagine she'd call me for any personal matter. If she'd been going to give me a barrelling about past behaviour, it would have happened a long time ago. Besides, she didn't need to. She had already punished and humiliated me in the best way she possibly could have – by being gracious, dignified and above it all.

I stared again at the cover of her black book. It must have been something to do with the story, surely. Maybe she thought I could help her with some facet of TB. God only knew what. Did she already have suspicions about something and want to sound me out about it? Nahhh. I was just going to have to stay terminally curious about that one.

The rest of her list was mundane: pick up computer, buy printer paper, new ink cartridges, book the car in for servicing ... Nothing to set the world alight. I squinted to make out one of the small pictures she'd drawn at the bottom of the envelope, and felt a tingle shoot up my spine as I recognised the shape. It was simple but clear – a skull atop a cross. A subconscious doodle? I shivered and pulled my eyes back up to the top of the page. At least I had a decent list of contacts. Where to start? Where to start? My own name on that list had really thrown me.

I started by reaching for the phone. There was no dial tone. The line didn't sound dead, though; it was all a bit strange. Gaby's reference to the Telemax man jumped to mind, and I couldn't resist the need to look over my shoulder. I was about to hang up when a tentative 'Hello?' just about made me wet my pants.

'Hello?'

A giggle I recognised lilted into my ear.

'Is that you, Maggie?'

'Of course it is, dumb-nut. What were you doing? The phone rang, then you picked up and didn't say a thing,' she said, her voice full of humour. 'You wouldn't get a job as a receptionist like that.'

'I'll bear it in mind. If you must know, the phone didn't even ring this end. I'd picked up to call someone else. You gave me a hell of a fright. It's just as well I'm wearing my Hanes self-cleaning underwear. Anyway, to what do I owe the pleasure?' Maggie never called during the day. The works telephone policy extended to lab staff too.

'A heads-up really. What's your worst nightmare?' There were plenty of those at the moment, so I picked one at random.

'Johnny Depp finally realises I'm the woman for him the day after I walk down the aisle with Joe.'

'Joe?'

'You know, Mr and Mrs Bloggs' boy.'

'Ah, yes. Well this trumps even that horror.' She paused for effect. 'You and your Tweety Pie pyjamas were on the midday news.'

It took me a few seconds before I could respond. Then: 'Oh, Jesus – Mum and Dad! They always watch the news.' But it wasn't my parents, plural, I was worried about. 'What will Mum say?' I knew what she'd say: that was the problem.

'I take it from that comment,' said Maggie, 'that you haven't called them at all, to let them know what's going on? It might have helped.'

I had thought about it, but something urgent to do with the case always seemed to come up. It was a bit late now; the shit and the fan had made contact.

'No, I was going to. God, I'll never hear the end of it now. Mum will think I didn't want to tell her. She'll blow it all out of proportion.'

'Sam?' Maggie interrupted. 'You were on national TV. That's a pretty big proportion to be blown out of. Everyone in the staffroom at the works saw it, probably half the people in Mataura saw it. Didn't make the best of impressions, I'm afraid.'

That took a while to sink in.

'What did they say, exactly?' I asked.

'They didn't say outright that you were a suspect, but made much of your being suspended from the case, and then linked in to recent cases of police officers on the wrong side of the law. It wasn't very pretty.'

I didn't need to look across to my mirror to know my face was a shade or two whiter.

'Thanks for the update, Maggie.'

'You be careful now. The majority of people won't believe that you could be involved. But there may be one or two—'

'Yeah, I know, I know.' There was always going to be some loony who might want to have a go at me. I'd have to watch my back, though I wanted to think a couple of years doing my best for the community would count for something. We would see.

'I'll come straight home tonight, OK?'

'Yeah, thanks, Maggs. See ya.'

It was cowardly, but I left the phone off the hook while I worked out what to do. Maggie's news had taken the edge off my urge for action. After a few minutes, though, I came to the conclusion I was damned if I acted and damned if I didn't. I wasn't that good at self-pity, so decided to carry on – I owed it to Gaby and, now, more than ever, to myself.

This time I didn't bother to disguise my voice when I rang the station. I didn't recognise the receptionist's voice and they didn't recognise mine, which suited just fine. I was transferred straight through.

'You just caught me, Sam. I was on my way out,' Paul Frost said. I could hear him rustle some paper and zip up a bag in the background. 'Have you found something else?'

I waited a moment, to see if he would make any reference to my recent fame. Didn't look like he would, so I ploughed on.

'No, no, just checking in. Off to anything exciting? Are there new developments?'

'This? No, I'm just off to follow up a cattle-rustling report, nothing exciting.'

'They're sending detectives for cattle rustling now?'

He chuckled. 'Yeah, there's a surplus here. Anyway, someone had to go, seeing as they got rid of the general dogsbody.'

He seemed to be in a good mood; I might be able to wheedle a bit out of him.

'So, how is the case progressing?' I asked.

'Nothing spectacular. I'm waiting to hear back from our British counterparts about our friend Dr Walden. Twelve-hour time lag is a pain. The tradesman lead has given us a bit more information to follow up on. By the way, I had to tell the Boss a little white lie as to how we got that lead. Didn't think it wise to give you the credit, considering he expressly forbade you from meddling. Didn't think it would help your cause any.' He got no argument from me there. 'Telemax didn't have any technicians in the area, or any records of faults on that day. We're following up with sign writers and graphics companies to see if they've had any requests for Telemax signage recently. There have been a few reports of sightings of a white late-model van with the logo on its doors in the area on Tuesday.'

'Someone really went to a lot of trouble. It sounds very professional.'

'It certainly does, which reminds me. They're getting a warrant to access your banking and telephone records. I warned you they might.'

'They're what? You can't be bloody serious. They still think I'm a suspect?'

'You know as well as I do no one truly believes you had anything to do with this, but it's procedure. If any of this goes to the Police Complaints Authority or Professional Standards, we can't be seen as favouring you. It's bullshit, but it's reality.'

'Bloody dismal reality.' That knotty feeling had made an unwelcome return to my intestinal tract.

'Just cooperate. Make an uproar, and they'll think you've got something to hide. You haven't got anything to hide, have you?'

I believe the term 'pregnant pause' was applicable here. He was helping me out, so a little trust was in order.

'Did you see the midday news?'

'No, should I have?'

'I had a visit from a reporter this morning. She caught me by surprise, so I wasn't at my best. Apparently they aired it at lunchtime and it didn't paint me in a good light.'

'Oh, great. Lucky you. They called by here too, for some official comment on the case. Frederickson dealt with it. Didn't occur to me they'd be banging on your door. I'd better watch the news tonight, then.'

'I sure as hell won't be. I have no desire to see myself condemned.'

'I don't blame you.' Paul's sympathy convinced me I might as well throw all my cards on the table.

'I should let you know that I've got the use of Lockie's vehicle.'

'How the hell did you manage that?'

'Well, he's decided I'm his best bet when it comes to uncovering Gaby's killer. I'm afraid he doesn't trust you guys to do it.'

'Thanks.'

'Also—'

'There's more?'

'He let me have a good look through Gaby's things and take away some of her journalism course notes. The forensics guys had already been through and they told him they'd finished at the house. He wasn't very impressed with their manner, by the way. They left a bit of a mess, and he felt they didn't accord Gaby's things the dignity they deserved. Anyway, that aside, I haven't found anything else obvious, but I've got a few leads I'm going to follow up.'

'Anything you'd care to share?'

'Not yet, but you'll be the first to know if there's anything worth pursuing.'

'Take care, Sam. The Boss won't look kindly on tampering with potential evidence. It could reflect badly on you.'

'God, Paul, you're starting to sound just like him. I'm not bloody stupid, you know. Give me some credit for brains. I've given you valuable leads, things the so-called experts missed, so you never know, I may well dredge up something important. I do know how to treat evidence and I am perfectly well aware of what's at stake here.'

I must have sounded pretty pissed off because Paul changed his tone markedly. 'Just watch your back, that's all I'm saying. Look, I'd trust you to solve this over these bussed-in goons any day, but there are a lot of politics involved here. Don't become a casualty.'

'I'm starting to think you care,' I said, and laughed.

'Yeah, well, I wouldn't get too carried away. I just want to make sure I don't get transferred to Mataura when they fire you. Got my own interests to watch.'

'Thanks. There I was thinking it was sentiment. Dash a girl's dreams, why don't you?' But I'd pushed the jest a little too far, and made a quick subject change to hide my embarrassment. 'So who reported the cattle rustling?'

'A couple of them were done last night. The Rawlings' property and Trevor Ray's.'

'Oh.' Those names had popped up a bit lately. 'Who are you off to first?'

'Trev's, it's closer.'

I'd give him an hour's head start, then I'd pay a little visit to Mr Ray myself.

I just hoped he hadn't seen the news.

31

The rough gravel driveway that snaked up from the road to Trevor Ray's farmhouse made me thank the powers that be I was driving a four-wheel-drive utility rather than a slick little city car that would have skittered all over the show. Another advantage of driving Lockie's vehicle was it didn't cringe and shudder as it traversed the river of cow shit that indicated the stock had recently been shifted from the paddock on one side to the other. It did mean that in the interests of common decency, I'd have to give it a good clean before I returned it to its owner.

I crested the hill towards the house, and two curious faces peered around the side of the tractor shed off to the right. I pointed the ute's nose in that direction and pulled up alongside the welcoming committee.

'Sam,' Cole said with his usual chattiness as I jumped down out of the cab.

'Hello, Sam.' Trevor wiped his rather soiled hands down his overalls and reached out and grasped mine in a firm handshake. 'Here on business or pleasure?' He gave me a wink.

I took it from the warm greeting they hadn't seen the TV news.

'Business, sort of, I guess.' Wow, that was authoritative. But how else to explain I wasn't here officially, but still wanted to pump him for information? When in doubt, be charming. 'Actually, I'm not here in an official capacity – I'm sure you've heard that I've been temporarily stood down. I'm doing a favour for Lockie, really. He was just wanting to understand a little more about what Gaby was doing in the days preceding her death.'

'Oh,' Trev said. He looked curious. 'How do you think we can help?'

'Lockie gave me access to Gaby's study notes. In it she had a note to ring you. I was wondering if she'd been in contact at all?'

'Oh that. Yes, yes, yes, she was out here last … Thursday, wasn't it, Cole?' He looked up at Cole, who nodded his agreement. 'Came out with that wee girl of theirs – she's a beautiful wee thing. Bloody tragic all round, really.'

'What did she want to see you about?' I asked.

'TB, of all things. She said she was working on a story on tuber-culosis in cattle for her journalism course. Can't see myself why she thought that would be an interesting story – it bores the shit out of me, if you don't mind my saying. But she wanted to know how all the regulations worked and what we had to do to keep the ministry on side. I was quite happy to show her all the certification and forms we have to fill in; took her over to the office and also for a look around the farm. We didn't get too far because she was carrying the youngster. Angel loved the cows, got very excited.'

Once he got going, Trev was a little difficult to shut up. It was no wonder his right-hand man, Cole, was so quiet – he didn't have a hope of getting a word in.

'Why do you think she chose to come to your farm, Trev?' I didn't think he'd be fazed by directness. I was right.

'Because of Cole, I imagine. Being Lockie's mate and all, I suppose you pick on who you know. Would that be right, mate?' He nudged Cole with his elbow.

'Yeah, she did ask if I thought Trev would mind. I said he'd be glad to help.'

That made perfect sense. Make use of the resources at hand. It was always easier to talk to someone friendly than to have to cold call.

'Do you want to come over to the office and see the bits and pieces I showed her?' Trev asked. With a guiding hand on my back, he directed me towards the house. 'Then I can show you where we went on the farm. Come on, I'll make you a cuppa. You want one, Cole?'

'No thanks, I'd better finish that tractor,' he said. 'Take care, Sam.' Then he disappeared around the corner of the shed.

'He's taking it really badly, you know, about Gaby. Lockie's his best mate and he's got a real soft spot for the girl. Doesn't say much, but I can tell he's hurting. So if there's anything I can do to help, you know, finding her killer, just ask. Cole's a good bloke; he's like a son to me. I don't like to see him so cut up.'

For all his affection for alcohol and lechery – his hand was still in the small of my back, slightly lower than was called for – I found it very hard not to like him.

'He's been a great support for Lockie. God knows Lockie needs him. It's good of you to give him the time off work,' I said, and stopped to pat the rather portly tabby cat that had appeared from the garden to greet us. The action also served to get Trev's hand away from the vicinity of my bottom.

'Off you go, Horse,' Trev said, and shooed him away.

'Horse? That pudding with legs is named Horse?' I couldn't help but laugh. Horse was the name of the most formidable fictional farm cat on the planet. I had been brought up with the *Footrot Flats* cartoons, as had generations of Kiwis. We all knew that Horse was not to be messed with and would happily take on and take down anything from dogs, wild pigs, and feral goats to humans of any level of scariness who dared cross his turf. Horse was a legend; this critter was a pat-and-tickle-seeking marshmallow.

Trev's face broke into a grin. 'Yeah. He doesn't live up to the standards of his namesake, that's for bloody sure. The only way he'd kill a mouse is if he accidentally sat on it. The vermin are pretty safe around here.'

He stumbled slightly as he went up the steps and had to lean into the wall to regain his balance.

'You right, Trev?' I asked. It was a bit early in the day for him to have been on the turps, though I couldn't smell any alcohol on his breath. As well as the stumble, I'd noticed his hands were a bit shaky again. Maybe it was just age and decrepitude.

'Yeah, yeah, caught my toes on the step. These boots are a bit big.' He kicked the gumboots off onto the porch and then held the front door open for me.

The farmhouse looked about 1930s' vintage, with plenty of exposed timber beams in its high-stud ceilings. Doors, windows and architraves had also been left unpainted to show the wood in all its warm glory. The décor was surprisingly feminine. Janice Ray's touch was evident in the details: a coat stand by the front door with a collection of old-style hats, a hall table displaying an antique miniature sewing machine and a collection of thimbles. There were fresh-cut flowers in a vase on the kitchen table. It was all very American Country.

'Janice still teaching at the college?' I asked, as Trev put the kettle on.

'Yeah, I don't think she'll ever retire – she loves it too much.'

I couldn't understand how anyone could love teaching a classroom of hormonal teenagers. I wouldn't have the patience for it and was pretty sure I'd end up in front of the disciplinary council for throttling the little buggers. I sat down at the table and savoured the delicious aroma that wafted through the room, its source an enormous hunk of meat roasting in the oven.

'You'll be a popular boy when she gets home,' I said.

'Eh?'

'Putting the dinner on. Janice will be pleased to see that.'

'Friday night ritual is the roast. The meat is easy enough to bung in. Janice deals with the vegetables when she gets home. I'd be in big trouble if I didn't have it cooking.' Trev poured the tea and brought over my mug. He hadn't asked me how I had it, so I was interested to see what he thought the standard mix was.

'Come down to the office,' he said, and I followed him back down the hall and into his den.

'Not a technophobe, then.' As well as a fax machine, which nowadays was a bit of a rarity and a nod to the old school, there was the latest model computer with an enormous screen, and a colour laser printer and scanner. 'You do actually use it, don't you?'

'Just goes to show you *can* teach an old dog new tricks,' he said, and gave me a wink. 'Farming is such a tight business these days, you've got to give yourself every advantage you can to keep profitable. I made it a policy years ago to keep up with the technology. I record all of the herd statistics, as well as business accounts in the thing. We've even got one of those tablets to use out on the farm. Just bring it back, hook into the network and download the information. Makes everything very easy. I tell you, I can't understand why the other old buggers are scared of the things. And the internet is great to stay in touch with the girls and the grandkiddies.'

I looked up at the photos on the wall as I took a sip of my tea – and cringed: he'd put sugar in it. The beaming faces of his four daughters looked back at me. There was no son for this farmer. Small wonder he was so fond of Cole. I'd gone through school with Colleen, his eldest girl. She'd gone on to university and studied to become a lawyer. In fact, all his girls had gone through university. Felicity, the youngest, was still at Otago, finishing her physiotherapy degree. He'd have been proud of their achievements, but who would take over the farm when he retired? Mind you, he struck me as the kind of old bugger who'd only hang up his gumboots when they chucked them into the coffin with him.

He was very fond of his cattle too. Interspersed among the family portraits were photos of his prize beasts. Trev was a breeder of Angus cattle, magnificent black hunks of walking steak. These must have been his stud cattle, sporting names like Romeo, Casanova, Samson and Raphael. It was all I could do not to snigger.

'Here's the TB information I showed Gaby,' Trev said as he plonked a folder full of material onto the desk. I had a premonition of being there for the rest of the afternoon.

'Oh,' I said, sighing as I turned the front cover. 'Could you possibly give me the condensed version?' I had gleaned some of the basics of TB control when I read Gaby's notes, but it would be good to hear it from the horse's mouth.

'It's all a load of bureaucratic crap, really. I mean, I can understand them wanting to be careful about TB and protect our export potential, but at the end of the day, it all comes down to more work for us cockies.'

'Bit of a sore point, I take it?'

'You just get sick of it. There's Health and Safety crap, Accident Compensation Corporation crap, Inland Revenue crap, Goods and Services Tax crap, Ministry for Primary Industries crap … this is just more of the same. Crap. We don't get paid to do it – in fact, like most of their great ideas, we carry the cost.'

Welcome to the world of compliance. I could sense this conversation would get us nowhere fast, so ushered him back to the point. 'So how does the system work, then? Can you give me the rundown?'

'Oh yeah, sorry. Got a bit carried away. Basically, every animal over one month old has to have an identification ear tag, particularly when it leaves the farm. You're a farming girl, aren't you? You'd know all about ear tags.'

I knew about ear tags, alright. Dad had made me help him when it came to tagging the calves. It was my second-most hated task, only outgunned by docking the tails off the lambs. I always had a soft spot for the baby animals.

'Yeah, seen it done, but I didn't pay much attention to what was on them.' I shuddered, even while acknowledging that my concern for the animals' welfare and comfort was a bit stupid, given that I'd had my own ears pierced voluntarily.

'Herd number, individual number and a bar code. Also, your herd gets a classification according to the testing and risk of infection. Of course, we have to pay for the MAF guy to come and do that.'

I got the feeling Trev didn't like to dole out money unless absolutely necessary, or for the latest gadget.

'How often does that happen?' I asked, as I put down the tea mug I had politely if unenthusiastically drained.

'We're low risk, so the animals are checked by the works at slaughter. So for now I don't have to pay. But if one of my beasts gets infected by some bloody possum or deer, then we have to go through all the testing rigmarole again.'

Possums were the scourge of this country. Introduced from Australia for their fur, they took to our climate with great enthusiasm and proliferated beyond all expectation and ability to control.

Consequently, they destroyed our native bush habitat for our birds, preyed on their eggs in nests and were carriers of bovine TB. Cattle were inherently nosey beasts, and oddly enough, if a sick or dying possum wandered out onto pasture, the cattle would come over for a look, a sniff and a lick. Most New Zealanders hated them. The only good possum was a dead possum. Nothing pleased me more than seeing one splatted as roadkill.

'So you'd do a bit of control then, would you?'

'Too bloody right. Traps and poison for the buggers. Bloody nuisance.' An expensive nuisance.

'So basically, each head of cattle has to be identifiable from birth to slaughter?'

'Yup. There are exceptions, but I won't lumber you with those.'

'Thanks – no need to tell me what a bore paperwork is. You should see how much we have to do in the police. Mind you, as you said, they have to keep tabs on it if too high levels of TB could affect overseas trade and drop meat prices. So it's in your best interests, I suppose. Does the disease cross over into humans?'

'Nah,' he said, and shook his head. 'Not nowadays. Well, only rarely. Now the milk's pasteurised and they're very careful at the slaughterhouse. The problem's more about being competitive in overseas markets. So, like you said, this whole TB business is a necessary evil – just another expense to complicate our lives.' He slapped his hand down on the folder. 'As usual, it's the farmers who have to carry the cost. We always do.'

'Yeah, but you'd be the first to complain if prices took a tumble, wouldn't you? And you'd feel really bad if some oversight on your farm caused everyone to be penalised. Export markets can be fickle things.'

'True, true. I guess we all have to protect our livelihoods as best we can.'

I could see Trev look off into the distance, pondering that one. I tried to lighten the tone.

'It's just as well the government didn't bring in that cow-fart tax they were proposing – you'd have been in the shit!'

Trev burst out with his characteristic chortle. 'You got that right, girl, you got that right. Thank Christ, they saw sense on that one. We'd have been the laughing stock of the world. How the hell do you count cow farts?'

I couldn't resist. 'It would certainly be a pretty stink job.' Trev doubled over, cackling, and for a minute I was worried he was going to wet himself.

'Christ, you're a dag, girl.'

'I'll take that as a compliment. I can't say I've been compared to the back end of a sheep before – well, not to my face, anyway.'

He laughed again. 'Come on, Sam, we'll have a look outside. I'll take you where I took Gaby the other day.' And, once again, his hand took up its customary position.

'Oh, that's right…' The sight of one of his framed photographs, of a rather magnificent bull named Romeo, reminded me. 'I hear you had some beasts stolen last night.'

'Yeah, rotten bastards. That really pisses me off.' He must have been upset by it, because he dropped the hand.

'How many did they take?' I asked.

'Five. Had near to a hundred head down in the roadside paddock. The bastards cut the padlock on the gate and just helped themselves. I don't know where people get off doing things like that. Farming's tough enough without some sod stealing your profits. And they got one of my stud boys – Jesus, I don't know how the hell I'll replace him.'

'One of these guys in the photos?'

'Yeah, this big boy. Bloody bastards.' He tapped on the picture of Samson.

'Ouch. Are you insured? How much would he be worth?'

Trev looked close to tears. 'A bomb, especially that boy. Irreplaceable. Big demand for his semen – it's been exported all over the world. But it's not just the money. That's my whole breeding programme thrown out of whack. I've spent years working on the bloodlines – damned good ones too. He was descended from all these boys, right back to Casanova here. Imported him specially from England. No, Samson was a star, and a bloody nice-natured bull too.'

I gave him a pat on the shoulder. 'You didn't hear or see anything?'

'No, the gate's out of sight from the house, behind the hill. Come out, I'll show you.'

We walked out of the house and across the gravelled yard, then paused at the top of the driveway that wound away before us.

'They were in that paddock,' he said, and pointed down to our right. 'The gate's around the other side of that hill.' The pasture stretched out, extending smoothly down to the road. It was pretty lush. We'd had a wet summer, so both hills and plains were dressed in verdant green, and a recent week of hard-out rain had created a surge in grass growth. The paddock extended around the base of the hill that rose up to the house and sheds. The hill was partially covered in shelter trees, poplars and eucalypts, so any noise from the nocturnal visitors would have been well and truly shielded.

I wondered how the hell they got them into the truck? I'd never known a cattle beast to voluntarily climb into one before.

'Where's your cattle race?' I asked.

'Unfortunately for me, there's an old one in that paddock, down from the original farmhouse. It's not one I use because it's a bit rickety. So they wouldn't have had any trouble getting them into a truck. Bastards.'

'But they only took five?' It seemed to me that wasn't a lot of stock for the effort. If the thieves were going to bring a truck big enough to fit five beasts, you'd think they'd fill it to capacity. It would have to be a sizeable vehicle; it certainly wasn't a trailer job.

'Five too many,' Trev said. 'Must have been taking them for meat, I reckon. Otherwise they would have taken more.' He stood there, hands in pockets, his usual amiable expression absent from his face. 'We haven't had rustling here since the mill closed. Then I could kind of wear it because people were suffering and had to find any way they could to feed their families. But things are good in the town now. The works are busy, there's no bloody reason for anyone to steal. It pisses me off. If I find the bastards, I'll show them just how pissed off I am.'

'You know bloody well you can't take the law into your own hands. Let us deal with it, Trev. Deal with it yourself, and the thieves would probably turn around and sue you for damages. And win them.'

He muttered something indecipherable to that, then perked up at the sight of a red-coloured vehicle slowing down on the road and about to turn into the drive. His face broke back into a grin.

'That's Janice. I haven't told her about the cattle yet. She won't be amused.' He added that last sentence with a distinct plum in his mouth.

'Ohhhh,' I said, with one in mine. 'I'd better be off, then. Thanks for your help, Trev. I hope you didn't mind me asking about Gaby's visit, but I thought if I followed her footsteps, so to speak, something might pop up to give us some clues.'

'That's OK, I understand where you're coming from. If I were Lockie, I'd be trying everything to find out what happened to my wife. I'm rather partial to my old bird, really.'

So, the lechery was a big front? He seemed very good at it.

By the time we'd walked over to the ute, Janice's car had crested the hill to the yard. She gave me a cheery wave as she drove past to the garage. Trev held the door open for me.

'Just yell if there's anything else we can do for you,' he said as he pushed the door shut.

'Thanks, Trev, I hope they catch up with the rustlers quickly.'

'Your guys better find them before I do,' he said with a wink. 'Anyway, I'm not taking any chances on a return visit. I've shifted the herd across to the other side. There's no gate onto the road there, and no race. If they want them, they'll have to work for their supper.'

I was certain that if the thieves wanted steak on their menu, it would take more than that to stop them.

32

I now knew a lot more than I cared to about the niceties of bovine TB, but I still couldn't fathom why Gaby would choose it as a subject worth writing about. It was topical for our area, but it was pretty technical, and I sure as hell wouldn't have classed it as human interest.

At the end of Trev's driveway, I slowed up and checked optimistically for traffic. As usual, there wasn't any. The only activity was a harrier hawk down to my left taking care of some roadkill. I pulled out and headed on to my next destination: Phillip Rawlings'. He was another feature on Gaby's follow-up list and also, curiously, another victim of the cattle rustlers. His property wasn't too far from Trev's, just a side road off from the main track back to town. I hadn't made an appointment, but I was happy to try my luck. So far it seemed to be holding.

As I drove, my fingers, unbidden, tapped along to some catchy, static-ridden country tune on the radio. Why would the rustlers do two properties in one night? Why not just fill up their truck at one farm and reduce their risk of being caught out? It didn't make sense. Unless they had some warped sense of social conscience that made them want to halve the burden of loss by sharing it around. Yeah, right.

My mind drifted back to Gaby, and the skull and crossbones on her to-do list. What if Gaby's death was linked to her investigation into TB? It seemed a bit of a stretch, and I had no real grounds to base the idea on, but I just couldn't think of anything else in her life that could cause someone to kill her. I couldn't, of course, completely rule out Dr Walden, but instinct told me he was a sideshow in this case, and that Gaby's research into TB was somehow important. So here was another item for research that night: look at the economic impact a higher rate of TB would have on the country. The disease was already present in a very small percentage of livestock, so it wasn't a high threat to biosecurity. There was the odd report in the newspaper about farms reporting an outbreak, but it was never front-page material. A phone call to the Ministry of Primary Industries might also be in order, to see if they were concerned about any particular farms in our area. I desperately needed to sit down and have a good hunt through Gaby's laptop – check her email and look at any websites she'd visited recently. The laptop was still sitting on the front passenger seat; ever the optimist, I'd brought it along for the ride in case I had a bit of time to kill.

Lockie's ute left a bit to be desired. It was an archaic piece of shit that lacked the creature comforts of air-conditioning and power steering, not to mention a decent stereo – I'd turned it off in disgust. The suspension was as hard as hell, and now the damned thing was starting to pull noticeably to the left. Somehow, I didn't think it was just the camber on the road. I pulled over onto the side, half on the grass, half on gravel, turned off the engine and hopped out to investigate.

'Oh, bloody marvellous.'

The bottom half of the left rear tyre was doing a pretty good impression of a pancake. A flat – and it was still a good ten kilometres into town. I could call for help. But who? Couldn't call work: I wasn't one of the in-crowd any more. Besides, the guys would never let me live it down. Trev's place was relatively close, but that somehow seemed a bit defeatist: after all, girls can do anything. I didn't think Lockie would appreciate it if I wrecked the wheel rim by attempting to drive it the rest of the way home. I'd just have to change the thing myself. I'd changed plenty of tyres before – on cars. How hard could it be? The ute was simply bigger. Surely?

One of my brothers had a similar type of ute, and it had a storage space behind the rear seats. I hauled myself into the driver's seat, clambered over to the back seat and pulled it down. Sure enough, there nestled behind it were the jack and toolkit. It was a good start.

I hopped out again and walked around the back to open the

canopy door and get out the spare tyre. Apart from a few grimy-looking rags and excess dog hair it was empty. OK, let's think. If I were a guy, where would I hide it? Of course, the most awkward place I could. Canopied ute; it must be...

'Underneath.' I crouched down and looked under at the chassis. Bingo, there it was.

'Oh shit.' I recalled the river of cow shit I'd just driven through twice at Trev's place. The underside of the ute, including the spare tyre, was plastered in it. Of course, being out to impress, I was wearing one of my best shirts and only decent pair of trousers. I stood up, and took a moment to adjust to the head rush. Then there was nothing for it. The deed had to be done. If I couldn't rely on anyone coming to my rescue, at least I could save the shirt. I took it off, folded it and placed it across the front seat of the cab. Thank God for singlets. They might not be spectacularly sexy, but they serve their purpose in keeping you warm. In light of the poo situation, I was pleased I hadn't gone for a lacy camisole. And at least I wasn't reduced to only wearing a bra.

'What are you staring at?' I said to a curious cow that had sauntered over, its face stretching over the wire-and-batten fence. 'Just 'cause I haven't got a twinset. You jealous?'

I poked my head back underneath the ute to see how the spare tyre was secured. Just by a couple of bolts, apparently; so I grabbed the spanner, lay down on my back and wriggled my way into position underneath the tyre. The odd bit of gravel that had sprayed off from the road bit into my skin. I gritted my teeth and kept wriggling until positioned directly under the bloody thing. I could see I was going to have to be careful the sucker didn't fall straight down and crush me to death. Wouldn't that be a marvellous way to go?

I set to and loosened the nuts with the spanner. Lying on my back, arms up, proved to be damned hard work. I had to pause and shake my arms out a few times before I finally got the nuts to the point where they only needed another couple of turns. The stench under there was not pretty and I was trying not to breathe too deeply.

How was I going to manage this? If I undid one nut first, then, as I undid the other, I could catch the wheel on my hands and knees. I'd then roll over to the side and get it on the ground. Sounded good in theory. In reality, manoeuvring the wheel in that confined space was difficult and my muscles strained under the awkward weight of the thing. My hands were slick with shit and I didn't even want to imagine how my trousers looked. Eventually, I got the wheel onto the ground without doing myself a mischief. I stopped for a quick breather, and then rolled over onto my stomach to wriggle back-wards and drag the poxy thing out. Whoever thought of putting the spare there should have been shot at dawn. Just about out, I cleared the edge of the bumper, then popped up onto my hands and knees.

Crack.

What felt like a baseball bat hit me squarely on the back of the head.

My face hit the gravel and I lay there, dazed, watching the display of fireworks that shot before my eyes.

'Fucking towbar!' I reached my hand to the back of my head, and felt dampness. I then realised it must have been the cow shit I'd just smeared through my hair. Fan-bloody-tastic.

With a little more care and a big swerve to the side I pulled myself up onto my hands and knees and stayed there swaying for a bit. There was going to be an industrial-sized lump on the back of my head. Getting up like that had been a stupid, careless thing to do.

'Bugger this.'

I eased myself up onto my feet and used the side of the ute as support to stagger back to the cab for the cellphone. I'd save my 'girls-can-do-anything' mantra for another occasion. I'd just have to suck up my pride and call for reinforcements. I'd ring Paul. He'd just love that. The whole station would.

I looked at the zero bars of signal on the useless flaming thing, and threw the phone unceremoniously back onto the seat.

'Bugger,' I yelled, startling the whole collection of cattle that had now gathered around for the show. Of course there'd be no bloody signal out here in the sticks. In this day and age it was crazy that there were cellphone reception dead spots, this wasn't the Third World – this was a flaming well-to-do nation. But there were, and Sod's law said there would be one here, today.

I looked back down the road towards Trev's place and tried to calculate how long the walk would take. Too long.

'Oh for God's sake, get hard, girl.' I marched around the back again and grabbed the jack. I wasn't going to be beaten by something as mundane as a bloody flat tyre. I positioned it under something solid-looking down the side and proceeded to do business lifting up the rear of the truck. The exertion didn't do my head any favours and I needed several pauses to clear the giddiness. Finally, I had the offending wheel raised in the air. A small victory. I grabbed the wheel brace, popped it over the first nut to hand and tried to loosen the damned thing.

'Oh bloody hell.'

All that succeeded in doing was spinning the wheel around. Even the cows laughed.

Use your brain, woman – of course I was going to need a bit of traction. I marvelled at how truly stupid I could be. I released the jack enough for the wheel to grip on the ground and tried again. It became apparent very quickly that the power my fifty-three-kilogram frame could exert wasn't going to produce enough force to loosen anything.

'Shit.' I tried another nut. All that straining on the wheel brace did was hurt my hands. And perhaps induced a haemorrhoid.

Desperate situations called for desperate measures. I swung the wheel brace around so that I'd apply the force in the right direction and not tighten the bloody thing: rightie tightie, leftie loosie rang inside my head – thanks, Dad. I leaned against the side of the ute for support, then carefully climbed up onto the brace and balanced precariously. I gave a small jump.

Nothing.

Tried a bigger jump.

A little movement.

That was hopeful.

Throwing caution to the wind, I tried the biggest jump I was game for. My feet came down on the bar; the bar shot down a few centimetres and threw my balance off. As my feet headed to the earth, I knew this was going to hurt.

'Bugger, bugger, bitch, bum, piss, cock, fart,' I roared, loud enough to send the cows scattering. Good as that statement felt, it didn't quite cut it.

'Ahhhh, fuck it all to hell.' I lashed out and hit the side of the door with my hand, which hurt me more than the ute, then slid down its side and landed in a bloody, dusty, shit-covered heap on the ground. The sobs burst out of their own accord; it was futile to try and control them. I rolled up my trouser leg and cringed at the sight of the gouge down the front of my shin that was now welling up with blood. Hot tears flowed down my cheeks and I angrily wiped them away, only to realise that I had now applied a shiny coating of cow shit to my face.

All that to move one nut.

There were five more to go.

33

It was some time before my ears caught the sound of an approaching vehicle. I scrambled to my feet and lifted up the front of my singlet to hurriedly wipe my face. I'm not sure why I bothered. The tears would have helped clean some of the cow shit away – the tears and the snot. I limped around to the roadside and looked towards the dust-shrouded vehicle. I didn't need to fake a damsel-in-distress look; it was pretty bloody obvious.

A ute pulled up alongside mine and a familiar face grinned at me.

'Sam. In a bit of trouble there?' Cole said.

I gave a big sniff, then realised how charming that must have sounded. 'Flat tyre.' I tried to hide the quiver in my voice by resorting to two-word sentences. 'Other side.' I turned and indicated the back of Lockie's ute.

I heard a sharp intake of breath.

'Shit, Sam, you're bleeding. Stay there.'

Like I was going anywhere. I turned to tell him I'd just knocked my shin, but Cole had already moved forward to park his ute in front of mine. Before I knew it, he had jumped out and was striding purposefully towards me, holding a cloth.

'Here, let me help,' he said.

I was just about to protest when he literally picked me up and leaned me across the bonnet.

'What are you doing?' I said, rather indignant. I tried to turn and look, but had my head forcibly directed to the front.

'Keep still. You've got blood pissing out the back of your head. What happened?'

I instinctively reached up to touch it, but Cole slapped my hand away. I felt his fingers part my hair, and winced at the jolt of pain that shot through my scalp. Now he mentioned it, the back of my head was feeling a bit sticky. It hadn't occurred to me I could have cut myself; I just thought it was more cow shit.

'Jesus, that's a good split you've got there. Might need a few stitches in it, not to mention a lot of disinfectant. You're a mess. What the hell have you been doing?'

I was surprised at the vehemence in his voice.

'What does it look like I've been doing? Trying to change the frigging tyre. I collected my head on the towbar, trying to get the stupid spare wheel out. I didn't do it for bloody fun.'

Once again I felt the need to justify myself to him.

'Why didn't you ring for help?' he asked. His voice had dropped to a more conversational level.

A huge sigh escaped me. 'I tried, but the cellphone had no reception.'

'You should have walked back to the farm, then. I'd have come out and changed it for you.'

He stepped back to give me room to stand up straight again. I turned around to face him, but couldn't quite meet his eyes. 'I would have, but my leg was a bit sore,' I said, lifting up my now rather gory-looking shin to show him.

'Christ. Get in my ute, we'll get you down to the doctor's.'

He grabbed me by the arm and started to drag me towards his vehicle. I tried to prise his fingers off as I remembered the precious cargo on the front seat.

'Hang on, I've just got to get something out.' I had no qualms about abandoning Lockie's hunk of crap to the wilds, but I wasn't about to leave Gaby's computer in it.

Cole let go and I hobbled back to the cab, grabbed the laptop, my bag and shirt. Then I limped my way back to Cole's ute and climbed up into the seat next to him. He must have found some water to dampen the cloth, because he reached across and proceeded to wipe at my face.

'Ouch, give that here, I can do that.' I grabbed the cloth from him and swung the rear-vision mirror around to get a look at myself. It wasn't pretty. The tears had tracked stripes down the smeared shit, and the gravel had bitten into my skin, leaving globs of blood on my cheeks and forehead. Still, after a bit of work with the cloth, I was vaguely fit to be seen in public. Pity I smelled like a sewer.

'What about Lockie's ute?' I asked as we trundled off towards town.

'It'll be alright there for a while. Nobody's going to steal it with a flat tyre. I'll come back later and fix it, then drop it back to you.'

I stared out at the belts of toetoe that rushed past the window. It shocked me to feel so small and vulnerable. I had always been able to handle any situation I'd got myself into – if I couldn't physically deal with it, I could talk my way out. Ms Invincible. It had been a rude awakening to feel so utterly useless. Even ruder to admit I needed the help of anyone, let alone a male. My traitorous eyes started to leak again.

As if reading my thoughts, Cole looked over at me and stated the obvious. 'You really should be more careful, Sam.'

An hour or so later, I was sporting three stitches in my head, courtesy of Dr Arnold. Of course, he had taken the opportunity to give me a lecture on looking after myself and told me in no uncertain terms that I did not need to act like a superhero. Sounded like a baritone version of my mother. I didn't have much choice but to take his words on board at the time – he was the one wielding the needle.

The medical-centre staff were up on my brush with TV fame. Francine had seen the news, so naturally, they had all been filled in on the gory details. Should have known my luck would run out on that front soon, but at least they seemed to be of the 'I-don't-believe-a-word-of-it' school of thought.

If there was one positive from the visit, it afforded me the opportunity to find out what had happened with Dr Walden. It had occurred to me that I might not be received enthusiastically after I'd sprung one of the surgery's doctors, but in fact, the welcome mat was warmly, if cautiously, extended. Perhaps I wasn't the only one who could see through Walden's apparent charms. The staff had been mortified to find that blackmail had gone on under their very noses. I think they all felt some level of guilt at having been blind to it. Ranjit, in particular, was most apologetic to me. Unfortunately, I wasn't the one who needed to hear it and Gaby was in no position to accept apologies.

While playing tailor with my scalp, Ranjit brought me up to speed on the doctor's activities. Officially, Dr Walden was on extended leave. Unofficially, he'd had his butt booted out the door and the Medical Council had been advised of his actions. Dr Walden had recently become a partner in the practice, so extracting him was going to be a bit messy. He'd already threatened to sue them for wrongful dismissal and, while he was at it, was going to do me for defamation, apparently. It was pretty clear we hadn't heard the last of that man.

Cole had done the chivalrous thing and waited while I was being attended to, then insisted on dropping me off at home. Not quite a knight on a white charger; more of a bloke in a tan ute.

'You sure you'll be OK?' he asked.

'I'll be fine. Maggie's home – she's good at playing Mum.'

He gave me that full-beam look, and I wriggled under his gaze.

'Thanks for coming to my rescue. I did make a bit of a mess of things. I don't know how I can repay you.'

'You could come out and buy me a beer later tonight,' he said, sounding casual.

'Oh, OK. Sure…' I was taken off guard. 'I won't be able to drink; the doc said I probably have concussion. But I can come out for a little while.' As I looked at him, I realised he had a bit of a glow rising up his cheeks. He didn't feel so casual, after all. It was quite cute on a grown man.

'I'll pick you up after dinner,' he said. 'Should have Lockie's ute sorted by then.'

I eased myself down out of the front seat and grabbed my things.

'I promise I'll have showered by then,' I said with a grin.

'Please.'

34

I fumbled with the key in the lock and literally fell into the house. Maggie sat at the table in the middle of what appeared to be the aftermath of a hurricane. She looked, to put it mildly, rather peeved.

I stood stock still as I took in the carnage around me.

'Jesus, what happened? Have you called the police?'

'This was the police,' she said dryly, and waved a piece of paper in the air. 'They had a warrant.'

'Oh, bloody hell. How much worse can today get?' I stormed over to the table and took the warrant to read.

'"To retrieve information relating to the death of Gabriella Patricia Knowes." Were you here? What did they take?'

I could see Maggie registering not only the state I was in, but also the halo of stench that surrounded me.

'Whoa, back, girl. You stink. What the hell happened to you?' She fanned her hand in front of her nose.

'It's a long story and I'd prefer to tell it after I've had a shower. Did they take much?'

'They took quite a few things from your bedroom – folders, a document box. They also took your computer. By the way, whose is this?' She tapped the laptop I'd placed on the table.

'Gaby's. Just as well I had it with me. I haven't even had a good look through it yet. Shit, that fink Paul Frost must have told them I had Gaby's things.'

The rather raised eyebrow and accusing look on Maggie's face reminded me I had a bit to explain to her yet. What was the most concise version of events?

'I went to see Lockie and he gave me access to Gaby's personal things. He doesn't have any faith in the police finding her killer, so he enlisted my help.'

'That's a rather curious development. Don't you think it poses a little conflict of interest?'

'Maybe, but the forensics team had already been through, so I wasn't disturbing anything they hadn't already had access to, if they'd thought about it.'

Maggie's voice took on a serious tone. 'I wasn't just talking about the physical aspects of the case. You're not holding any hope that this might help you get back with Lockie, are you?'

My jaw dropped. What an awful thing to say. Even coming from Maggie the suggestion was offensive to the point of disgust. How could she even think it?

'Of course I'm not. I have got some sense, not to mention taste. I'm only doing a favour for Lockie and trying to clear my own name.' I indicated the shambles. 'God only knows I need to.'

I stormed off to the sanctuary of the bathroom and slammed the door shut behind me.

An indescribably divine shower and a set of fresh clothes later, I began to feel vaguely human and perhaps a little more rational. I owed Maggie a conciliatory cup of tea after my display of pique. She had only my best interests at heart and it galled me mightily to realise there was probably an ounce of truth in her comments. My rational being could never conceive of the idea of Lockie and me reuniting in the aftermath of Gaby's death. In fact, the thought was really quite repulsive. But I had to admit some small fantasy self viewed Sam Shephard as a shining knightess on a white charger, restoring domestic bliss and happiness to Lockie Knowes and his shattered family. Life could continue now that Sam was here. It was truly ego run amok in Disneyland. Oddly, I was more embarrassed at the thought of Gaby – wherever she now was – being aware of those fantasies than Lockie. My, how the loyalties had shifted.

As well as getting my emotions on an even keel, the shower had also revived the need to address a particularly glaring betrayal. Paul sodding Frost! I couldn't believe he'd dobbed me in, after all I'd done to help him. That sure as hell was going to be the last information I shared with him, bloody ingrate. I slumped down onto my bed and pulled out my mobile phone.

'Frost.'

'What the hell did you think you were doing? I do not appreciate having my home ransacked by your bloody mob. If you wanted Gaby's stuff, why didn't you just bloody well ask?' I thought that dispensed with the pleasantries nicely. Next, I'd give him both barrels.

'I presume that's you, Sam. So kind of you to introduce yourself.'

'Don't go and get all high and mighty with me, you bloody rat. I've had a shit of a day and the visit of Lightfingers McGraw and his merry band of demolition men was not what I needed. I suppose you were there too? You could have at least tidied up after yourselves, or was that just your sick little way of getting back at me? An added bonus for no extra charge?'

'Have you finished yet?' he asked calmly. He may as well have invited me to stampede.

'Oh, I'm only just warming up. If you think—'

'Well, let me just save you the bother of wearing out your delicate little voice and say I had absolutely nothing to do with it. I haven't told a soul.'

That left me gawping somewhat, but not for long.

'Well how the hell did they know to search my house, then?'

'This is a small town, Sam. You didn't stop to think someone might have noticed Lockie's ute parked outside your house? This place thrives on gossip. A little phone call here, innuendo there, and before you know it Lockie's being accused of having an affair – with you. The Boss rang him up to find out what was going on and, considering the circumstances, Lockie wasn't about to lie.'

My impending tirade screeched to an abrupt halt. There wasn't much that could be said to that. How could I have been so naïve? Poor Lockie, the last thing he needed was to have tongues awag and his reputation tarnished. You could almost hear it: 'It's always the husband, the husband always does it. Got the Mrs out of the way so he could shack up with the ex.' I could hardly blame him for covering his butt.

'Oh.' It was all I could muster. I was glad he couldn't see the heat that had edged its way up my face.

'Oh, is bloody right,' Paul said.

'Well,' I said. 'I haven't had a good look – not that I'd be able to tell anyway with the mess they left behind…' I was working on the principle of changing the subject. 'Did the boys take anything other than Gaby's stuff?'

'Your computer, diary and several notebooks. They didn't find Gaby's computer. I take it you have that with you.' Paul had a thanks-for-not-telling-me tone to his voice. Lockie must have fessed up about that too.

I chose to ignore the tone. 'Yes, thank God.'

'Well, might I make a small suggestion, then? In the interests of public relations and any chance of ever getting your job back, check out her computer and then turn it over to us, pronto, tonight. The last thing you need is a return visit from the Gestapo. Also, yet another warning: I suspect the Boss may be undertaking formal disciplinary proceedings against you … Are you still there?'

My world was starting to go a bit fuzzy around the edges again.

'Yeah, I'm still here,' I said quietly. 'I didn't think today could get much lower, but I'm on the fast track to hell.'

'Hey, don't be too down on yourself. This lot, for all their rank and brains, haven't come up with a single useful lead of their own. If you hadn't found the Telemax note we'd all be pretty bored and embarrassed right now. As it is, the Boss has been given the hard word from the bean counters and the staffing allocation has halved. So basically, we need any help we can get. Have you found anything of interest today?'

I pondered momentarily on the question. I didn't have anything I could substantiate, just a vague sensation of a connection between Gaby's death, her researching bovine TB and the sudden rash of cattle rustling. It was too coincidental to me. But I didn't think Paul would want a hunch: proof was what he was after. I'd keep my feelings to myself for now.

'No,' I replied, 'but I'll let you know if I find anything of interest in Gaby's computer. For now, I have a few ideas but nothing concrete. Can you do me a favour?'

'It depends,' he said, and I could hear the humour in his voice. At least I hadn't offended him too much with my earlier outburst. 'Can you come around in about an hour and pick up Gaby's computer? I'm not in any fit state to face the Boss right now.'

I could feel the relief from the other end of the line. 'Of course, Sam. In an hour, then.'

35

The only blip in an otherwise productive time exploring Gaby's laptop was a hang-up phone call. God, I hated those. If you dialled a wrong number, at least have the common courtesy to apologise.

Lucky for me, Gaby hadn't bothered to password-protect her computer, so I didn't have to waste precious time figuring it out and was able to rip straight in. An hour passed in a wink. I was no expert, but I could navigate my way around computers and find things that were supposed to be hidden.

There were no emails of note, other than the query Gaby had logged to MPI about TB. Evidently, they hadn't replied. Her electronic calendar didn't show any other appointments in addition to those she had scribbled on the envelope. Examination of Gaby's documents folder showed only assignments and a few webpages she'd saved for future reference – these, unsurprisingly, related to TB. Where things got a little more interesting was when I looked back to see what webpages she'd looked at recently. They were not limited to TB. Her research into livestock diseases had also extended to the foreign and positively catastrophic – foot-and-mouth disease, BSE, scrapie, brucella, mycoplasma bovis, anthrax. As a list it made scary reading, and several diseases had made their way onto the international stage in recent years. Anthrax had been used as a terrorist weapon post 9/11. Once upon a time, white powder in an envelope was likely to be an A-class drug; now it triggered a decontamination alert. There were still new cases of BSE or mad-cow disease cropping up in countries other than Britain and Europe. Canada and Japan had had recent cases; another case in the United States had been on the news the other night at the pub. Even New Zealand had had a potentially disastrous brush with foot-and-mouth: some sick bugger claimed to have released the disease on Waiheke Island. It was most likely a hoax, but the shock waves were felt throughout the world. Trading partners threatened to close borders to our meat, and an obscene amount of taxpayer money had to be spent on containment and testing – just in case. All thanks to a suspected university capping stunt. No one had laughed at the joke.

These thoughts led me back to Gaby, and why she'd been looking at these websites. Thoroughness, morbid curiosity or suspicion?

I didn't get the opportunity to look further into it before someone knocked at the door.

'Hey, square eyes, you've got a visitor,' Maggie called as she showed Paul into the house.

I was back in Maggie's good books again. Making her a cup of tea and providing conciliatory chocolate biscuits had done much to repair any potential rift in relations. Not that the risk of that was large: Maggie knew me too well. But hey, any excuse for Toffee Pops. She waved bye-bye as she made herself scarce.

I stood up and awkwardly shook Paul's hand. I don't know why I felt the need to do that. Conditioning?

'How's it going? Find anything interesting?' He came around to look at the screen. 'Whoa, what happened to your head? Are you OK?'

His concern was gratifying, but the afternoon's escapades were still a bit of a sore point, so I shrugged it off.

'It was just an accident. It's nothing, I'm OK.' The frown told me he wasn't too convinced. 'It's nothing.' I shot him an end-of-conversation look, to which he merely raised his eyebrows. I continued on. 'Now, I'm sad to say I haven't found anything startling on Gaby's computer. I take it by now you guys have worked out she was studying journalism, and the article she was working on when she died was about bovine TB.'

'They had mentioned the journalism course, and the TB. Not a very exciting topic to feature. You think there's a connection?'

How much did I tell him? I wasn't sure.

'I think there must be some connection, but it's probably very vague or indirect. I can't for the life of me think why someone would be threatened by her writing about TB. It's hardly the stuff of conspiracy, after all. All I've found on her computer is general background research that you'd expect from someone writing about livestock. Ministry of Primary Industries regulations, diseases – not just TB. She's looked at several others as well, identification, things like that. Her email correspondence is mainly chitchat with friends and family, jokes forwarded, the usual mountain of spam. The only email relating to her work was a query sent to MPI which hasn't been answered yet.'

'That's disappointing. I'd have much preferred to find a great big arrow pointing to her killer on her desktop.' He sighed. I noticed the dark rings under his eyes. The staff who'd remained had been putting in long hours. Tough – but weren't we all?

'Sorry, no neon signs. Looks like we're just going to have to solve this one the old-fashioned way with lots of legwork.'

'Bugger,' he said.

That summed it up nicely, really.

'I like the way you said *we're* going to have to solve this one. Need I remind you that you are currently under suspension and quite a bit of scrutiny? I think it would be in your best interests if you just let us handle it from here. The CIB guys might be able to pull a bit more information out of the computer that could be helpful.'

'Yeah, 'cause they've been really successful at finding other leads so far.'

All that comment got me was a withering look.

'Don't knock us too much. Some of us have been working hard and, despite what you may think, we're not the Keystone Cops. We're a professional bunch who want to solve this case as badly as you do.'

The last thing I wanted was to get off side with Paul. I muttered a quick 'Sorry.'

'Gracious apology accepted,' he said. 'As I was saying before you decided to slag off your profession, I've come up with some interesting information on our Dr Walden which keeps him firmly on our suspects list.'

I took the proffered opportunity to get my foot out of my mouth. 'So, what did you find?'

'Did a bit of digging into his past activities in Britain. I always had a bad feeling about that man.' He wasn't alone there. 'I could never fathom how Mrs Knowes could have got herself into a blackmail situation in the first place. She seemed to be an intelligent woman, and, as far as we can tell, didn't have any history. To me, the whole scenario seemed so improbable. But maybe not. It now appears that Dr Walden has done this before.'

'Really?'

'Really.' Paul pulled up a chair and sat down next to me. 'He was under investigation for inappropriate sexual relationships with a patient. With several patients, it would seem. He left the country rather hurriedly once the accusations came out and hasn't fronted up to his Medical Council disciplinary hearings. Needless to say, his registration has been revoked.'

'OK, but if that is the case, how did he get to practise medicine here?'

That must have been the question Paul was hoping for. The glee in his eyes told me he was building up to the show-stopper. He literally rubbed his hands together.

'That's where things get really interesting. Our Dr Anthony Walden is not Dr Tony Walden at all. He is in reality Dr Christopher Walden, repeat sleaze and banned from practising in Britain. Dr Tony Walden is, in fact, his older brother, also a doctor, and practising as a GP somewhere in northern England.'

'So big brother bails him out of a spot of bother by lending him the paperwork to get registered here. What a caring, sharing family they have.'

'Either that or the brother didn't know. From what I can gather, they are very close in age – just over a year's difference. They studied medicine at the same university; hell, they may have even flatted together. We don't know that yet, but we will. The British police are pretty keen to have a word with him.'

I bet they were.

'But surely someone would have picked that up when he was applying for registration here? There must have been discrepancies in his documentation. It can't be that easy to fool the Medical Council. And surely the Medical Centre here would have checked his references before they employed him?'

'Well, you'd think that, but no, it slipped through. It probably wasn't helped by the fact that Christopher Walden's full name is Christopher Anthony Walden, so it would be easy enough for him to say that he goes by his middle name. Must be a family name.'

'He must be a very convincing liar, then.'

'Well, yes, he certainly had everyone fooled. The ladies at the Gore station who'd met him thought he was wonderful. I didn't think he was all that good-looking.'

I looked at the expression on his face and laughed. Fancy Paul, the ladies' man, feeling jealous of some competition.

'It isn't all about looks, Paul. It's about charm. And that's the same feedback I got from the locals – that he was very charming. All the ladies liked him.'

'I suppose he had you fooled too?'

'Ooh no.' I visibly shuddered. 'I found him sleazy. Creepy. Yuk.' I thought about that for a moment. 'So you have to ask yourself, what's wrong with Angela Walden, then? Why would she follow that bastard to the other side of the world when he was in trouble for shagging his patients? She must hate him for it. Actually, it could explain her being such a bitch.'

It was Paul's turn to smile.

'Perhaps your comment the other day about a big inheritance isn't too far from the truth. The repeated names in the family could be a major suck-up to a rich grandfather or uncle. She might have decided she could put up with anything to get a slice of that pie.'

'Unless she had her own little misdemeanours she wanted to leave on the other side of the world. Maybe she had her own demons to escape.'

'Could be, she's scary enough,' Paul said.

'And Mataura is as far away as you can get from England and still be on the planet. We do define the back of beyond.'

'No argument there.'

'So what happens to Dr Walden now?' I asked. 'Is he in custody?'

'We've got some final checks to make with our colleagues in Britain. We want to make sure he can't wheedle his way out of this one on a technicality. He'll face charges in the morning relating to practising without a medical certificate. And, of course, we're still looking for any involvement in the Knowes case. Either way, he's going to be experiencing some of Her Majesty's hospitality.'

Good bloody job too. That rat had to pay for what he did to Gaby and those other women.

'So do you really think he had anything to do with Gaby's death?' I asked.

'Do you mean professionally or personally?' Paul cocked his head to the side.

'Is there a difference?' I asked, curious that he'd separate the two.

'Professionally, he could still have paid a third party to have Mrs Knowes killed, so the case is still open there. Personally, even with this new information, I don't think he did it. His game is about lies and power. Paying to have her killed so it looked like suicide is not a display of power.'

'So where do we go with the investigation from here?' I asked.

Paul looked at me as if I was mad. 'I've told you, there is no "we", Sam. You need to stay out of it. You're still under the microscope, or have you forgotten that? You could still get into serious trouble, especially after pulling stunts like this.' He tapped on Gaby's computer, which had flicked over to its screen saver – a family photo including the dog.

My face reddened, and not just because of the reprimand. 'How could I possibly forget? But I still think I'd be useful with the locals. I know the…'

'Stay out of it. I'm serious. The Boss is under a lot of pressure from above to get this case solved and tidied up. He's as grumpy as hell and he hasn't taken kindly to your extracurricular activities.'

'Is he really putting me up for disciplinary?'

Paul reached over and put a hand on my shoulder. 'He's started the paperwork. But to be honest, Sam, he has a soft spot for you. I'm sure he wouldn't go through with it unless he absolutely had to. He has to be seen to be maintaining discipline and standards. My message is don't push his patience too far.'

I suspected I already had.

36

I looked at the empty space on the table and contemplated my next move. Now Paul had taken Gaby's computer into custody, and mine had been commandeered by the police, I was going to have to sweet-talk Maggie into letting me use hers for a bit more research. I could have used my smartphone, but peering into that little screen wasn't going to do my eyes or my headache any favours.

The landline phone started to ring. Maggie was busy concocting a stir-fry in the kitchen. It sure as hell smelled good. Not counting the chocolate biscuits, I'd hardly eaten all day. I picked up on the fifth ring.

'Hello,' I said in my usual I'm-expecting-a-friend manner. What I got was silence, then a deafening click, followed by beep, beep, beep, beep.

'God, that's annoying' I hung up and tossed the phone back where I'd found it on the sofa.

'What's your problem?' was the call from the kitchen.

I wandered on through. 'Second frigging one of those today. You'd think if people dialled a wrong number they'd just say sorry, instead of hanging up in your ear. Either that or someone thinks it's a real grown-up way of expressing their delight at my television appearance.'

'Give them a piece of your mind,' Maggie said, and emphasised her point with an animated wave of the implement in her hand. 'Knowing the mentality around here, it will be someone's sick idea of a joke. You could probably trace the call to the pub. There'll be a group of guys rolling around on the floor laughing, thinking they're oh so clever after seeing you on the news. In fact, I find it odd *you* haven't wanted to watch it.'

Maggie got my yeah-yeah-yeah look in reply. First off, I hadn't wanted any distractions while I explored Gaby's computer; then Paul had called by. And despite being curious about the report on the rest of Gaby's case, I didn't feel like being witness to my own moment of glory.

'Yeah, well, my day has sucked enough without putting myself through the extra torment. It would only put me in a worse mood.'

'That's possible, is it?'

I shrugged. 'I don't really want to find out. I think—' My words were cut off by the telephone again.

'I'll take care of this one,' I said as I strode over, grabbed it off the sofa and hit the talk button. 'Now piss off, you fucking bastards. This is not bloody funny. Just grow up.'

There was a brief, stunned silence before my heart hit my boots. I recognised who was on the other end purely by the sharp intake of breath. Oh, shit.

'Well I never. What sort of a way is that to greet anyone?'

My eyes scrunched closed and my free hand did an immediate face-palm.

'I've never heard anything so rude in all my life. Now what is going on with you? First I get to see you sprawled all over the news, then I get this kind of reception when I call to see if you're alright.'

'God, Mum, I'm sorry, I didn't realise it was—'

'Well that much is obvious. What is going on? And why is it that the first I hear of this is through the telly? When were you going to bother to tell us?'

Oh Lordy, she had her hurt voice on. I knew from bitter experience this conversation wasn't salvageable. I may as well resign myself to fate and take the blows.

'I'm sorry, so much has been going on, I just haven't had the chance—'

'Well it's good to know where we rate on your list of priorities. For heaven's sake, they're saying that you had something to do with the death of this woman, Lockie's wife. Is that true? They wouldn't say things like that unless there was something to it. I hope you didn't have anything to do with this.'

I could not believe my ears – from my own mother.

'Mum, how can you even think that? Of course I didn't have anything to—'

'Well, I don't know what to think, Sam. It's obvious you've been keeping things from us. They were saying you've been suspended. Everyone's been ringing to see what's going on, and what have I been able to tell them? Nothing, not a thing, because my daughter hasn't even seen fit to give me a call.'

She was on a roll, and I knew there was no point trying to insert my side of the story now. The direction of the conversation was inevitable.

'And your father. You know he's not well. This could kill him, you know. He was back at the hospital for tests again this morning, so we found out from everyone else that you were on the news, and in your pyjamas. Sam, what were you thinking? What will other people think? We had to wait till tonight to see it because you didn't have the decency to call, and you weren't answering your phone.'

Too right there. This was precisely what I'd been trying to avoid. Look how well that move had paid off. My head was aching on too many different levels.

'So when are you coming home? You can't stay there. You can help out on the farm. Thank heavens Stephen is here – he and Sheryl are basically running the place for us now. We couldn't do without them.'

And there it was. Saint Steve had married their perfect daughter-in-law – the one who stayed at home to raise their perfect grandchildren. A point that I was reminded of in every conversation. How could I possibly compete?

'I know your dad would love to have you back. We said you should never have gone into the police. Look where it's got you. You should have married that man when you had the chance; you were a fool to let him get away. Things could have been so different. If you'd married him, that girl would never have died.'

Oh bloody hell, now it was my fault that Gaby had been murdered, instead of her being tucked away safe in some civil-service job in Auckland. God only knows how Mum had come to that conclusion – although, in the addled state my mind was in, there was some morbid kind of logic to it.

'Mum, Mum, look, I had nothing to do with Gaby's death. I'm only off duties because of my former association with Lockie, that's all.' That wasn't all, but there was no point in explaining further. That thought was proven as when I finally got to put an end to the torturous conversation and get off the phone, ten minutes later, she still didn't know anything, because she hadn't given me a chance to get a further word in.

'Could today get any worse?' I still had my hands wrapped around the mug of tea Maggie had shoved into them after she'd prised the telephone off me and extinguished my burning ear. She was parked next to me on the sofa.

'The way it's going, I don't dare answer that question. Have you never heard of tempting fate?'

'Fate, karma, whatever, I must have done something dreadfully bad in a previous life to deserve this.'

'Was this when you were Cleopatra or Helen of Troy?'

'Catherine the Great.' She'd managed to wheedle a smile out of me. 'Do you think it would be too rude if I rang up and cancelled on Cole. I don't think I can face going out now. I just want to curl up somewhere and quietly die.'

'Well you could, but he's probably already on his way. And if you were counting on my company, I've already promised the work girls we'd go over to Gore for a night out. I'm the wheels, so I can't bail out, sorry.' She reached over and patted my knee. 'A night out might take your mind off things.'

Maggie was right. I had kind of been counting on her company. 'Everyone's going to have seen me. They'll be talking, staring. I'll never be able to live it down. What if someone decides to have a go?'

'I don't think you have to worry there. Cole doesn't strike me as the type of guy to let anyone have a go at a lady, much less you.'

'Thanks for the compliment,' I said as I clipped her one on the arm.

'Oh, don't be stupid, you know what I mean. He'll look after you. Anyway, you can't sulk for ever. If you get out there and show your face, people will give you credit for it and think you've got nothing to hide.'

'You really think so?' I wasn't so sure.

'Yes. Best thing you can do.'

I put the mug down and slouched back into the chair.

'God, I suppose I should. It will be an early night, though. I feel like crap.'

'Look a bit like crap, and I hate to tell you, still smell a bit like it too. But I suppose you have had a bit of a shit day.' If I'd had more energy I'd have thumped her properly. 'So, what are you wearing out on your date?'

Argghhh. She kept calling it a date. It was nothing of the sort.

'It's not a flaming date, we're just going out for a drink. I think it's the least I can do, considering. In fact, I probably owe him more than one. I'm just being polite.'

'Whatever you say, sunshine.' Maggie could be a cow when she wanted to be. 'But if you want to look the part on your being-polite non-date, your red V-neck top makes quite an impression.'

37

Friday-night revelries weren't yet in full swing when we entered The Arms. Most of the tables were adorned with drinkers, but the volume was still at semi-sober.

'You look really nice tonight. That top suits you well,' Cole said. The hint of colour that rose in his face gave away his self-consciousness.

I brushed at some non-existent crumb. 'Oh, thanks. Yeah, I think I spilled some dinner on it.' I was never very good at taking a compliment.

There were several raised eyebrows as we made our way through the pub. A few people stared momentarily before turning back to their drinking companions – to fill them in on the gossip, I was sure. Cole must have noticed them too, as he put his arm around my shoulders and gently ushered me towards the bar.

'Good to see you, young Samantha. What will you have?' Pat Buchanan always had a handle on what was happening in the town. If he was genial towards me, it was a good sign, though my choice of chaperone probably helped. I was just about to reply when I caught a glimpse of Lockie in my peripheral vision. My pulse jumped and the atmosphere in the bar suddenly became very close.

'Oh, just an IPA,' I stammered as I craned around to make sure I had seen correctly and wasn't on a codeine-induced hallucination.

'Ahem,' rumbled a deep voice beside me. 'I thought you weren't supposed to be drinking.'

'Oh, shit, yes, that's right…'

Lockie was working his way over to the bar.

'A lime and soda, then, thanks.'

He was making slow progress as well-wishers came up to him and shook his hand. I supposed it was his first public outing since Gaby's death.

'Ahem,' came the voice beside me again. I tore my gaze away from Lockie to see a frown disturbing Cole's face. 'I believe you're supposed to be shouting me a drink.'

A blush crawled its way up mine.

'God, sorry Cole, I just saw,' I gestured towards Lockie, 'you know. What will you have?' I couldn't meet his eyes. That was really good form, Shep.

Cole looked over, saw who was coming and said, 'Why don't you find a seat over there?' He pointed in the opposite direction to Lockie. 'I'll bring the drinks over.'

I grabbed the opportunity for a dignified retreat and headed for the armchairs. Shit. Lockie was the last person I expected to see. Surely Cole wouldn't have brought me here if he knew Lockie was going to be in attendance. They were mates, and I was absolutely certain Cole would have filled Lockie in on his opportune rescue. It had probably provided Lockie with some welcome comic relief.

None of the other patrons seemed to pay me any attention now; curious eyes instead followed Lockie. I hastily reapplied some lipstick and rearranged my clothes. I eased the fabric of my skirt straight with my hands. I always felt slightly exposed in a skirt, but Maggie had insisted. She'd also insisted on me wearing my long boots to cover up the decidedly unattractive gouge down my shin. Alas, there wasn't much that could be done with my hair other than try to hide the lovely split down the back of my head.

I looked about to see where Cole and the drinks were. They were over talking to Lockie. I saw Cole indicate, beer in hand, in my direction and Lockie pat him on the shoulder as he turned to make his way back.

Jesus bloody Christ, what the hell did Cole think he was playing at?

My eyes must have been laden with accusation, because he started to explain as he sat the drinks down on the table.

'Lockie just wants to pop over for a second. He's come in to finalise a few arrangements for tomorrow. He's not staying.'

Of course, I should have figured that one. The funeral. It would be a big one, at the Catholic church. As well as his and Gaby's families, Lockie had a lot of loyal friends and acquaintances who would be there to support him. There would be his workmates, members of the local community, professional mourners and opportunistic morning-tea eaters, as well as the straight-out curious. A high-profile death invariably brought out the rubberneckers and vultures who feasted on the misfortune of others.

It was also common for the perpetrator of a murder to make an appearance at the funeral – to add a final insult to their victim. To gloat over the destruction and grief their act had created, and savour the mourners' homage to their work. Would I recognise them if I saw them there? Would I be able to look Gaby's killer in the eyes and identify the evil that inhabited them? I would certainly be paying close attention to those present.

Lockie had almost woven his way over to our possie when a new song began to drawl through the speakers.

'Stand By Your Man'. Just perfect.

Cole excused himself as Lockie took up position perched on the edge of a chair.

'How's the head?' he asked, immediately breaking the tension.

'It's letting me know it's still there,' I said, and smiled at him. 'I'm sorry about abandoning your ute. I'm rather grateful no one flogged it.'

'Yeah. I hope you didn't get into too much trouble with the Boss. I had to tell him about your involvement.'

'I know. I'll deal with it, but I'm still going to keep looking into things. How does the saying go? In for a penny?' We sat in silence for a while. Lockie looked around the room and jiggled his leg up and down. I recognised the mannerism from our years together. Besides driving me nuts, it was a sure sign of something on his mind.

'What's the matter?' I finally asked. What wasn't the matter was probably the more appropriate question.

Lockie looked up at the ceiling, then with a big sigh looked me dead in the eye. 'I need to ask you a favour,' he said.

Was that all? It couldn't be that bad.

'What do you need? Of course I'll help.'

'I need you to stay away from Gaby's funeral.'

I felt the blood drain out of my face, only to surge back as the rest of me registered the kick to my solar plexus. I fought back the tears that leaped into my eyes, unbidden.

'Why?' I managed to choke out the word.

'Ah, Christ,' he said as he looked back up towards the ceiling. He took a deep breath, then exhaled slowly through pursed lips. 'There's no kind way to say this. People are talking. The police still view you as a suspect, there's the TV thing. I want...' He ran his hand through his hair and that tortured look which had become a familiar feature of his face twisted further. 'I want tomorrow to be about Gaby. I don't want any distraction, any unwanted attention. I don't want anything to taint this for her. I'm sorry, I just can't have you there.'

He stood up abruptly and retreated back into the hubbub of the room. Tears prevented me from seeing where he went. There was a roaring in my ears, too, and I barely registered someone sitting next to me, the arm around my shoulders.

'Sam.' A voice filtered vaguely through the murk.

'Sam?' A large hand turned my face and I registered Cole's concerned eyes swimming inches from my own. 'Sam, are you OK?'

I didn't know if I would ever be OK. The blur of noise refocused into the sound of voices, the clinking of glasses, Tammy's lament more mournful than ever. I remembered to breathe.

'Do you want to go?' he asked.

I shook my head. The thought of getting up and walking through that room of pitying eyes was unbearable. What I wanted was an anaesthetic.

'I need a drink,' I said.

Immediately a glass was thrust into one hand.

'What's this?' I asked, as I wiped beneath my nose with the other.

'Whisky.'

It looked like a big one, and I downed it in one gulp – then coughed violently as the fumes hit me square in the sinuses.

'You knew what he was going to say?' I spluttered.

'Yes,' was the simple reply.

Of course he did. I tried to feel some resentment, but the only sensation I could really muster up was exhaustion. I leaned heavily against his shoulder.

'Did he ask you to look after me?'

'Yes.'

'Can I have another drink?'

'No, but I'll get you a coffee.'

I tried to resent that too, but instead felt a flicker of gratitude. He propped me back up into the vertical, and then cupped my cheek with his giant hand before he uttered, 'I'm sorry, Sam,' with surprising tenderness, then disappeared off. My hand reached up to where his had been and I squeezed my eyes tight shut against the confusion that boiled in my head.

It took a couple of coffees before I was outwardly calm enough even to consider moving. For once, I was actually grateful that Cole was not the talkative type and didn't need to fill my silence with hollow conversation. He sat, content to sip on his beer and assume the role of minder. On the odd occasion, when someone went to approach me, he subtly turned them away with a simple shake of the head.

Inwardly, I was still a writhing mess. How had it come to this? I was a suspect in a murder; I'd probably completely screwed my career; I felt a physical and emotional wreck; and now the man I still cared for most in this world had banned me from his wife's funeral. That kind of thing only happened to social lepers and pariahs. My brittle veneer of composure ran the risk of fragmenting again.

'Get me out of here, please.'

Cole helped me to my feet, then took my hand and led me to the door by the most direct route possible. I studied my footsteps the whole way, not daring to meet curious or accusing eyes, but I was acutely aware of the wane in conversation as we passed, and the crescendo that followed in our wake.

As the door shut behind us, that small part of me that had maintained some degree of strength succumbed to the strain. I stumbled my way down the steps, then collapsed to my knees, my body no longer able to contain the sheer size of my desolation.

'Come on, let's get you home.' Cole's hands grabbed me under the armpits, and he lifted me up and over his shoulder, then rearranged me so he could carry me like a child. With one arm around the back of his neck and the other around the front, I clung on and wept into his collar.

'Hey, hang on there!' A voice hailed us from the other side of the car park. I heard running footsteps approach.

'What's going on? Sam, are you alright?'

I lifted my tear-streaked face out of Cole's neck and saw Paul Frost's troubled features wavering before me.

'She's a bit upset,' Cole said. 'I'm just taking her home.'

'Are you OK with that, Sam? Or do you want me to take you?'

I nodded my head at the first question and shook it for the other.

'Hang on a second, mate.' Cole opened the door to his ute and carefully lowered me into the seat. He rummaged in the glovebox and handed me a grimy man-sized handkerchief, then shut the door. I leaned my head against the window and watched the two men in discussion. Their voices were low; I couldn't catch what they were saying and I didn't really want to. It was fairly obvious who the topic of conversation was. They both stood stiffly, hands thrust in pockets except when pulled out to point or gesture, feet slowly shuffling. Several minutes later, I saw the conversation end as Paul waved his finger at Cole. Cole threw his hands up in the air, then strode around to the driver's side of the ute. He climbed in and closed the door with enough force to make me jump.

'What was that about?' I asked. God, my voice sounded foreign.

'Nothing,' Cole said, and turned the key in the ignition.

38

The house was dark except for the porch light, a lone beacon. Maggie's little Honda hatch wasn't in the driveway. Shit, the last thing I wanted was to be alone. Cole pulled up close to the door and left the engine idling; I didn't make any move to get out.

'Are you going to be OK?' he asked. 'Is Maggie home?'

'She went out with some work friends.' I didn't look at him and hesitated before asking a question I wasn't sure was wise. 'Do you mind coming in for a bit, till she gets back? I just need some company.'

'Yeah, of course.' He edged the ute forward, killed the engine and the lights, then hopped out and came around to open my door. 'Do you want a hand?'

'Thanks.' I swung my legs around, took his hand and descended from the vehicle as gracefully as I could in a straight skirt.

My fingers fumbled the key into the lock. I opened the door, reached my hand around and flicked on the light switch. Everything looked in the same tidy order in which I'd left it, and the sense of relief made me realise how nervous I had been that the police would come back for another go.

'Come in, please,' I said as Cole hesitated in the entrance. 'Have a seat, I'll make a cup of tea.' I filled the kettle, turned it on, then excused myself to the bathroom.

Once there, I got brave and looked at my reflection. The face in the mirror was in dire need of repair. My supposedly waterproof mascara had failed dismally. Tears had washed pale tracks down my foundation. Lipstick was nowhere to be seen, only the drawn outline of my mouth where I had traced it with lip liner. Then there were my eyes. Even I didn't like looking into those. God only knew what Cole thought: that was twice today he had seen me at my less than best.

I turned on the hot tap and idly splashed my fingers through the stream as I waited for the heat to come through. All I wanted to do was collapse into my bed and hope that the oblivion of sleep would fix all my woes. Who knew, I might get lucky and never wake up. I soaked a facecloth with the now scalding water and held it against my face: the warmth was wonderful. I held it there till it started to cool, then heated it up again. Eventually, my face glowed bright pink – it was an improvement.

I took a few deep breaths and opened the door to return to my company. I had begun to feel a little odd about having him in my house.

Two mugs of tea emitted ribbons of steam on the side table; Cole sat in an armchair. I settled myself into the corner of the sofa and, with as much dramatic flair as I could muster, patted my hands against my cheeks and announced that I was 'a bit more human now'.

'It's a definite improvement,' he said, then resumed his study of the room, his body language a translation in discomfort. I reached forward and gingerly tested the tea he'd put in front of me. I gave a little sigh as its tannins registered on my taste buds; I appreciated its comfort. This Kiwi bloke had turned out to be a very thoughtful man. 'Thank you,' I said.

'That's OK, I found everything.'

'No, not for that … I mean, yes, for that too. I mean thank you for tonight and for caring. I didn't expect that from Lockie. It threw me.' I shrugged.

Cole gave a small smile to show he knew just how much it threw me. I was slightly embarrassed by that. I wanted to think that if my day hadn't been such a disaster up to that point, I would have handled Lockie's request a little more objectively. He had every right to ask me to stay away from the funeral. Well, that's what my brain said. My heart held an altogether different opinion, and the mere acknowledgement of that set me to sniffing again.

'Look, you've had a hell of a hard day. Why don't you go to bed? I can wait out here till Maggie gets back.'

My eyes began to overflow again. 'Shit, Cole, I've got myself into such a mess. I don't know what to do.'

He looked over, and then with the great deliberation of having made a decision, he got up and came over to sit next to me. He enclosed my knee in his hand.

'Look, why don't you get away for a while? Go home to your folks?'

Christ, my family. As much as a part of me wanted to run home to my mother's arms, another part knew too well the failure that would admit. My pride could never let me do that. And I could not subject myself to the inevitable lectures that would come my way. Oh yes, they would give me a day or two's grace to recover, then the insidious little comments would start – the wee hints here, suggestions there, and all in my best interests, of course. Mum had already made her opinion quite clear, so it would only be Dad's presence that would hold her back from a full-on launch: 'You don't have to go back, permanently. You could stay here. We could find you work. Maybe the police isn't really for a girl like you.'

A girl like me.

I didn't really know what kind of a girl I was any more. I burst into tears again, and then tried to utter an apology when I saw the look on Cole's face. The poor man was just trying to be helpful and all he had was a pathetic, hysterical, snot-covered female on his hands.

I was so busy with my self-flagellation, it took a few moments to register that Cole was picking me up, lifting me onto his lap, and enveloping me in his long muscular arms. I stiffened; then, with a howl, leaned in to his chest and gave myself up to the sobs.

I don't know how long I sobbed or how long Cole sat there cradling me like a hurt child, but at some indefinable point the dynamic changed – a vertiginous shift that confused my senses. The chest that had offered tender comfort now offered the promise of strength; the arms that gently rocked me to ease my tension now created a tension of a different kind.

My self-pitying, hazed mind made an abrupt lurch into the here and now. My hand that had rested on Cole's shoulder now caressed it. I watched it as it ran up the side of his neck and paused, cupped on his cheek. He stopped rocking me, and I could feel his breath hold, his muscles tense, as if poised for … what? I slowly lifted my eyes up to meet his. The look that bore down on me was a perfect fusion of uncertainty and hunger and I just had to consume it. I slipped my hand behind his neck and pulled his mouth down onto mine. His lips were uncertain at first, but they did not pull away. I felt any resistance drain away, replaced by hot, urgent need. I pressed myself hard in against his body and his hand reached up into my hair, to pull my mouth impossibly deeper into his. White light and pain erupted in my mind and I screamed out, the sound muffled by Cole's lips and tongue.

Cole leaped up and I fell in a heap onto the floor.

'Shit, fuck, what?' He stood poised for action; his head whipped around ready to fight whatever foe might be there. I groaned and sat up, then leaned forwards with my head between my knees and my hands around my wound.

Realisation dawned and he dropped to his knees in front of me.

'Shit, I've hurt you. I'm so sorry, I shouldn't have let that happen,' he said, and pulled his hands through his hair. He sat back on his heels and let out a sigh that sounded as tired as I felt. 'I'm sorry, I'll go. I shouldn't be here.' He stood back up slowly and started towards the door.

I couldn't let that happen.

'Cole, wait.'

He stopped, but didn't turn around.

With the help of the sofa for support, I stood up, then walked over to him on unsteady legs. I wrapped my arms around his waist and rested my cheek against his back. I could hear his heart pound beneath my ear.

'Please don't go. I need you here.'

He grasped my hands and lifted them to his lips, then kissed the knuckle of each thumb in turn. Then he separated my hands and placed them down at my sides.

'Look,' he said, 'I don't want to take advantage of you. I don't know what you want.'

No single word was complex enough to express what I wanted. But there was something he could give me that would assuage some of my needs for the moment. I turned him around to face me, then reached up my hand and, once again, guided his lips down to mine. When he eventually pulled away, he again offered me the opportunity to stop what was apparent from becoming inevitable.

'Are you sure this is what you want?'

His chivalry only made me more certain.

I smiled, took his hand and led him towards my room.

39

I lay on my side, tense and wary, and listened for any indication that he was awake. The monotonous, regular breathing and slight nasal whistle signalled Cole was in a state of blissful slumber. It really pissed me off how men could fall asleep at the drop of a hat after sex, while we women lay wide awake, minds enlivened, going over everything from shopping lists to recriminations. Mine worked on the latter.

What the hell had I been thinking, sleeping with Cole? I had answered my own question really – thinking was precisely what I hadn't been doing.

My eyes studied Cole's bulky outline in the semi-darkness. They traced a line from the curve of his head to the fall of his neck, the sharp rise of muscular shoulder to the gentle falling away of his back. It was a silhouette that oozed solidity and an earthiness that in a strange way felt strong and safe at some primeval level.

I released a sigh and risked an examination of my motives. Put in blunt terms, I'd just screwed my ex's best friend. Lockie had hurt me terribly last night, then left Cole to pick up the pieces. End result? Well, here we were.

Was Cole my Lockie substitute? Was I trying to make him jealous? Surely, I wasn't shallow and manipulative enough to do that. I couldn't have turned into that hated and spiteful creature – the vindictive ex.

Cole let out a small snuffling snort and I smiled despite myself. I certainly had an affection for him. I'd always been curious about him, with his undeniable physicality teamed with an endearing reserve. He had a manner and an economy of speech which was common among Kiwi heartland men. It did not reflect a lack of imagination or brainpower, rather the self-assurance brought about by being one in a line of generations who made a life on this land. Perhaps we'd had sex simply because I needed him and he was there. He wasn't an unwitting participant in my game of tit for tat. I'd screwed him, but I hadn't screwed him over. He wasn't Mr Charisma. He might only be a good, solid kind of a man, but what was wrong with that?

I smiled. It felt as if I'd passed some important self-diagnostic. I leaned forwards, kissed him gently between his shoulder blades, and at last went to sleep.

I woke to the sound and movement of Cole getting up. The early-morning light crept in around the edges of the drapes. We kissed goodbye, parting with the awkwardness of people who didn't know what to say or what was to come next, if anything.

I stayed on in bed, nursing my headache and contemplating the night's unexpected turn of events. I replayed it all, over and over. I was, in the end, surprised to find that I seemed to be in a much better place, emotionally speaking. My assignation with Cole hadn't messed up my head the way I'd expected. If anything, I felt more centred and calm. Would I see him again? I didn't need to decide that here and now. And it certainly wasn't the kind of decision to be made before coffee.

I could hear Maggie clanking around in the kitchen and hollered out my regular refrain. 'Need coffee, bring it to me, please, ta, please.' I seemed to be doing that a lot lately.

Her morning-shamble-haired head poked around the corner of my door. 'Was that who I think it was skulking out of here at some ungodly hour?'

'Maybe, and he wasn't skulking, thank you.'

'Ha, I told you you liked him!' Maggie's glee was obvious.

'Oh, what a load of crap.'

'Oh, so you don't like him, but slept with him anyway. What a nice girl you turned out to be.' A school-ma'am look was plastered across her face.

'If I wasn't so lazy, I'd get up and kick you.'

'That's kind of what I was counting on,' she said, and smiled. 'But really, what happened? I thought you were just going out for a drink.'

'Yeah, well, so did I. But it was all your fault, anyway. If you hadn't abandoned me and gone off gallivanting around the countryside, if you'd been at home where you belonged, none of this would have happened.' All I'd needed was some company. As it turned out, I had got a whole lot more than that.

'Oh, I forgot, I'm not allowed a social life. News flash for Sam Shephard: I'm not going to hang around home on the off chance you have a dud date and an early night. I'm not your bloody mother. Anyway, you're not the only one who gets offers from eligible young men,' she said, and waggled her eyebrows up and down. 'And, I've seen the way Cole looks at you, and you flirt back. It's subtle, but it's there. Don't think I haven't noticed.'

I did my scoffing indignation act. I did not flirt; flirting was for teenagers.

Maggie pressed on with her point. 'I think something would have happened whether I was here or not. I'm just glad I wasn't here to hear it.' I threw my pillow across the room at her. Its aerodynamics left much to be desired, as did its effect as a deterrent. Maggie laughed, picked it up off the floor and flung it back.

My reflexes were a bit off and I caught it with my face.

'See, the truth hurts, doesn't it?'

'You're lucky I didn't throw the alarm clock. I could hit you square between the eyes, ya know.'

'And I can catch, ya know. But after seeing your astonishing skills there, I think I would be quite safe.' She had a point.

'You'll keep, girl, but you definitely owe me coffee for mortally hurting my feeling.'

'Feeling?'

'Yeah, feeling. I'm only capable of one, and right now it involves caffeine.'

My attempt to distract attention from my nocturnal visitor with humour was failing badly. Maggie gave me the look that signalled a lecture was headed my way.

'Seriously though. Are you sure you know what you're doing with Cole?'

I pulled the sheet up over my head.

'No,' I said, feeling like that angst and hormone-challenged teenager. 'That's part of the charm.'

40

'Mataura Station.'

'Paul Frost, please.'

'He isn't on duty today. Can I help you with anything?'

Ah, damn it all. I really needed to touch base with Paul. He was entitled to a break like anyone else, but it was bloody inconsiderate of him, and majorly stuffed up my plans. I wasn't about to trust anyone else at the station.

'No, thank you, I'll contact him when he's in next. Can you tell me when he'll be on duty?'

I heard some paper shuffle. 'He's on duty Monday, morning shift. Can I take a message?'

Like I wanted them to know who was calling.

'No, that's OK, I'll talk to him Monday.'

Shit. I really needed to know what was happening in the murder investigation and whether there had been any progress on the cattle rustling. I put the phone down, and contemplated my next move. Monday. It was too far away, but there really wasn't anyone else at the station I felt I could convince to information share. The phone beside me started to ring and I automatically reached out, hit the talk button and raised the handset to my ear.

'Hello.'

Nothing.

Shit, not again.

'Hello?'

There was silence. No, not quite silence. I could just make out the sound of breath, regular and steady breath, not excited breath, not hesitant breath, just steady, measured, even breath. A click followed by the familiar beep, beep, beep broke the spell.

'Ah, piss off, idiot,' I muttered out loud.

'I hope that wasn't your boss you were talking to, otherwise you need to do some serious work on your communication skills.' Maggie had walked into the lounge just in time to catch the end of the call.

'You're probably right about the people skills, but no, it was another one of my favourite hang-up callers – someone who still thinks it's a good idea to play silly buggers.'

It didn't surprise me. Some of the looks I'd received at the pub last night weren't altogether charitable, and it wasn't as if I was in a position to get the call traced and do something about it. The police weren't about to do me any favours. The calls were majorly pissing me off though, and even more annoying was the fact I had to admit they were beginning to get to me. There was a little worm of disquiet starting to make its way into my thoughts. The shadow it cast on my mood made me regret even more the fact that in one of my darker moments I'd been the one doing the hanging up and Gaby had been the one on the receiving end.

I didn't have time to dwell on it, and self-flaggelation would serve no purpose. I got on to the task at hand. The second phone call I needed to make was to Darryl Fletcher, the local vet whose name had featured on Gaby's contact list. His inclusion there was an obvious choice: if you wanted to know more about a disease state, why not go straight to the horse's mouth, so to speak. Much better than Google. He'd been helpful a few days ago when I followed up on the avail-ability of Midazolam; I hoped he'd be as forthcoming today.

'Hi Darryl, it's Sam Shephard again.'

There was a slight hesitation. 'Oh. Hi. What can I do for you?' His voice was measured, his tone guarded. I knew what that meant. Well, I had him on the line, I may as well press on.

'I was wondering if you'd be able to help me out with some more information regarding the Gaby Knowes case?'

Once again, the hesitation, and when he spoke his discomfort was audible.

'I don't know if I can do that, Sam.'

I could picture him squirming on his seat while he tried desperately to think of a polite way to get me off the phone. I'd be direct. It was a simple request really, and not one that required him to extend himself in any way.

'I was just wanting to know some background information on bovine tuberculosis. I'm following up on some work Gaby was doing before her murder.'

'You're putting me in a bit of a position here. You know I'd like to help, but, well, you're not working for the police any more and they've said that they don't want you involved.'

Well, at least it clarified one point. My colleagues were doing a hatchet job on my reputation. Bloody charming. Still, if they'd spoken to him, perhaps it meant they were following up on the TB connection themselves, and that someone had bothered to read through the material they'd seized from my house. That, at least, was a good thing. The more heads trying to piece this puzzle together, the better.

The silence was getting decidedly uncomfortable. Darryl was not going to elaborate any further.

'I won't trouble you any more, then. Thanks for letting me know, all the same.'

'I'm sorry I can't help.' He sounded earnest.

'Yeah, I know, me too.'

41

It had just occurred to me there was a fundamental flaw in the next part of my plan and there was only one person I could think of to remedy it.

'I need to ask you a big favour,' I said as I walked up to the table and fluttered my eyelashes at Maggie.

'Oh God, now what? I shudder to think.' Her eye roll was so spectacular I could almost hear it.

'Did you have any great plans for the day?'

'No…' Her voice inflected up somewhat, making her suspicion-o-meter sound quite high.

'Good. Can I borrow your car for the morning, then?'

Maggie scoffed a derisive laugh. 'Oh, I don't know. Your track record with borrowing vehicles isn't too hot right now.'

She had a point. I was going to have to seriously consider investing in my own wheels, instead of relying on the work vehicle or the charity of long-suffering friends and acquaintances. And the acquisition of a car was likely to be needed sooner rather than later, considering having a work vehicle was rather dependent on having a job, and that wasn't looking too hopeful at the moment.

'I promise I won't abandon it if it breaks down. Cross my heart.' I made the appropriate actions. 'And I won't baptise it in cow shit, honest.'

Maggie's nose wrinkled. 'No, no, no, that's old hat for you. You'd probably torch the thing, or park it in the river, something grand and dramatic.'

'Well, I could. How much are you insured for? I could cut you a deal.' I flashed her my best orthodontic specials.

'You're a funny lady. Tempting, but no, I'm not that desperate for an upgrade. You can take the car and swan off. I was only planning to spend the day with a book and with you, in your hour of need,' she said, making my request sound like a major imposition. Passive aggression at its finest.

'And I really appreciate you wanting to keep me company today, especially when the funeral is on, but I feel like I have to do something to keep sane. I need to check a few things out before I come home and wallow in my outcast status.'

'It's not that bad. It's not like everyone in the town will be there except you and, of course, me.'

I had to laugh. Yup, most of the town would be there, and they would probably notice the glaring omission of my presence. I was about to make some quip about the gossip mill going into overdrive, but then I noticed the wodge of papers she had on the table.

'What are you reading?' I asked.

She held up the novel so I could see the cover of the latest Stephen King.

'No, no, I mean the other things. What are you looking at there?' I pointed to the big white envelope with the coat of arms in the top left corner and the large brochures she was trying to conceal.

'Ah, those. I don't think you want to know right this moment.'

'Try me.'

Maggie, with a look of great reluctance, held up the brochures in each hand, so I could see them.

I took in the title of the publications – *University of Otago Undergraduate* and *Otago Postgraduate Prospectus*. The University of Otago? That meant she'd have to move to Dunedin.

'Oh.'

Shit, she was right, I did not want to see those right now.

'So, you were serious about getting the hell out of Mataura.' The wind was most emphatically sucked out of my sails.

She set the brochures back down on the table and indicated for me to take a seat. 'It's not as simple as just wanting to get away from this place. There's the whole job-security thing, the industry is struggling and there are constant rumours of the meat works being closed down and production moving elsewhere. But mostly, I feel like it's time to change tack, anyway.' She angled her seat around to face me as I pulled up a chair. 'I don't want to be doing the same old thing in twenty years' time. Hell, I don't even want to be doing it in twenty days' time.'

I could understand that sentiment, given the crap I was going through in my career at present.

'So, you've pretty much made up your mind, then?' Somehow, this news, piled on top of everything else, made me feel incredibly weary. It was a good thing: I was too flat to cry.

'Yeah,' she said. 'I need to get away. I enjoy it here, but I want more out of life than spending all day at the works, then having nothing to do in this one-horse town. Admit it, it's not exactly scintillating here. When I went over to Dunedin at New Year's, I didn't want to come back. It reminded me how much I missed the place from my student days. There was so much to see and do. The people were really interesting, not so blinkered as they are here – present company excluded, of course. Anyway, I've always wanted to do more study, extend myself. I feel like I'm stuck in a rut. So, heading back to Otago seems the way to go.'

'Did you have anything particular in mind?' I asked the obvious question to disguise my surprise at how keen she was to leave. Maggie was my best friend and I'd had no idea she was so dissatisfied with her lot. How was that? We always joked about leaving this hole, but I never thought she'd do it. God, what would I do? Life here would be intolerable without her.

'Couple of ideas,' she said, sounding more excited as my heart sank. 'I always fancied the idea of getting back into psychology. I did first-year psych as part of my B.Sc. and really enjoyed it. I like the idea of figuring out what makes someone tick, and it seems a natural progression of my science background. So that's one option. Or…' She paused as if expecting a response.

'Or?' I said, playing her game.

'Or, I thought I might do something completely different,

something in the arts. I always loved the arts – English, history – but did sciences at uni because I was good at them, and they worked towards a career. All hail the almighty career.' I cringed at how appropriate that line was right now. 'It would be great to study something purely for interest.'

'You must have more money than sense. What on earth would you do with an arts degree? You'd still have to earn a crust.' They didn't call it a B.A. – Bugger All – for nothing.

She smiled. 'I'd thought about teaching, or even research and academia.'

The laugh I was trying to contain snorted its way out.

'Teaching? You? But you can't stand the snotty-nosed little brats around here.'

'Oh, that was elegant, Sam,' she said, referring, I presumed, to the snort. 'And yes, I'd have to get over my desire to strangle some of them, but it's something I've often thought of, and all the people I've talked to about it say teaching can be hugely rewarding.'

All the people? She'd been talking to people, but hadn't even mentioned it to me. She'd been checking things out behind my back.

'Why didn't you tell me any of this earlier? I had no idea you were even interested in these things.' My voice wasn't exactly neutral.

'I didn't want to upset you. And I can see that's worked really well.' Maggie leaned forwards to tweak my nose. 'I wanted to be sure of myself before letting the cat out of the proverbial, and anyway, there hasn't been an opportune time to drop this on you lately. It's not like there's anything else big happening in your life.'

Granted.

'I suppose.' I managed a brave kind of a smile. 'Good for you, and I am pleased for you, but please excuse me if I decide to take this badly and wallow in self-pity. When do you think you would start?'

'I could do a mid-year intake, so July. But that's still a way off. We'd be able to get plenty of partying and living it up in Mataura done before then.'

'We'd have to pace ourselves, though, so we don't burn out.'

'Too right. I'm glad you understand. God, I'll miss you, though.'

Saying I understood was stretching it, but my brain had taken in enough. 'I'd better get on with it, then. Thanks for the use of your car.'

'I'll see you later, then,' Maggie said.

'Yeah, I'll get going.'

'Be careful out there, Sam,' she said. Maggie, ever the camp Mumma, looking after everyone.

I wandered over to the bench and grabbed the car keys with no great enthusiasm.

This day couldn't really get much more shit.

42

If I hadn't already made a morning appointment with Phillip Rawlings – a replacement for the one I'd missed when I had my run-in with the solid bits of Lockie's ute – I would never have got out of the house. Pride dictated I wasn't going to ring and cancel. It was just as well: a bit of action would stop me thinking about Maggie's planned desertion and, more to the point, stop me analysing the previous night's events to death.

Maggie's old Honda Civic was a different kettle of fish from Lockie's ute, but under the circumstances, he'd called in his loan, and I was grateful to be riding anything that involved four wheels and an internal combustion engine, rather than two and a lot of sweat. Maggie had obliged and you didn't look gift-horsepower in the mouth. Still, I was thankful this morning's visit was on a proper sealed road and I didn't have to skitter around on gravel.

As well as farming cattle, Phillip operated a stock-trucking firm from his property that serviced most of Southland. He owned several truck and trailer units himself, and also contracted out work to owner-operators. This made him one of the larger employers in Mataura, other than the meat works. It was my guess that it would have been the trucking arm of his business that had attracted Gaby's interest rather than the cattle.

Like all aspects of the TB prevention programme, stock transportation involved a paper trail and identification of each beast. It was all part of the package.

Phillip had given me instructions to come straight on down to the house – a more comfortable environment to talk in than the business. I turned into the driveway and went to bypass the substantial truck yard on my left. Aesthetics evidently weren't Phillip's priority. The yard was littered with the rusted hulks of trailer units that had clearly seen their day, a couple of used-tyre mountains and several barrels of dubious vintage. Overnight rain had rendered the normally hard-packed earth a shiny mud brown. Waving arms caught my attention. I slowed up as I recognised Phillip's pie-inflated figure – he must have been waiting in the office to catch me. I leaned over and manually wound the passenger-side window down as he walked up alongside – Maggie's car was a bit of an antique. He leaned over and placed a grimy hand on each side of the door frame.

'Shall I park over there?' I said, pointing to the large corrugated-iron shed that served as an office and repair shop.

'No, that won't be necessary, Sam,' he said, his voice curt. His weather-beaten features were cemented into a rather dour expression.

'Are we going up to the house, then?'

He shook his head. 'No. I want you to get the hell off my property.'

I was a little too taken aback to muster a prompt reply to that. I didn't get the chance, anyway.

'I have nothing to say to you. You're not even in the police any more – that's what I've heard. You're suspended. And I saw the news. They're saying you're a suspect in the bloody murder. Hell, no. I have nothing to say to you, and you can get the hell out of here before I call the police myself and tell them what you're up to. You've got a bloody cheek coming here to ask me questions. Now get off with you.' With that last statement he stepped away from the car and made a series of rude and aggressive gestures that left me in no doubt of his anger.

Argument was pointless, so I leaned over, wound up the window, turned the car around and headed back in the direction I'd come from. A glance in the rear-view mirror showed him standing there, feet spread, hands on hips, glaring after me.

Shit. My reputation had preceded me. If I was going to get that kind of welcome every time I tried to talk to someone I was going to get nowhere fast. Bloody media.

At least the sensations of rage and heat that now bubbled up inside me made a change from my recent range of emotions. Now what was I going to do? I drove a bit further down the road, and when I was quite sure I was out of view pulled over into a lay-by and turned off the engine.

'Shit, shit, shit and bugger!' I yelled and banged my hands against the steering wheel. All that succeeded in doing was hurting.

It was clear that any attempt to interview the others on Gaby's list was out of the question. My recent TV exposure ensured anyone who had missed the gossip through the normal sources would be well up to date on my alleged activities. But how much of Phillip's knowledge was direct? He said he'd 'heard' that I was on suspension and a suspect. Had someone rung him and had a word? Like they had to Darryl? My friends at the police again?

'Wankers!' I banged the steering wheel again in a pointless display of frustration. If I was going to make any headway on this case, I had to figure out how it was all connected: TB – Gaby – cattle rustling – murder – me. It was all linked, but how, specifically? God, I wished I still had Gaby's computer. Or my own, for that matter. What I needed was some old-fashioned information, and the only place I was going to find it at 9.30am on a Saturday was at the library. The Mataura library didn't open on the weekend, but Gore did, and it had free internet access. I could get Maggie to come with me. She'd probably be keen for a jaunt to get some new books. And that way, not only would I have some welcome company but, as an added bonus, it would get me out of Mataura while Gaby's funeral was on. The last thing I needed to do was hide myself away at home feeling rejected.

Between being ordered away from funerals and thrown off people's properties, I was starting to feel like an outcast in my own town.

43

A wodge of junk mail was half sticking out of the letter box and a couple of extra brochures had escaped onto the ground at the base of the post it perched on. Good to see the 'No flyers' sticker was being taken seriously. I parked Maggie's Honda in the carport and wandered back up the drive to the box to empty it out. I couldn't believe how much crap advertising found its way into it from such a small town. It wasn't like we were flush with supermarkets and big-ticket retailers. I picked the bits off the ground and pulled the remainder out of the front. No wonder they were hanging out – when I peered through the slot I could see a parcel occupying most of the space. What had Maggie been buying online this time?

I swung open the flap at the back and extracted the brown-paper-wrapped package. The name Shephard was scrawled across it in what looked like permanent marker. Strange, I wasn't expecting anything. I turned it over to see if there was a name on it and noted the dark stains on the underside about the same time as I noted the rather unpleasant smell. I stood staring at it a while, my curiosity about what it could be fighting with the sense of dread that was starting to build in my stomach. I crouched down and placed it on the ground, took a breath and pulled away the pieces of tape holding the parcel together. Then, with as much courage as I could muster, I pulled back the flaps.

The rabbit was curled up like a soft toy, except that this was no toy. Toys didn't ooze blood. Toys weren't stiff with rigor mortis. And toys sure as hell didn't have a miniature noose around their necks.

A cold sweat broke out across my face and I leaped to my feet, staggering back away from the gruesome sight. I could hear the blood rushing in my ears, my heart racing. The irrational part of me wanted to kick it away, get it as far away as possible. But the stone-cold-sober part of me was transfixed. Who the hell would do this? If this was a joke, it had gone way too far. I looked up and down the road, imagined a set of eyes observing me, laughing. Get a grip, Shep. Whoever did this would be long gone. My eyes flicked towards the house. Thank Christ it was me who found it, and not Maggie. She couldn't know about this; it would freak her out completely. But what to do? I couldn't toss it in the wheelie bin. The stench would be enough to give it away. Besides, the cop in me was thinking evidence. This was an out-and-out threat. There could be fingerprints, trace. But where the hell could I hide it? I grimaced in distaste as I bent back down and folded the edges of the paper back over, then wrapped it in a few of the larger brochures that had been in the box. There was a ramshackle shed down the back of the section where we kept the lawnmower. It would have to go in there for now.

That was the easy part. The hard part was going to be pretending to Maggie that, apart from being a murder suspect, a pariah in my own town and now shit-scared, there was absolutely nothing wrong.

44

I had almost forgotten how liberating the regular beat of pounding the road could be. Although it had only been a couple of days since I'd last gone running, I had a vague tinge of guilt, as if I had neglected a friend and needed to make a special effort to make up for it.

My head was awash with information. My trip to the library and the information superhighway had only added to the congestion, and offered no enlightenment. My hope was that if I voided my overloaded conscious with the hypnotic trance of a run, my subconscious would get to work and map things out. It had often worked in the past. I'd experienced many an epiphany while running in the fresh air and wide open spaces.

I made a concerted effort to blot out thoughts of the case, Cole, the battle zone that was my life, the now constant urge to look over my shoulder, and instead concentrated on the smaller details at my feet: the chunkiness of the chip in the road, the texture created by the white paint of the centre line as it melted its way around each stone, the reflective matchsticks standing to attention like oversized toy soldiers guarding the verge.

My eyes feasted on the gentle contours of the land, the lush green pastures peppered with a seasoning of grazing sheep and cattle. They followed the path of the river as it meandered through this fertile land fringed with willow and birch. The feathered heads of the toetoe hedges waved a syncopated rhythm against their flaxen bodies.

My lungs gorged themselves on the fresh, earthy, country air, flavoured with a hint of – what was that? Smoke? I pulled up, panting hard, and tried to pause long enough to inhale through my nose. It was definitely smoke, with a decidedly acrid edge to it. There was no visible sign of it, but I was climbing up to a bend that would open out to a valley. Perhaps I'd get a view of it there. I picked up pace again, curious about what anyone could be burning to create that kind of stench. There were no farmhouses in the vicinity, so it was unlikely to be a rubbish fire. Perhaps some campers by the river, flouting the fire ban?

After I crested the hill, I could see a plume of blackish smoke rising from a stand of willows that bordered the river below me. It looked to be a good two kilometres away by the circuitous road, but I was intrigued now, and it wasn't as if I had anywhere else to be.

I came to a gated access way to the river. The track, to use a very generous description, wended its way in the direction of the smoke. It was well overgrown with spindly grasses and weeds, although it did look like a vehicle had been down recently. You'd need a sturdy truck or four-wheel drive to negotiate that one. I climbed over the gate and made my way towards the pyre, but not before having a good check up and down the road. It was pretty isolated down here, and the spooked part of me had got in the habit of scoping everything and planning an escape route. Through the screen of trees, I could now make out the outline of a smoking mass the size of a van. The stench that came from it was enough to turn my stomach. The flames had died down to a few small licks amid the glowing bed of embers at the bottom, but it was the strange, angular projections jutting out of the pyre that really caught my attention.

'Oh, bloody hell.'

I now knew what had happened to the stolen cattle. Legs, stiff and lance-like; ribs; heads: it was enough to turn a girl vegetarian. I put my hands over my nose and mouth, and skirted around the fire from upwind in the futile hope the stench would be less eye-watering, but it did nothing to curb the charred smell of death. I was glad I hadn't eaten recently.

A rough estimate accounted for six beasts, but there could have been others at the bottom of the heap. The carcasses were by no means intact. Muscle and tissue had been carved away, leaving exposed bone covered in loose chunks of charred meat. It didn't look like a professional butchering job, so chances were whoever did this wasn't on the production line at the works, but they had scored a good haul of meat.

I stared at the forlorn sight of a cow's head that had partially escaped the effects of the fire. Half of its face was blackened and crisp, the other relatively unscathed, other than the hair being singed off and the muzzle blistered. Whoever had done this had not done a very good job of burning this lot. Why, I wondered, did they go to the trouble of burning them at all? This spot was isolated enough that you could have just left the carcasses in a rotting heap and no one would have discovered them for weeks, months even. By then the flies and maggots would have done the dirty work. Burning the carcasses only attracted attention – I was here, after all.

I walked around the pyre again, giving it a wide berth. It seemed an undignified and downright wasteful end for these beasts. The wind made a slight shift and I found myself in the path of the smoke trail. I moved over a bit and crouched down on my haunches. My mouth was parched and dry, and not helped at all by the smoke, but I wasn't desperate enough to go over to the river for a drink: the sight of these cattle beasts dumped so thoughtlessly made me wonder what had made its way into the Mataura's flowing waters.

Besides, there was something that really bugged me about that half-burned animal, other than the obvious nastiness of the whole scene. I cocked my head to the side and peered closely at one of the other beasts; then I got up and quickly walked around the rest in the pyre to confirm it.

Ear tags. None of them had their ear tags. I scanned around the base and the embers, looking for ... I wasn't quite sure what. Little puddles of yellow plastic? But old Half-Face still nagged at me.

I had to get a whole lot closer to the pyre than I wanted to, and the heat and the stench drove me back a couple of times, but at last I was able to get close enough for a quick but targeted look. It was all I needed. This beast's ear tags had been ripped off. I could make out the telltale tear.

I retreated to a safe distance, sat down and leaned against the trunk of a willow to ponder the significance of it all. I was grateful for the breeze and the sound of it rustling the leaves above me, adding to the chorus from the river. I swatted at a sandfly on my leg – unfortunately, the smoke wasn't acting as a deterrent to the pesky blighters.

Why would you want to hide the animals' identities if you had only stolen them for meat? For that matter, why would you burn them? It didn't add up. If you were desperate enough to rustle cattle and hack them up, why not just dump the carcasses on the side of the road? Hell, you could dump them in the middle of the main street early on a Saturday morning and no one would see you do it. I idly pushed backwards and forwards on my heels, digging little trenches in the river shingle.

Identity. This had to be all about identity. What was special about these particular cattle? I thought about Trev and his breeding stock. They were valuable; could this be an inside job for the insurance? What would a top stud beast be worth? Five, ten thousand dollars? But Trev didn't strike me as being financially challenged. The equipment in his office was not your run-of-the-mill, package-deal stuff. There was a fair investment in technology parked on his desk, and he was pretty business savvy and up with the play. Likewise, Phillip Rawlings wasn't short of a dollar. No, it couldn't be about money.

Another memory of my visit to Trev made me laugh out loud. That was a very large chunk of beef roasting in his oven on the day I called by, and it was a damned sight better cooked than the burnt offerings here. He could have arranged for a few head of cattle to be taken, and a few from down the road to throw the scent off. I could imagine him being too Scottish to waste perfectly good meat, even if it was for a good cause. But what cause? Was he a gambling man? Had the odds played against him recently? Was he a bit skint? I'd seen him in the pub displaying all the signs of intoxication often enough, but couldn't recall ever seeing him at one of the pokie machines, gambling his life savings away.

I picked up a pebble and tossed it up and down in my hand a

couple of times to test its weight. Then I threw it hard, enjoying the thwack as it hit the sapling I had taken aim at. I followed it up with another: perfect shot. The product of a misspent youth trying to keep up with my brothers. Thwack. Give me a target and I could hit it with anything: rock, ball, bullet. My brothers didn't enjoy being beaten by their little sis. I'd even won an axe-throwing competition at the local Agricultural and Pastoral Show when I was a teenager. I didn't think the boys had ever forgiven me for that. I pulled my mind back to the case and Gaby's enquiries for her journalism course.

These beasts could have had TB. But so what? That wasn't the end of the world – it just meant more intensive monitoring. A pain in the arse? Yes. An impact on profit? Yes. Catastrophic? No. I didn't think it was serious enough to provoke someone to commit what was basically fraud. I tried to replay as much of my conversation with Trev as I could remember. Each animal was tagged to track its whereabouts from cradle to grave – an audit trail for potential disease testing and control…

A tingle shot up my spine, accompanied by an uneasy sensation growing in my stomach. All along, I had felt there was a connection here – a connection between Gaby's research and her murder – but TB was too mundane a threat to lead to that. Had I been too narrow in my thinking? There were plenty of nasties other than TB.

I jumped to my feet again, rubbed the numbness out of my bum, then started to pace around the remains of the fire, my mind working to piece it out with each step.

Trev was passionate about his beasts, to the extent of having portraits of his prize breeding stock on the walls – and that included his beloved stolen bull, Samson, over whom he had even shed a few tears. All sentiment aside, I would wager that Samson had finished up on this pyre. The only reason you'd go to this much trouble and actually burn the carcasses would be to prevent identification of one or more individual animals. Prevent any possible identification from photographs. Lose them in the crowd. To hide what, though? Disease? Or, perhaps more importantly, to destroy the bodies and prevent any post-mortem tissue testing. But testing for what? DNA? How would that be useful?

I stared at the beasts as my mind flipped through the internet pages Gaby had looked at recently – and a dawning possibility whacked me straight between the eyes.

'Holy shit and Christ Almighty.'

There had been more than one disease state listed on those pages, and many had scary consequences. There had been an outbreak of mycoplasma bovis recently, and its spread was causing concern, to the extent that farmers were having to slaughter stock en masse. An inconvenience, yes, and tragic for the poor farmers concerned, but it wasn't the worst. The most catastrophic of these diseases related to cattle, but had ramifications for humans as well. I shook my head – this was far-fetched, but it had to be it; I couldn't think of anything else that would scare a man enough to do all this and even commit a murder.

BSE, bovine spongiform encephalitis. Mad-frigging-cow disease. The more I thought about it, the more I thought it could be the only thing that could provoke someone to go to so much trouble, to react so extremely. Look at what was smouldering before me. It was the perfect way to hide an outbreak, really: fake the cattle rustling, so the affected beast or beasts just happen to be taken. Make it look like a heist for meat, burn the carcasses, so the brain and spinal tissue is useless for testing and no one need suspect a thing. Except that someone did suspect, or had come too close to discovering the truth. I found my eyes welling up at the thought of Gaby being murdered for the sake of a few rotten bloody head of cattle.

But Trev? How could Trev do something like that? He'd been so friendly and helpful; Jesus, he even helped me search for Gaby's body. Perhaps it was Phillip Rawlings: his cattle had been stolen too. But no, he didn't breed. It had to be Trev.

Anyway, what was I thinking? BSE? That was impossible. New Zealand had never had a case of BSE; our domestically bred cattle were free of the disease. The only risk of it entering the country was through imported stock, and imports had been banned from Britain and Europe for years. But what about those other countries – Canada, Japan, the United States? They'd all had recent scares. Shit, Trev had said Samson was bred on the farm, but was descended from an import – I couldn't recall exactly where from. Somewhere in Britain, maybe? I was going to have to find out.

BSE couldn't have got here in stock feed. New Zealand had strict regulations on what farm animals could be fed, so the disease couldn't spread by animals eating contaminated meat meal. Anyway, we didn't have all those wide open spaces for nothing – our animals fed on pasture. For BSE to get here it would have to have been pre-existing in an imported animal. It could only be Samson's grandsire or great grandsire, or whatever generation it was. Which was another point. If BSE had come in with an infected import, then that was generations ago. It didn't spread easily, and surely it would have been picked up on post-mortem testing of the original animal. Maggie might be able to help me out there – perhaps her lab had tested that beast?

My mind seemed to lurch from one far-fetched idea to another. Could it be another disease altogether? Foot-and-mouth? I discounted that idea straight away. Foot-and-mouth spread like wildfire; the external symptoms were obvious, with blistering on the mouth and feet and frothing at the mouth. You'd never manage to hide it. BSE seemed so unlikely, but it was the only thing I could think of that was major enough to trigger such an extreme response – something worth killing for.

Christ, what to do?

First, I had to get in touch with Paul, let him know about this pile of burning cow flesh and sound him out about my theory. Then, I had to go back and see Trev. I'd have to tread carefully. If I could confirm where that import came from, what year it arrived and ultimately what had happened to him I'd have enough evidence – well, not evidence, but potential motive to get a warrant and get him arrested and in for questioning.

Rotten bloody cows. Gaby was dead, Lockie without his wife and Angel motherless, all because of some rotten bloody cows.

Out of impulse I picked up a large stone and threw it at Half Face's head, hard.

'Christ, I'm going to get the bastard who did this to you Gaby.'

45

By the time I had run back to the house, it wasn't just the physical exertion that had me hot and fuming. The more I thought about it, the more incensed I was that some two-faced, slimy old bastard could have killed Gaby for the sake of a lump or two of cattle beast and the potentially nasty financial consequences of BSE. I wondered what price he had put on her life. Was there a monetary value which made it possible for him to crunch the numbers and think, 'Yep, it's worth me killing her'? But no, technically speaking, he did not kill Gaby; he was too lily-livered to do the deed himself and had paid someone else to do his dirty work. I bet that fit into the monthly ledger tidily: 'Payment to hit man'. Described as what? 'Professional pest-removal services'? 'Acme bug eradication'?

By now I didn't give a toss that Paul Frost was having a day off. I stormed into the house and headed straight for the phone. I punched in the numbers and waited for it to ring, but instead the phone skipped straight to his message service.

'Damn it all.' I hurled the phone straight into the sofa cushions.

'My, my, that was very adult.'

I turned to see Maggie in her bedroom doorway, still clutching her novel. I just scowled at her, then picked up the phone and, with exaggerated calmness, hit redial. I listened to the pre-recorded voice with the American accent, and the beep, and I obediently left a message.

'Paul, it's Sam Shephard. I have some vital information for you. Please call me as soon as you get this. It's urgent.'

'That was better,' she said, and headed over towards me. 'What's happened?'

What hadn't happened? I sat the phone down on the table and tried to sort my thoughts and questions into some logical order.

'What can you tell me about BSE testing?'

Maggie's eyebrows shot up. 'Here?' she asked, pointing at the ground. 'That's a pretty heavy-duty question. Do you think BSE has got something to do with all of this?'

'Maybe, yes, I don't know.'

'OK, well, sit down.' She pulled up a chair. 'What do you want to know?'

'Does the plant do random screening? When do you test for it?'

Maggie thought for a moment before replying.

'No random screening. A few years ago we did targeted testing based on an animal's age and how they'd died – you know, if they'd been dead in the yard or were emergency slaughter, that kind of thing. I take it there's a point to all this?'

'Yes, there's a point, but humour me for now. What testing do you do – you know, how's it done?'

'The test involves taking a sample of brain-stem tissue, which is prepared and preserved and then sent away for examination. Prionics Western Blot test, if you want to know the official jargon. BSE is what's called a prion disease.'

'So burning an animal's carcass would prevent you getting a sample?'

'Not necessarily. It would depend on how badly it was damaged. It certainly would make it more difficult. Are you going to tell me what's going on?'

My mind was a whirr. I wanted to clarify a few more points before I enlightened her.

'Soon, my impatient friend. What about BSE testing on imported animals?'

'Imports? There wouldn't be any; I mean, there wouldn't be any imports. No one's been able to bring live animals into the country since at least the nineties, probably before then even, the mid-eighties, say, because of the BSE disaster in Britain and Europe. I think you can bring them in from Australia under special circumstances, because Aussie's guaranteed BSE free too, but not from anywhere else.'

Bugger. That's where my theory of an outbreak on Trev's farm fell over. Trev's import would have been years ago, decades ago. Surely they'd have noticed if the beast had symptoms of BSE before now.

'Damn, that scotches that theory.' I rubbed at my forehead. 'OK, what about testing on an imported beast way back whenever? Say, twenty plus years ago?'

'Any imported beast would have had the Western Blot test performed as a matter of protocol. In fact, the Ministry went to the trouble of tracking every single one. Just who are we talking about here?'

I relieved Maggie's curiosity.

'Trevor Ray had a stud bull imported from, I think, Britain. It would have been years and years ago, but I was thinking it may have come over with BSE and infected other beasts and – la, la, la.' I illustrated the la, la, la with hand actions. 'Anyway, I must have been wrong. I can't see how it could possibly lead to an outbreak now.'

'Did you say Trevor Ray?'

'Yeah, Trev.'

'And am I leaping a bit too far here to think you suspect him of killing Gaby because of a BSE scare on his farm?'

'Well, that's kind of what I was thinking. When I was out on my run I came across a pile of burning carcasses that had had their ear tags removed, so were unidentifiable. They'd have to be the same animals that were reported stolen from Trev's and Phillip Rawlings' farms, and so I put two and two together and got rather more than four, as you do.' It all seemed pretty preposterous now.

Maggie actually laughed; she must have thought I'd really lost the plot. I sighed and moved to get up, but she reached over and grabbed my arm.

'Sit, sit. I wasn't laughing at you,' she said. She must have read the despair on my face. 'Let me tell you a little story about Trev that might help with your maths. When I first got the job in the lab, the supervisor, as one of his cautionary tales about risk management, talked about Trev and his bull – Casanova, I think it was.'

That name caused a flashback to the gallery of photos on his office wall.

'Casanova was imported from Britain, for Trev's breeding programme. He was brought in before the ban came into effect and that was fine. Under the national protocol, all imported beasts had to be monitored and then tested for BSE at slaughter or death, to be safe. That's where it got interesting. The bull got very ill, to the point where Trev put it out of its misery: didn't think, and did it the old-fashioned way with a bullet between the eyes. Well, did the shit hit the fan. This was an imported beast, so BSE testing was mandatory, but that was rather impossible now the thing's brain had been mashed by a bullet. The bull, in actuality, had a serious kidney infection and that was listed as the cause of death, but not before Trev and his vet had signed affidavits saying that the beast had not displayed any of the signs of mad-cow disease – you know, staggering, tremors, odd behaviour.'

'Hang on, hang on, hang on.' The jumble of information in my head had begun to take some form. It was all starting to make a scary type of sense. 'So Casanova could have had BSE but no one could confirm it.'

'That's right. Trev and his vet, who'd seen the bull reasonably often, vowed that it hadn't displayed any symptoms. The carcass was disposed of according to protocol, but the brain tissue was too badly damaged to get a usable sample.'

'And he had a kidney infection?'

'Yes, it would have killed him, anyway. The kidneys were quite damaged apparently, so he must have had the disease for a while. Probably had some genetic predisposition.'

That snippet of information was the last piece that might support what had seemed a crazy idea.

'Hear me out and tell me if this sounds too far-fetched. Gaby had been looking at a few webpages about BSE as well as TB. One of the pages – I remember it because the ramifications were pretty scary – was on a study of mice infected with scrapie, which is a similar disease...'

'Yep, I know about scrapie, another prion disease.'

'Yeah, anyway, these mice had kidney inflammation, and the end result was they excreted the infectious agent in their urine, and that then infected other mice.'

'Shit,' said Maggie. I could see her brain ticking away. 'Extend that possibility to cattle and if Trev's beast did have BSE, and it kept having kidney infections, it could have infected other cows.' She was damned quick on the uptake.

'Yes, but that would have had to have happened across several generations for us to have a current-day problem. And surely if they had BSE they'd display symptoms? Someone would have picked it up earlier.' The argument still wouldn't quite stack up.

'Not necessarily so.' Maggie was tapping her finger on the table like she always did when her brain was working overtime. 'If we're going to talk about remote possibilities, picture this: Casanova has mad-cow, has kidney inflammation, pees everywhere, infects other cattle. BSE has a hell of a long incubation period – we're talking five-plus years – so what if none of these beasts showed clinical signs before they were sent to slaughter? Another what if: Casanova was a stud bull; chances are he was infecting some of his progeny, and they may also have inherited his kidney disorder. You see where this is going?'

Unfortunately, I could. 'So they too had dodgy kidneys and, to put it how you so politely did, peed everywhere, infected more cattle. Oh my God, it is theoretically possible that mad-cow disease could have been passed down for generations and gone on for decades on Trev's farm and no one would ever have known.'

It was a fantastic idea, and not in the good sense.

'Theoretically,' she said. 'The odds would have to be incredible, but it is possible. If none of the animals displayed the staggers, you'd have no reason to suspect it. Especially in New Zealand, where we've never had an outbreak of anything nasty, and certainly not BSE.'

Another cog went clunk, and this one made me gasp. A dreadful thought had crept into my mind.

'You OK?' Maggie asked. 'You've gone even pastier than usual.'

'Maggie, tell me the symptoms of mad-cow disease – no, I mean the human version.'

She shot me a worried look. 'You mean variant CJD?'

I gave her a nod.

'In humans you would see staggering, tremor, odd behaviour, neurological symptoms.' She looked apprehensive. 'What are you thinking?'

'Oh my God.' I thought back to Trev tripping up steps, his shakes, being so emotional. I'd attributed it to alcohol, but what if it wasn't?

'I think Trev. He'd have killed the odd beast for home consumption. What if…? And what about Janice?'

And not just Janice either, there were the girls too. It didn't bear thinking about.

'There's an even bigger "what if?" here,' Maggie said, her face a strange combination of alarm and solemnity. 'If this has been present for years, and no one has picked up anything wrong with his cattle, Trev's stock would have gone to the works for slaughter as usual and we could have been eating it. Everyone could have been eating it.'

I suddenly felt very queasy.

'That is one hell of a shit-scary thought.'

'And that is one hell of an understatement.'

We both sat in silence for a while, our minds trying to digest the information.

'Jesus Christ. Now what do I do? Those are some pretty serious theories based on very slim odds. Who would ever believe it?'

Maggie took it upon herself to reply.

'Someone's got to, unlikely as it may seem. You've done your bit, found all this out, now you've got to hand it over to the police.'

I looked at her sideways.

'You know what I mean,' she said. 'The real police.'

I gave her a frown.

'Stop it, you know what I mean.'

46

For one last time, I went over the spiel we'd decided on in my head. I picked up the phone and dialled the Mataura station number. I recognised the series of clicks and clunks that meant the call was being transferred over to Gore. Damn, everyone must have left for the day or, more likely, they hadn't switched the phones back since the funeral.

'Gore Watch House.'

'Hi, it's Constable Sam Shephard here. I need to talk to Senior Sergeant Thomson. It's urgent.'

There was a measured pause on the end of the phone that could only have come from some knowledge of my circumstances. 'One moment please,' came the equally measured reply.

One moment for what? Half a minute of echoed silence passed before I again heard a few rings and another voice on the phone. It wasn't the Boss's.

'Constable Shephard. Detective Inspector Johns.'

Oh, bloody marvellous, the stiff they brought in from Dunedin.

'What can I do for you?'

How much did I tell him? I pitched another shot for the Boss. 'I was really wanting to speak to Senior Sergeant Thomson. Is he available?'

'No, he is not available to take your call right now. What is it you want?'

The man really had to work on his telephone manner. I was in no mood for his curt, clipped tones. Despite my best efforts at self-control, I could feel my dander heading well and truly up.

'I don't want anything. It is important that I speak to the Senior Sergeant. If he is not at the station, may I please be transferred through to his cellphone?'

I thought I'd worked hard to suppress the annoyance in my voice. DI Johns did not agree.

'Might I remind you, Ms Shephard, that you are currently under suspension from the police force and will be facing disciplinary action for your repeated interference in this case – for which, I might add, you are a suspect. You are in no position to demand to speak to anyone.'

'I am not demanding, sir. It's just very important that I speak to my boss.' There was something about this man and his stubborn refusal to listen to anything I said that got my goat.

'Well, that is completely out of the question, Ms Shephard. You may direct your comments to me. I am your appointed liaison in this case.'

Like fun. That was it. One push too far. The floodgates opened.

'Well, you can just bloody well go and rot in hell. I'd rather talk to a real police officer, not some brought-in hack with a flash paper degree who couldn't bloody well solve a mystery if the answer was tattooed across his forehead. Go back to reading your bloody manual, or your comic book or whatever it is you carry around in that poncy briefcase of yours.'

The unfortunate thing about portable phones was that you couldn't hang up with a good, hearty slam. Firmly pressing the talk button just didn't cut it, so once again, I made do with launching the thing into the sofa cushions. It bounced off and hit the side of the coffee table before coming to rest not too far from where Maggie stood. She stared at the projectile for a while before loosening the barb I knew would head my way.

'How old did you say you were?' She gave me a look that would normally make me feel abashed. 'I would also like to make reference to my earlier comment about your people skills.' That was quite restrained on her part.

'Did I get a bit personal?'

'Just a tad,' she said, and held up her hand to show me the tiny gap between her thumb and forefinger. 'You have a bit to learn about public relations. I take it you don't ever want your job back?'

I didn't need to be reminded about that.

'Oh shit and bloody hell. Why can't I get to talk to the right people? It's all I ask.' Frustration mutated itself into a need for action. 'I'll just have to sort it out myself. Can I borrow your car again?'

'What exactly are you going to do?'

'I haven't got time to go into details.' Not that I had any. 'If Paul Frost rings back, tell him I've gone out to Trevor Ray's. He might want to meet me there. If he asks why, tell him Trev rustled his own cattle. I think the rest of it he'd need to hear face to face.'

'Sam?' Maggie's voice was strange.

'Yes,' I said, as I ferreted around for my bag and cellphone.

'What about Cole?'

I stopped dead still, could barely breathe. I'd been so preoccupied with the idea that Trev was the instigator of this affair that the implication of others on his payroll hadn't occurred to me. I gawped like some stranded fish, and a heat that became rapidly uncomfortable seared up my body and into my face. My hands flung themselves up to my cheeks.

Cole.

'No, no, no, no, no. No. I can't even think about that right now. I … just … please can I use your car? I have to sort this out. Now.'

'Shouldn't you hand this all over to the police to deal with now and stay out of it? If Trev had Gaby killed, don't you think it would be safer for you—'

'What do you think I was just bloody well trying to do? They're not even prepared to listen to me.' I finally located my cellphone and rammed it unceremoniously into the bag. 'I'm only an annoying piece of shit stuck to their heel. They don't care about anything I might know. So what else can I do? I have to sort this out for myself.'

Maggie knew me well enough to realise arguing was pointless. She went over to the fridge and retrieved her car keys from the top.

'And what if Paul doesn't ring back?' she asked, holding them out for me.

'I'll keep on trying him on my cell. I just hope he hasn't gone away.'

Concern was written over every available surface of Maggie's body, and I felt a momentary pang of guilt for putting her through this. I reached over and gave her a hug.

'Look, I'll be fine. I know what I'm doing. I need to check out a few things, then that's it as far as I'm concerned. Paul can have the whole kit and caboodle. Well, when I can bloody well get hold of him he can.'

I gave her one last squeeze and headed for the door. I'd only lied a little. After the events and threats of the last few days, there was no guarantee anything was going to be fine, and I had no idea what I was doing; but hey, improvisation was my forte. And as far as I was concerned, I had nothing left to lose.

'You be bloody careful out there, Sam. For the record, I think you're being irrational and reckless. If you're not back in an hour, I'm calling the police.'

I turned and gave her a tentative smile.

'Hell, if I'm not back in an hour, you can probably call the morgue.'

I wasn't quite sure it was a joke.

47

'What the hell am I doing?'

My perception of the idyllic countryside had taken on a more sinister tone, even the antics of a couple of magpies strutting in the grass verge couldn't deflect from the palpable sense of dread. I turned into Trevor Ray's driveway. It was a wonder I'd made it here at all, as I'd concentrated more on practising my pitch than my driving. It was only luck that there had been no other cars to contend with. Even after all that rehearsal, I had major reservations about how well my questions would be received or even what those questions would be. Perhaps I'd start by asking about TB – take the angle of still following up on Gaby's story, throw him off the scent. Then I'd gently steer towards questions about Casanova and that bloodline. I wondered how far I could push it without tipping him off. Mind you, if Trev had the disease I thought he did, he might not be thinking that well, anyway. His decision to kill off Gaby was testament to skewed thought processes. Still, this would be a good opportunity to get a good look at him and check for further evidence of his CJD. Not that I was any kind of doctor.

CJD, BSE, TB – so many acronyms just added to the generalised spin in my head. What was I doing here again? If I had half a brain, I'd turn the car around and head straight back home. Only now, somehow, I was in too deep and this had to be done. There was no going back. There was always a risk Trev would run me off the property like Phillip had, but so far he'd been keen to help – overly keen, doing a bit of scent-throwing of his own. I would have to count on his continued cooperation. Maybe my association with Cole might ease the way somewhat.

Cole. That was another thing altogether. I pushed any thoughts of him out of my head and ordered the butterflies that charged around my stomach into formation.

This was probably the most foolhardy thing I'd ever done in my life. But then, what choice had I been given? I headed slowly up towards the house.

When I crested the last rise of the drive and entered the yard, I was surprised to be confronted by a herd of parked cars and utilities. There were six vehicles in the car park, including Trevor's and Cole's; Janice Ray's car was notably absent. It looked like quite a gathering, and thus probably not the ideal time to quiz Trevor on the whereabouts and origins of his prized stud bull. Again, I seriously contemplated turning around and going home, but sheer curiosity got the better of me. It may have been coincidental, but I recognised several vehicles here as belonging to people whose names had featured in my investigations.

I parked as close to the driveway entrance as I could without actually blocking it, and with the nose pointed in the right direction just in case I needed a quick exit. It didn't hurt to be careful. I almost laughed out loud as the idiocy of the idea hit me. Here I was on my own, in the middle of nowhere, about to question my suspected murderer, on his turf, with his mates present. Careful it wasn't. Bloody stark raving bonkers it most definitely was.

At least no one had come out to investigate my arrival. I decided on a quick reconnoitre around the outside of the house. If anyone challenged me, I'd just say I'd knocked at the door and no one had answered. It sounded pretty convincing to me.

The gravel crunched unbearably loud under my footsteps, and when I tried to walk quietly it seemed to have the exact opposite effect. I knew a little of the layout of Trevor's house from my earlier visit. Instead of heading towards the front door, I skirted around the side and along the southern wall; I crouched low at windows and checked out each room. The southern side consisted of bedrooms, with the kitchen down the furthest end. I recalled a large farmhouse table in the kitchen, and I assumed this was where they'd all be. A peek through the window by the sink told me they weren't there, or in the lounge beyond. It must be the formal dining room then, on the north-facing side of the house.

As I neared the window I could make out the murmur of voices, though none was distinct. A handily placed kowhai tree afforded me some cover as I cautiously peered through the window. I need not have bothered with the subterfuge: the faces were in such intent discussion I could probably have paraded across in the nuddy and they wouldn't have noticed.

I took inventory of the men gathered there, attired in their very best suits. They must have called for this war council to occur straight after Gaby's funeral. And war council it was. I was close enough to catch some of the more heated comments, and my pulse picked up pace as I heard not only Gaby's name but my own bandied around in not too complimentary terms. A roll call of those present made a disheartening list of people at the very heart of the Mataura community: Trevor Ray; Phillip Rawlings; Edgar Pride, one of the vets from the meat-processing plant; John Fellows, management from the very same plant; Henry Purvis, a local farmer from the property that adjoined Trevor's and a popular local character known as Mataura's unofficial mayor. It hadn't occurred to me that Gaby's death had been a committee decision made by town council. I had only thought of it in terms of Trevor protecting his interests, not…

A hand dropped onto my shoulder and another wrapped itself across my mouth to stifle the scream that threatened to explode. I flailed and kicked out as I was grabbed and dragged away from the window and around the side of the house. There, I was abruptly dropped onto the ground, where I gasped for air and then almost threw up as my chest pounded up into my larynx.

'What the hell do you think you're doing?' Cole towered over me, his teeth gritted as he hissed out the words. 'You shouldn't be here.'

I skittered away backwards like some panic-stricken crab. All I had been trying to deny about this man ripped through my conscience like a knife. He was here and he was part of it.

'Keep away from me, you bastard. Don't think I don't know what's going on here. They killed her, didn't they? Shut her up to stop her telling about that bloody bull. Shit, you killed her. I can't believe you did this.'

'Sam, no, I swear I didn't have anything to do with it.' He reached down to grab my arm, but I slapped his hand away, hard, then flipped over onto my front, leaped up and ran like hell around the back of the house. 'Sam, let me explain…'

The words trailed after me as my feet flew across the grass. There was no way he was going to get close enough to explain anything. He could explain to the bloody police. I could hear his footsteps pounding behind me as I broke across the car park, threw myself at the car door, ripped it open and hurled myself inside. I flicked the door lock just as he banged against the side, trying to get in.

'Sam, stop. You have to let me explain.'

I fumbled around in my pocket, located the keys and jammed them into the ignition. It might have been old, but Maggie's car was reliable and I wept with relief as the engine fired with first turn of the key. I didn't dare look at the face at the window; I heard only the thump of fists on the roof as I threw the car into gear and skidded off straight down the driveway.

'Shit, shit, shit.' Hindsight was a bloody marvellous thing, and it told me I was mad to have come out here alone.

'Stupid, stupid, bitch. What were you thinking?'

My chest ached, and so did my head as my body processed an overdose of adrenaline. The car skittered over the gravel as I wound my way recklessly down the drive and then floored it as I hit the straight. My wet hands struggled to keep grip on the steering wheel. I pulled out onto the road and let out a monstrous breath as the tyres gripped the security of the tarmac.

It was then that the shiver plunged down my spine and the heart that had been in my mouth plummeted to my boots. Without the roar of tyres on gravel, a noise other than Maggie's engine whining had begun to register on my radar, and it was increasing in volume as it got closer. I glanced rapidly over my shoulder to see a motorbike, and the dust trail it threw up had just hit the straight bit of the driveway. The form astride it could only belong to Cole.

I threw the gear stick down a gear to try to get some speed up, and chopped it up again when the engine was finally screaming enough. The speedometer climbed and climbed, but the mass in the rear-view mirror still got larger and larger. Maggie's car was no match for a motorbike – but then what could he do? He couldn't run me off the road. He couldn't stop me. I steeled my gaze ahead and kept driving.

Even over the din of the car's straining engine the wasp-like drone grew louder and louder until, in a flash of movement and noise, he was past me.

'You're OK, you're OK, he can't stop you, you're bigger than he is,' I kept telling myself.

I considered turning around and going back the other way, but quickly dismissed the idea. The others in the house must have heard me leave. They could have been following too, for all I knew. Cole, meantime, had disappeared around the bend ahead, and I eased back on the accelerator; it was obvious speed wasn't going to get me out of this one. I'd just have to work my way into town and straight to the station. If it looked like nobody was there, I'd head right on to the Gore…

'Oh shit, shit, shit.' I took my foot off the gas and coasted forward. 'I don't bloody believe it!' I had forgotten about the one-lane bridge.

Cole was positioned sideways across it, still astride his bike, his hand out, beckoning me to stop. I could roar the engine and run him down. But no, in reality, I couldn't. Despite everything, I couldn't deliberately harm him. Capitulation was the only available course of action. I slowed down and came to a halt a few metres from where he stood, my hands gripping the steering wheel, the engine still running. He climbed off the bike, left it smack in the middle of the bridge and slowly walked over to the car. His face twitched and moved, as if it couldn't decide on which of a thousand emotions to portray.

'Sam, you have to let me explain. I need to talk to you. You don't have to be afraid of me.'

'Well, I'm not bloody well getting out of the car, so if you're going to explain, hurry up and get on with it.' If he wanted to talk it would have to be through five millimetres of toughened glass. I would not give up my fortress.

He leaned forwards, his hands on either side of the window frame, and placed his forehead against the glass. When he spoke it was with a voice battered by grief and guilt.

'I didn't have anything to do with Gaby's murder,' he said.

'So you've already said.' I wasn't in a mood to be charitable.

'Trev was worried she'd figured out about the bull.'

'Oh, so you were just conspiring to hide something of major importance to the whole damned country.' Once again, the rage that had built up over the course of the week pushed aside any fear.

'Yes. No. We just wanted to wait, have him tested, make sure it was BSE before we alerted the whole world. Even a rumour of it could have screwed the country, screwed us all.'

'Well, was it worth it?' I asked. The contempt split my voice.

'Christ, we didn't think he'd kill her. He said he'd take care of it. We thought he meant talk to her, bribe her, for God's sake, not kill her.'

'But you knew, you bloody well knew who killed her. Why didn't you just tell me? Jesus Christ, you bloody well slept with me and you didn't think to mention it? What, you thought you'd score some points with the good guys? Sleep with the cop, see if she goes easy on me. Or were you just keeping an eye on me, making sure I didn't get too close? You're a worthless piece of shit.'

He lifted his head and looked at me then, his face ravaged by emotion.

'I was in an impossible position.'

'Oh yeah, poor little you. Gaby's dead, Lockie's lost his wife, Angel her mother – and you were in an impossible position? Well, wake up, sunshine. She was your best mate's wife. You were best man at their fucking wedding. How could you betray them like that? Where did your loyalties lie? Obviously not with your friends or anyone who really mattered. Why did you shield Trev? Why didn't you just dob him in?'

'Who would believe me? I was too close to him. I'd be tarred with the same brush.'

'Yeah, well, you sure as hell are now. Any plea of innocence will just be laughed at by the law. At best, you're an accessory to a murder. The police know everything; I've filled them in. What? Did you think I wouldn't find out? Poor ditzy little Sam, she wouldn't figure it out. Was that what you were counting on? Well, tough shit, guys, I did find out. I have got a brain. So you and Trev and the rest of that pathetic gang back there can bloody well go and rot in hell. Now, get that heap of shit out of my way before I run it over.'

I glared at him with a hatred that threatened to melt the glass barrier between us, but he couldn't meet my eyes. Shoulders slumped, he pulled himself up and walked over to move the bike.

I loosened my cramped fingers off the steering wheel and extracted my fingernails from the cuts they had made in the plastic. Then, with a purposeful calm that belied my inner emotions, I put the car into gear and drove on past him without a second look.

48

'Argghh, bloody hell.' I tossed the cellphone back on the seat. 'Useless bloody thing.' I had broken the law and my personal rule of not using the phone while driving, but hell, if this didn't define extenuating circumstances, I didn't know what did. I had to get hold of Paul, and fast. No fucking signal.

I flicked my eyes up to the rear-view mirror again and licked my parched lips. I'd spent more time looking at what was behind me than at the road ahead, on the lookout for any sign of pursuit. I only hoped Cole had bought my bluff.

I'd have to go to the Mataura command centre now, damn it. That meant dealing with the Boss, or worse. I knew who I'd rather deal with. Paul at least would listen. I didn't know if the others would even let me on the premises.

'Where are you, Paul?' I uttered. Wouldn't that be right? The only cop in the area I actually trusted, and he chose now to have some R & R.

Despite my reservations, I felt hugely relieved to finally clap my eyes on the Mataura Elderly Citizens Centre and see that the lights were on. I pulled up into the vacant car park a little too quickly and cringed as the tyre and wheel rim hit the kerb. Sorry, Maggie. Then I couldn't get myself into the building fast enough. In fact, I could have got down on my knees and kissed that hideous carpet. Even I had to admit I'd never been so bloody scared in all my life. How could I have been so reckless? If Cole had been of a murderous disposition I wouldn't even be here right now.

I'd made some very poor judgement calls lately and I wasn't about to stuff up again. I took a few moments to compose myself in the foyer, and then swung open the main doors to track down the Boss. God, please let him be there.

At first glance, I could only spot one officer on duty.

'Sam, what are you doing here?'

Make that two. I looked around to my right and was pleased to see one of the Gore constables transferred over for the case. She was always a friendly face.

'Mel, hi, I'm glad it's you. I've got some information I need to get to the Boss right away. Can I see him?'

'He's not here. Got the rest of the day off after the funeral.' My face must have dropped, because she put her hand on my shoulder. 'You OK?'

After the rollercoaster ride that had been my day, my week, all I wanted was for something to be straightforward for a change. Was it so much to ask for the person I wanted to speak with to be there, have them listen, no fuss, no drama? Why did everything have to be so bloody difficult? My eyes filled with tears.

'Sorry,' I said, wiping them away. 'It's been a hard week.'

Mel smiled at the understatement, and she only knew the half of it.

'Who's in charge, then?' I asked, although I already suspected the answer.

'Detective Inspector Johns, the guy from Dunedin.'

'I'd better see him, then.' My dread told in my voice. Mel looked at me, then ushered me gently towards one of the corner rooms.

'Do you want me to sit in?' she asked.

'It might be an idea.'

We reached the room and Mel gave me a moment to wipe a few more tears, pull at my clothes and take a big breath. I nodded at her, then she knocked at the door and we went in.

DI Johns' eyes widened, then narrowed, when he saw me. A good gauge of the reception I would get, I was sure.

'Constable Shephard would like a word, sir. Says she has some information you will be interested in.'

She walked straight to one of the chairs and sat down, so I did too. The DI frowned. I thought he was about to ask her to leave, so I tried to get straight to the point.

My voice caught in my throat. 'I have some very important information regarding the Gaby Knowes case.'

I could tell by the way he changed his posture he'd decided to be an arsehole.

'Do you really think I would want to listen to anything you have to say after the way you spoke to me this morning? You have been insubordinate and disrespectful. And I seem to be spending a lot of my time reminding you that you are under suspension and still a suspect in this case.'

'I understand that, sir, and I'm sorry, but I've found out some information you need to know.' I tried to sound subordinate and respectful.

'I should have you thrown out of the building. In fact, by all rights, I should get the constable here to escort you across the road and put you under lock and key. I have half a mind to have you arrested for obstruction of justice and—'

I'd been trying to keep it together. It was pointless.

'For Christ's sake, get down off your bloody high horse and just listen to me,' I exploded.

'Don't you bloody well speak to me like that. Get the hell out of my office before I have you thrown in jail.'

I jumped to my feet and started to storm out. Then I realised that at that moment I had to be heard above all else, no matter how much I hated the DI and wanted to rip his throat out. So I let out an 'Arggghh', turned back around, strode over and banged my fists on his desk.

He and Mel both jumped.

'Now listen to me.' I leaned over towards him as far as I could, fixed him in the eye and spat it out before he could interject again. 'Let's stop the stupid games and just shut up and listen. I know who killed Gabriella Knowes.'

There was an awkward silence as I glared at him and he glared straight back.

The deadlock was broken by an 'Ahem' from Mel.

'OK, we're listening,' she said. 'How about you sit back down, Constable, and tell us exactly what you know.'

I slowly sat down, and DI Johns leaned back into his seat.

'Alright, then, who do you think killed Mrs Knowes?' His voice was still full of condescension.

'I think that Trevor Ray was behind the murder of Mrs Knowes.'

The DI laughed in my face. It took all of my self-control not to swear at him again.

'No, don't laugh. Come on, be fair, hear me out.'

So I told him everything. I told him that Gaby had been killed because she'd figured out, or Trev thought she'd figured out, that he had cattle infected with BSE on the farm. I told him of the burning carcasses and how it tied in with the recent spate of cattle rustling. I told him my theory on how an outbreak could have happened and how long it could have been going on. I told him my suspicions about Trev having the human equivalent of mad-cow disease, and lastly, I told him of my visit to the farm, who I'd seen there and my conversation with Cole.

When I'd finished, he sat there for a moment, taking it all in. At least he didn't tell me I was mad. When he did speak, his attitude and his tone had utterly changed. It was serious and level.

'You took a huge risk going back there. You shouldn't have done that.' He twirled a pencil on his desk.

'I know, it was dangerous in hindsight, but I felt it was my responsibility to clear this all up. I had to sort it out.' That, and he'd given me no choice, but I didn't verbalise that thought.

Now I'd offered everything I knew, it felt like my plug had been pulled out. Events of the last week had taken their toll, and I felt brittle and flat.

'If what you're saying is true, then Mr Ray had Mrs Knowes murdered over a few head of cattle. That's a bit of an overkill.'

'God, yes,' said Mel.

It was. I tried to imagine it from Trev's perspective.

'I suppose all he could focus on was his stock being slaughtered, losing money, losing his livelihood. He could see the potential ramifications locally and nationally, so got the vet involved – and the meat plant, transporters, the people who had a lot to lose – but on a hush-hush level. He had them all caught up in it. When he made the decision to have Gaby killed, he made them all accessories.'

'They made themselves accessories if they didn't come forward as soon as they knew.' That was Mel.

'Mad-cow disease. Shit. You do realise that if it's confirmed, our export beef market is going to be obliterated, so the farmers are going to suffer, and the works, the town – hell, the whole country. Meat plants will close, jobs will be lost. It will be the end of some towns.' The DI looked me in the eye. I knew exactly one of the towns he was alluding to. It was a scary thought, but not half as scary as the thought of how many people were exposed to the disease, how many could be infected. 'That kind of thing could throw the nation into complete crisis.'

'Trev must have known that too, which is why he tried to keep it a secret, even to the extent of killing an innocent woman,' I said.

'It doesn't make sense, though. Something that big was always going to get out, and at some point, the authorities would have to get involved. It would be inevitable. And anyway, if he'd gone straight to the authorities, they could at least have had a chance to minimise the damage to the country and everyone concerned. Our world-class reputation and our clean, green image is going to be shot to hell. The foreign media are going to have a field day – young mother killed in back-country town to cover up conspiracy of silence over mad-cow disease. We'll be seen as trying to hide it. He must have been insane to think killing her would hide it all, make it go away.'

He got that right.

'Well, that's the crucial point,' I said. 'In a way, he probably is insane. He may not even realise he's got CJD and the awful effect it's having on his brain and his mind, and he certainly isn't making sane decisions.'

God only knew what else he had wrecked. I could never excuse him for what he'd done, but I was surprised to feel a twinge of pity for Trev.

'So now what do we do?' I asked.

'I'll be calling in reinforcements. We've got a fair few people to round up and question. We'll start out at the Ray farm, see how many we can catch still there.'

I was pretty sure Cole would have gone back and told them what had happened. They would have cleared off by now.

The DI had thought of that. 'We'll send cars out to their residences as well, make sure no one gets by us.' He'd stood up and was already reaching for the phone. 'As for you, I want you to go home ... No—' He held his hand up as I started to protest. 'Listen, you will go home, and then when I need you to come back and identify the people present at the farm I'll send someone around to pick you up.'

I could see he would not be open to debate on the matter. He'd already moved on to the business of calling in officers.

Mel tapped me on the elbow and indicated towards the door, so I got up and followed her back out into the main hall.

'Well done,' she said, 'though I don't know that solving this case makes me any happier.'

'No, it raises some pretty unappetising questions.' I inclined my head back towards the room. 'Are you sure he won't let me tag along for the ride?'

Mel laughed. 'I think he made it quite clear he wanted you out of the way. Go home, Sam. Someone will come pick you up when we need you.' She patted me on the back and then headed back to the action.

Thought of home made me suddenly realise I hadn't let Maggie know I was safe. I felt a pang of guilt: she'd be worried sick. I hopped into her car and called the home number on my cell. It went straight to answerphone. I flicked her a text message to tell her to put the kettle on, I was on my way.

All I wanted to do was get to the safety of my own home for a cuppa, some Toffee Pops and some Maggie therapy.

49

After my shit of a day I felt positively delirious driving up to what I usually considered to be our dump of a flat. Today it looked like Buckingham flaming Palace. I knew I'd get a bit of grief from Maggie for not getting in touch with her sooner, and causing her so much worry, but I'd take what came. Right now, all I cared about was her company, that cup of tea and as many chocolate biscuits as we could muster. Then, when it was a more socially acceptable hour, we could hit the wine.

I closed the front door behind me and called out as I turned back to the room.

'Maggie! I lived to tell the tale, but you're not going to bloody believe this.'

I stopped dead. Maggie was seated at the table – that was normal. The ropes, the gag, the gash seeping blood into her left eye were not. For a moment I floundered for something to say, some way to act, but was held in suspension by the terror that screamed from her eyes. They flicked from me to behind my right shoulder, and reflex kicked in as I threw myself in the other direction, avoiding the full impact of the human missile that charged at me. Even the glancing blow was enough to knock my breath away. I hit the ground, rolled and came up on all fours, my limbs moving in an uncoordinated frenzy to get distance from my assailant. I watched as a brown steel-capped boot attached to navy-blue drill trousers swung towards my chest.

Survival instinct made me try to jump upwards as the boot connected with skin, but the force still lifted me completely off the ground. My ears calmly noted a crunching noise before the rest of my brain logged pain and acted accordingly. My vision swirled and tunnelled, the roar of blood filled my ears and my body began to succumb to the irresistible force of gravity. I hit the ground with a bone-jarring crash that I didn't feel inclined to get up from.

I lay, face down, my lungs screaming against their broken casings.

I was going to die. It had to be easier than breathing. In fact, dying seemed like quite an attractive option for a second or two before I realised that if I was going to die, Maggie was going to die, and I couldn't let that happen. Somehow, I had to think, and lucidly.

The man lifted me up and threw me over his shoulder, folded in half like some casually slung beach towel. My mind, off on a tangent of its own, made an uninvited comparison with being carried away by a young Arnold Schwarzenegger. The reality, of course, was far less appealing, and the pain that ripped through my torso cleared my mind like a whiff of the salts.

From this vantage point he had to be at least six foot six and hardened with muscle. My feet were too high up to deliver a blow to anywhere personal and vulnerable, but if I was outgunned for size, I was buggered if I was going to be outgunned for brains.

He was carrying me over towards Maggie, and it didn't require a crystal ball to know how I was going to be dealt with. I had to find a…

My eye caught sight of the phone sitting atop the sofa and I reached out and grabbed it as we brushed past. With all the force I could muster I reached my arm back and rammed the phone as hard as I could, antennae first, towards his rectum. I felt a gratifying rip of fabric and slide before it anchored against firmer flesh or bone. I didn't care which. He roared and threw me off, head first, over his shoulder. My legs flicked over and I landed flat on my back on the floor. I wasn't going to get much of a reprieve, so rolled over onto my stomach and up onto my knees as he reeled around to face me, hands clutching at his arse. My mind photographed the moment: the giant towering over me, the navy zip-up coveralls, the name 'Dave' embroidered in contrasting yellow on the chest pocket, the close-shaven, dimpled chin, the thin lips snarled back into a grimace, the impeccably straight teeth, the neat scar beneath the left nostril, the strong but slightly askew nose, the watering and murderous green eyes.

'You fucking bitch!' he bellowed, and I knew in that instant that any hope of mercy had evaporated. With his right hand, he reached into his hip pocket, pulled out a flick knife and activated it in one deft movement.

'Oh shit,' slipped out of my mouth as I tried to scrabble up and out of the way, but I was too slow. The arm swept down in a terrifying, graceful arc, and I watched fascinated as the blade disappeared through my trouser leg and into the flesh of my thigh. I felt it slice its way through muscle before it came to an abrupt crunch against bone. The blow knocked me on my butt and I heard a scream as I tried to shuffle away from him, staring at the incongruous sight of the knife, haft high, still sticking out of my left leg. My back met the wall and I leaned hard against it for support before I finally raised my eyes to see what was coming next. The knockout blow I expected never arrived. Instead he just stood there, his face a grimace, hands rubbing at his backside; his laboured breaths matched mine. The nausea I had tried to suppress ripped free, and I leaned over and threw up on the floor beside me. He stood over me, observing me wiping my streaming eyes and nose, then he walked away and turned his attention to our gas heater. He appeared to be attaching some small device, and a premonition of our planned demise flashed into my head.

'I was going to make this painless for you, but now I'll enjoy knowing you got to sit and enjoy the fireworks. Your friend too.' He nodded towards Maggie, who watched, mortified, from her enforced front-row seat. 'This is going to look like a tragic accident. I'm sure you'll get a nice obituary.'

Maggie writhed and strained against her bonds, pushing back with her feet. Then, with a sickening thud, she toppled over backwards.

Where terror had once gripped my heart, calculated calm took control. This man deemed me as no longer being a threat, and it was his second mistake. The first had been to leave me with a weapon.

'I suppose you worked for Telemax last week, Dave.' He turned to look at me and curled his mouth into a chilling smile before he focused his attention back on the task at hand.

I shuffled forwards slightly to give myself space. With both hands I took a firm grip on the handle of the knife and then, steeling myself with a huge breath, I pulled. White searing heat exploded through my thigh and I cried out as a wave of nausea and giddiness washed over me. I sucked air in through my teeth and forced back the greyness encroaching on my vision.

I watched as he swung his head around at the noise, and saw him register the presence of the knife in my hand. I saw him turn and start to stride in my direction. I kept my gaze on his face as I drew back my arm and threw the knife with every ounce of strength I could muster. I watched as it flew straight and true, covering the three metres or so between us in a blink, before it buried itself up to its haft in his throat. His eyes reflected his astonishment as his hands lifted to his neck to clutch at the foreign object protruding from it. In a ballet of warped choreography, he spun around several times before landing, less than gracefully, face up on the floor, the knife in one hand, the other still clutched at his throat. I watched dispassionately as an extraordinary amount of blood spilled out onto the carpet; I wondered about how difficult it would be to get the stain out. He had probably made it worse by pulling out the knife. Now he was making a bigger mess, trying to sit up. Fool.

A sharp smell of sulphur pulled me back from my parallel dimension into this one. Gas.

'Maggie,' I called out. 'Hang on, I'm coming.' I tried to stand, but couldn't put any weight on my leg without it collapsing out from under me. I set out on hands and knee, dragging the other leg behind me, trying to ignore the stabbing pains that shot through my chest.

The man's movements had slowed down somewhat, but I had seen enough movies in which the 'should-be-dead-by-now' villain had miraculously leaped to his feet and had another shot at the hero. I wasn't about to take any chances, and skirted around the far side of the sofa. I had no idea of the extent of Maggie's injuries and was desperately afraid for her, especially now, with the thick stench of gas. Somehow, I had to find the strength to get us both out.

The graunch of the forcibly turned door handle and the crash as the front door slammed back into the wall made me jerk my head up in terror. The door swung back so hard that the handle went through the wall.

What the hell now?

Cole stood semi-silhouetted in the doorway.

All hope sank. I knew I was beaten. I couldn't fight him too – I just didn't have anything left to give. I felt hot tears spill down my face as I watched him survey the scene: Maggie, unmoving, on her back, still strapped to the chair; the gigantic man clutching the knife, twitching and bleeding all over the carpet; and me, at the end of a trail of blood, trying to crawl across the floor towards my friend.

Swiftly, and with no hesitation, Cole strode over to the man, drew back his leg and delivered him a sickening, full-blooded boot to the side of the head. The head whiplashed to the other side, and all movement stopped instantly. He kicked the knife away, and then he was at my side. His hands tried to pull me up.

'Sam, Sam. Are you alright?'

Of course I wasn't alright. What a stupid bloody thing to ask. I wanted to hit him, and to fully inform him of how stupid that question was, but a vision of impending doom filled my mind. There was someone else who needed his help more than me.

'Get Maggie out, get her out now. He was going to blow up the house. Can't you smell the gas?' He hesitated, so I screamed at him: 'Go!'

He leaped into action, reached Maggie in a few bounds, shoved the table out of the way, picked her up, chair and all and made for the door. I turned myself around and scrambled towards the door with the speed that only fear could impart. I dragged myself down the steps and across the driveway towards where Cole had laid Maggie down on her side. He was about to leave her to come back for me, but I waved him away and kept up under my own steam, spurred on by the mental image of the blast I knew had to be coming.

At last, I was at Maggie's side, at what I hoped was a safe distance from the house. I tore at the last remaining bonds around Maggie's shoulders while Cole pulled away the chair. Then I ripped the gag out of her mouth and wept as I felt her breath on my cheek, her pulse sure and steady under my fingertips. I ran my hand through her hair and could feel an egg-sized lump on the back of her head. It must have happened when the chair fell over. The gash above her eye was deep; the glistening white of bone peeked through the tissue and gore.

I was about to lean over and kiss the top of her forehead when the explosion finally came.

Knowing that it was going to happen did nothing to prepare me for its magnitude. It overwhelmed my senses; the shock wave threw me forward as I tried to shield Maggie with my body. Even at this distance, I felt the shrapnel of shattered glass rain onto my back. The blast reverberated in my skull long after the silence of its aftermath descended.

I realised then that Cole had tried to shield us as well, and the mere fact that he had touched us sparked back to life the maelstrom of hate and anger within me. I shoved him away, hard. A look of hurt and surprise crossed his face, quickly replaced by resignation as he leaned back and sat on his heels.

'Get away from me, Cole,' I said.

'I'm sorry, Sam. I'm so sorry.'

I said nothing and kept staring my contempt.

He shifted uncomfortably before he continued. 'Honestly, I never thought … never meant for you to get hurt. I tried to warn you, keep you away from Trev.'

'When? When was that, Cole? I don't seem to recall you saying, "Hey, he's a murdering bastard, watch your back".' As I spat out the words, and saw the feeble expression on his face, something clicked into place. 'Oh, you're kidding. That was your idea of a warning – a few nuisance phone calls. Oh, my God, and the fucking rabbit?'

'I wanted to scare you off. And the tyre. But I didn't want you to get hurt. I'm sorry…'

'You've already said that and I'm sick of hearing it. Did you care about me at all, or was all that apparent concern just to ease your own damned conscience? In fact, why did you bother coming back here at all?'

He looked away, and spoke so quietly I had to strain to hear him over the ringing in my ears. 'I went back to the house and told them you knew everything, and Trev just smiled and said not to worry 'cause he'd taken care of it. After the way he took care of Gaby, shit, I couldn't let it happen again.'

'Well, if you think you're the bloody great hero, you were too bloody late. Tell that to Maggie.' I stroked her bleeding, broken head. 'Tell it to Lockie. See if he thinks you're the good guy, Cole. I'm sure it will make him feel much better to know that you're sorry. Get the hell out of my sight.'

He didn't move.

He might have arrived just after the nick of time, he might have come back for me, but whether motivated by guilt or affection I didn't care. I could never forgive him for putting Maggie's or my life in danger. I could never forgive him for not stepping in and stopping Gaby's murder. I could never forgive him his duplicity.

'Get away from us!' I screamed at him. 'Just get the fuck away.'

He stood up and walked slowly back to the front fence, before he slid down against it and held his head in his hands.

My shell-shocked ears picked up the muffled and distant sound of the civil-defence siren calling up the volunteer fire brigade. Help was on its way – but it was too late. My home was gone, my best friend lay unconscious and injured in my arms, my body was battered and broken.

Nothing could ever be the same, and I didn't want it to be.

Epilogue

The door clicked smoothly into place on the shiny red rental that carried all that remained of my earthly goods. It was ironic that I had the police to thank for having anything other than the clothes on my back – not that they were fit for any use other than being burned. They had confiscated my computer when they still considered me to be public enemy number one, so that was the sum of my possessions – an outdated computer and a set of very second-hand running gear. It was not a lot to show for my life's work.

I retrieved the small bunch of roses I'd placed on the car roof. My intended destination was not difficult to spot, and I picked my way towards the mound of freshly turned earth that indicated the final resting place of Gabriella Patricia Knowes. The funerary bouquets were past their best, and their fading glory was reflected in the colour of the surrounding trees, turning with the march of autumn. I sighed heavily to push back the lump that formed in my throat when I saw the grubby, well-loved toy rabbit nestled among the wilted blooms.

'Well, Gaby, we got the bastards who did this, not that it makes any difference to you here.' My voice was thick and stilted, and my eyes lingered on the spare white wooden cross that bore her name. I felt on hallowed ground and, despite the discomfort, knelt to place the roses next to Rabbit.

My thigh was heavily bandaged. The knife hadn't done too much in the way of damage, but its tip had broken off when it hit bone and a surgeon's knife had been required to retrieve it. The man who had wielded it still lay in the morgue, his true identity a mystery, his business persona still being pieced together. Our only hope of discovering who he was lay in the hands of anyone concerned enough to file a missing persons report. Perhaps a family whose husband or father or son had never come home. That hadn't happened yet.

As for those who hired his services, I hoped they were going to rot in jail where they belonged. Trevor Ray for procuring a murder and attempting to procure a murder; the others, including Colin Avery, for being accessories after the fact. How many lives had been destroyed, how many futures ruined because of that one unfathomable decision: Trev's precious cattle and bottom line taking precedence over the sanctity of human life?

'Oh, it could have ruined us financially,' he'd said. 'It would have been a death knell for the town, crucified the nation.' Something in that disease-ridden brain of his had thought it better to take matters into his own hands rather than alert the authorities to the possibility of BSE and let them deal with it through official channels. For some unknown reason, his disciples followed blindly, and here, beneath me, lay the result.

It was perhaps some small comfort that Trevor Ray had a life sentence of his own. The disease he had contracted from his beloved cattle would kill him, and soon. There was a natural kind of justice to that.

As for his predictions of national doom, we would see.

To the incredulity of the scientists, our highly unlikely scenario had proven accurate. Edgar Pride, the vet who was in on Trev's activities, had taken a brain-stem sample from Samson, the suspect bull, before they'd torched the carcasses. That sample had tested positive for BSE, as had one salvaged from Half Face, the beast that had partially escaped the flames. New Zealand beef was banned overseas and the farming community was reeling. The Government was in crisis mode, attempting to allay a nation's fears about CJD in people exposed to the contaminated meat, and warning of a new and difficult era for agriculture. A small consolation was the assertion from scientists that the outbreak was most likely localised to Trev's farm, but the whole scenario was making people rethink how BSE spread, worldwide.

As for me, I could not stay in Mataura. My life here was destroyed as emphatically as my house. Maggie had it right: it was time to move on. In fact, she quit Mataura the day she got out of hospital and went to stay in Dunedin with her aunt. Like me, she was left only with scars to show for a life here, and she had a plan: to try something new, extend herself.

The beginnings of a plan of my own had begun to take shape in my head. Despite everything, I still held the firm belief I was meant to be in the police. The fact remained I had found Gaby's murderer, had pieced together the puzzle. And that was a good feeling. I'd often toyed with the idea of becoming a detective. It was time to consider it more seriously. I wanted more of a challenge from my work, and striving for detective could bring it. Of course, I did have a bit of bridge-building to do with my colleagues; my future was at the mercy of my superiors. Paul Frost had been doing his best to smooth the way there, as had the Boss. I felt confident my suspension would be lifted and I'd be allowed to get on with my life.

My life. The more I thought about it, the more appeal Dunedin had. Detective training would be possible there. Maggie had gone as far as to invite me to move there too. Her aunt and uncle would put me up, she said, and apart from my appalling taste in pyjamas, I made a halfway decent flatmate.

For now, my immediate future lay in the direction of my parents. I knew full well there would be lectures and recriminations, but I really needed a chance to heal, and to be with my loved ones. Even if they did nag.

Life in Mataura was over for me. I was on my way home.

The cemetery was my last stop, my last goodbye. A chance for a peace offering and belated prayers for forgiveness from a woman I had wronged through petty jealousy and immaturity. It was a recognition of her worth as wife, mother and human being. An affirmation that her death would not go unavenged.

'Rest in peace, Gaby.'

I lifted myself back to my feet, and then gave her a sad smile as I turned and walked away.

Acknowledgements

A writer's path is never a solitary journey. There are a myriad of people who contribute to and support our writing habit in some way, from the obvious – those wonderful people in the publishing industry, to the not so direct but also appreciated – such as the person who made the perfect flat white coffee on that morning when I needed a little chemical inspiration.

Huge thanks to Karen Sullivan and Orenda Books for taking a punt on a Kiwi gal, and to Craig Sisterson for being my cheer leader and telling Karen, 'There's this New Zealand author you should read…'

Thanks also to The New Zealand Society of Authors, and their assessment programme funded by Creative New Zealand – in the early days it was invaluable having the canny eye of Stephen Stratford critiquing the manuscript. I will always be indebted to Geoff Walker and Penguin New Zealand for taking that first leap of faith in a new writer.

How can I express my immense gratitude to my husband and children for their patience, and for having a good sense of humour those times I got sidetracked by writing and burned the dinners or forgot to pick them up – love you guys.

If you enjoyed *Overkill*, you'll love
Steph Broadribb's Lori Anderson Series

'Like *Midnight Run*, but much darker ...
really, really good' IAN RANKIN

DEEP
DOWN
DEAD

'Fast,
confident and
suspenseful'
LEE CHILD

STEPH BROADRIBB

'A real cracker ... Steph Broadribb kicks ass, as does
her ace protagonist' MARK BILLINGHAM

'An adrenaline-fuelled, brilliant
thriller. Trouble has never been so
attractive' A K BENEDICT

DEEP

'My kind of book'
LEE CHILD

BLUE

TROUBLE

STEPH BROADRIBB

'A real cracker … Steph Broadribb kicks ass,
as does her ace protagonist' MARK BILLINGHAM

Coming soon…

DEEP
DIRTY
TRUTH

STEPH BROADRIBB